Never Keeping Secrets

Also by Niobia Bryant

Mistress, Inc.
Mistress No More
Message from a Mistress
Show and Tell
Live and Learn
Red Hot
The Hot Spot
Give Me Fever
Make You Mine
Hot Like Fire
Heated
Heat Wave (with Donna Hill and Zuri Day)
Reckless (with Cydney Rax and Grace Octavia)

Never Keeping Secrets

NIOBIA BRYANT

Kensington Publishing Corp.
http://www.kensingtonbooks.com

DAFINA BOOKS are published by

Kensington Publishing Corp.
119 West 40th Street
New York, NY 10018

All Kensington Titles, Imprints, and Distributed Lines are available at special quantity discounts for bulk purchases for sales promotions, premiums, fund-raising, and educational or institutional use. Special book excerpts or customized printings can also be created to fit specific needs. For details, write or phone the office of the Kensington special sales manager: Kensington Publishing Corp., 119 West 40th Street, New York, NY 10018, attn: Special Sales Department, Phone: 1-800-221-2647.

Dafina and the Dafina logo Reg. U.S. Pat. & TM Off.

First trade paperback printing: June 2013

ISBN-13: 978-0-7582-6531-9
ISBN-10: 0-7582-6531-X

10 9 8 7 6 5 4 3 2 1

Printed in the United States of America

Thank you, Lord, for blessing me with the gift of story-telling; for the wisdom to utilize that gift; and for the readers who seem to enjoy it.

Prologue
Ladies

2013

Friendships end. Shit happens. Be it personal growth or a silly argument or physical distance or hurtful betrayal . . . sometimes friends just stop being friends.

Stop calling.

Stop relying.

Stop depending.

Stop expecting.

Stop caring.

Stop giving a fuck.

Just stop.

Danielle Johnson, Monica Winters, Keesha Lands, and Latoya James had been the very best of friends since their days back at University High School in Newark, New Jersey. But that was during the nineties and plenty of time had passed since then. Plenty of shit had happened since then. Some good. Some bad. Over the years they had been through it all together. Love. Heartbreak. Loyalty. Betrayal. Hurtful lies and even more devastating truths.

They thought there wasn't a thing created by God that could end their friendship. Nothing in the world. But they were wrong. Somehow petty arguments, misunderstandings, and distance had done them in. Fucked their friendship—their closeness—all the way up.

Sometimes friends just stop being friends.

Stop calling.

Stop relying.

Stop depending.

Stop expecting.

Stop caring.

Stop giving a fuck.

Just stop.

Three women stood side by side in front of the open casket, their bodies pressed close together as they sought comfort from one another as they looked down at the face of a friend. There was a peace on her face that could only be found in death.

The one in the middle cried out suddenly in anguish and her body went slack. The other two rushed to hold her upright as their own tears coated their faces, their hearts pounded in distress, and their bodies trembled with grief. Grief and disbelief.

"Oh, God, why?" one questioned, her voice barely above a whisper more for the lack of resolve to speak louder than out of respect for being in attendance to the wake.

"We wasted so much time being mad and now this?" another said, her eyes filled with a mix of confusion and sadness as she looked at the faces of her two friends.

The last woman remained quiet. There were no words in existence to express the emotions that rushed through her. None. There weren't enough tears for the pain. Not enough sadness for the grief. Not enough consoling for the healing.

Their friend was dead. Gone. There was nothing they could do about it.

Chapter 1
Monica a.k.a. Alizé

Five Years Earlier

"What happened to the good old days when a married man kept his dirty mistress a fucking secret?"

Monica Winters didn't know whether it was the sarcastic words or just the very presence of Serena Lockhart-Steele that made her back go stiff like it was filled with a dozen shots of Viagra just as she was kissed and held tightly by her man, Cameron Steele—Serena's husband. Serena and Cameron were very separated—separate homes, separate lives—but it was clear that just like the many times before when he asked Serena for a divorce that she wasn't willing to accept the end of their marriage. Monica shared a brief look with Cameron that was filled with all kinds of unspoken words before they stepped back from one another and looked over at his wife standing in the open doorway of his office.

Serena shook her head like a chastising parent as she stepped inside and then slammed the door.

WHAM!

Monica winced.

Cameron released a heavy breath.

This particular threesome spelled nothing but trouble and the fact that it was going down in the New York corporate offices of Braun, Weber made the whole situation even more precarious. Possibly embarrassing. Just dead damn wrong.

Serena was very aware that Monica and Cameron were in a relationship; just as Monica was painfully aware that Cameron was still legally married. The tension in the room was as palpable as the racing pulses. It was clear no one wanted to be in the presence of the other. A fucking monkey could figure that shit out.

Notching her chin high, Monica smoothed her hands over her hips in the fitted linen dress she wore before leaning back against the edge of Cameron's oversized, neatly arranged desk. Eyeing the other woman unflinchingly, she crossed her legs at the ankle. She hated to admit to herself that she looked beautiful. Tall and slender with fine features and even finer designer garb that fit her body like a second skin.

In that moment, Monica had never felt more like a grad student/intern. Serena Steele was established. Monica was months from graduating with her masters of business administration and determined to get there.

"Hello, Serena. I wasn't expecting you," Cameron stressed politely as he straightened his double-knotted silk tie and made his way around his desk to claim the leather executive chair behind it.

Serena gave him a tight smile as she continued to walk over to his desk. "Since when does a *wife* need an appointment to see *her* husband, Cam?" she asked with a meaningful arch of her brow as she eyed Monica.

Monica glanced away from the slightly older, sophisticated woman as she fought hard not to grab Serena by the throat and slow-walk her ass out of both the building and Cameron's life. She hated the insecurities that claimed her. And regardless of Monica spending every night in his arms, this woman had more right to him than her. She was his wife. Plain and simple. Like it or not.

Monica wanted those fucking divorce papers signed, sealed, and delivered to the courts as quickly as possible.

"Cam, I need to speak with you . . . in private," she insisted, folding her tall and slender frame into one of the leather chairs before his desk.

Monica's heart pounded as she bit the inside of her mouth to keep from snapping at Serena as she eyed the way the hem of the pencil skirt she wore raised up her thigh. Rolling her eyes, she looked over her shoulder at Cameron.

His eyes met hers for a few moments that seemed like forever.

The message in Monica's eyes was clear: *Don't fuck with it.*

"Hammering out the details of our marriage in front of your mistress is asking a bit too much, Cam, don't you think?"

The tension levels in the room shot up a thousand notches as he glanced away from Monica and cleared his throat.

No, this motherfucker ain't . . .

"Monica, will you excuse us for just a moment?"

Yes, this motherfucker did.

A sharp and intense pain radiated across her chest. A pain that was fed by disappointment, anger, and jealousy. And those emotions were fed by the smug look of satisfaction on Serena's face.

Monica's shoulders were squared up and as stiff as a linebacker's as she rose up on her five-inch heels and turned to look for the keys she had dropped just moments before when Cameron's kisses had distracted her. *If I knew I was going to run into this bullshit I would have taken my black ass straight home*, she thought, fighting the urge to pull a cliché "mistress" move and kiss him in front of Serena.

Cameron rose from his seat and came around his desk to walk her to the door. "Just give me a few minutes with Serena and then we'll go to Cipriani for dinner before we head home," he said in a low tone, his hand lightly touching the small of her back.

Monica was too deep into her emotions to give a fuck about his words, his emphasis on the word "home," his apologetic tone, his presence, or the warm and spicy scent of his cologne. Without a glance up at him, Monica opened the office door and stepped out onto the tiled hallway, closing it securely behind her and in his face. "Fuck you, Negro," she muttered, avoiding the awkward glances of his executive assistant, Georgia.

Monica felt the heat of shame warm her cheeks as she imagined Georgia's thoughts on the girlfriend exiting right after the wife entered. It made her feel like she was sneaking around with Cameron. And they weren't.

They damn near lived together. They attended events together. They introduced each other as a significant other. They were together.

But she is legally still his wife.

Taking a deep breath, Monica headed straight for the elevator. She held her keys tightly in her hand as she waited for the doors to open and tried not to imagine just what was going on behind the door of his office.

Cameron and Monica met during her first year of interning at Braun, Weber. He was the Vice President of Mergers and Acquisitions for the investment firm. She had been deep in a world mixed with what she wanted—her desire to earn her MBA and take over corporate America—and what she had, which was shitty relationships with thugs from her Newark neighborhood. The two definitely didn't mix—especially when her ex Rah had beat her ass and broken her leg while he was high off dope and angry from news that she had cheated on him in the past. The craziest part of that drama was his anger over her betrayal topping that she just walked in on him deep between the thighs of one of her closest friends. She had been more than happy to get him out of her life and into a prison facility for aggravated assault charges.

To her, men like Cameron were the real threat to her career and her heart because she knew a thug wasn't good for shit but his money and dick. And when Cameron revealed he wanted to take their relationship further, she hadn't gone for it, choosing his friendship instead.

Five months later she received an invitation to his wedding to Serena—a woman he started dating after Monica turned him down. He did eventually marry Serena . . . even after Monica boldly went to the church just minutes before the ceremony to finally admit to him that she loved him. The happily ever after she wished for did not happen.

By then she had lost him and she left him alone to be happy with his wife—his *choice*.

Serena's anger at her was misplaced but Monica had zero fucks to give about setting the woman straight. "Fuck her," she muttered, releasing a heavy breath as she stepped onto the elevator.

Monica felt sweet relief when the doors closed behind her. Licking her lips, she pressed the button for the lobby before she used her other hand to squeeze the bridge of her nose. She remembered the night they were trapped on this very same elevator together and the words he said to her.

"I care for my wife. I do. But you can only love one person at a time and I try to deny it but deep down I knew you were the one I loved. I shouldn't have married her. I shouldn't have hurt her . . . or you."

After weeks of him ignoring her at work. After kissing her with all of the passion and conflict he felt for still loving her even as he was married to another woman.

"I fucked up. I thought I was over you. I really thought I could make this marriage with Serena work. This drama. This bullshit. This triangle shit ain't me. I fucked up."

Monica shook her head as she pressed away at the lobby button like it would make the trip down any faster.

If Cameron thought she was going to sit and wait like a duck while he huddled up in his office with his *wife* cooperating in all of that drama and bullshit he claimed wasn't him, then his ass was certifiably crazy. "Never that," she said aloud as the elevator slid to a stop and the doors opened to set her free. Love was hard enough—risky enough—without an extra person floating all through a relationship.

She couldn't get out of that building fast enough, but she couldn't run. She didn't want to attract any attention—she did have an image to maintain. The pounding of her heart and her heels against the pavement of the streets didn't stop until she finally slid behind the wheel of her used Toyota Camry that had seen better days when her mother used to drive it.

Monica reached inside her purse and pulled out her cell phone. She pressed number four on her speed dial. After her mother, her father, and her man, her three best friends filled the next spots. The six most important people in her life.

The phone rang twice before Danielle answered. "Hello, Alizé," she said, using Monica's nickname from high school. Danielle's nickname was Cristal, Latoya's was Moët, and Keesha's was "Dom" Perignon. The nineties and their fascination with The Notorious B.I.G. had them all the way fucked up.

"You off from work?" Monica asked, as she let her head fall back against the cloth headrest.

The line went quiet for a few ticks before she said, "Yes."

Monica made a face. "What's wrong with you?" she asked, her Newark accent suddenly heavy and pronounced.

"Does it matter?" Danielle asked, almost sounding like she sighed. "Because I can tell something is wrong with you."

Monica sat up straight in the driver's seat. "Yes. I just left Cameron upstairs in his office with his wife. And do you know he asked me to leave? I was so ashamed strolling out of there trying to pretend my ass was cute and confident."

"What exactly do you think is going on in that office?" Danielle asked, crossing the t's and dotting the i's with her pronunciation as always.

Monica shrugged and hated how helpless she felt as she looked through the lightly tinted windshield at the summer skies above. She tasted her lip gloss as she bit her lips. "I don't think they're fucking or nothing," she finally answered her friend.

"You sure?" Danielle asked.

Monica froze as she pressed her cell phone closer to her ear. She heard some inflection in her tone and she couldn't put her finger on what it was. Sarcasm? Doubt? Mocking?

"I am glad you called actually because I really would like my Yves Saint Laurent dress back that you borrowed," Danielle slid in, her voice sounding slightly breathy.

Monica frowned again. "Did you just change the subject?" she snapped.

"Yes, I did because you are holding it hostage," Danielle returned smoothly.

Monica didn't want to talk about a dress when she was in the midst of a personal mini-storm and needed Danielle to play her role in the friendship. Monica was clear that she was the friend to call to party. Keesha stayed ready to jump in and fight if called on. Latoya was all over prayers and church. And Danielle was the go-to girl for advice. Period. Point blank.

But this bitch tripping.

"Damn, you're acting up about a dress?"

"Same way you keep telling me about that money Dom owes you. That dress cost me way more than three hundred dollars, Ze."

Monica arched a brow. "I'm in grad school. I need my money!" she retorted.

Danielle did sigh this time and it was loud and clear on the phone. "Ze, you need to talk to Cameron about what you expect from him. His obligation was to his wife and he decided to move on from that. Your obligation is to yourself and you can never move on from that. Fuck stressing about something you cannot change and focus on what you can . . . like moving on if it is not moving right."

Monica felt relief at the return of the friend she was looking for in the first place. And she knew Danielle was right. She couldn't control Cameron or Serena and it was *their* marriage that *they* had to end.

But I have total control over me and what the fuck I do about my role in this bullshit.

"Oh and put my dress in the cleaners and then in my closet. Seriously, Alizé."

Click.

"I will . . . as soon as I find it," Monica mumbled, dropping her cell phone on the passenger seat before she slid her key in the ignition and started her car. The entire vehicle rumbled to life and shook for a few moments before it idled down.

Suddenly the sound of "Need U Bad" by Jazmine Sullivan filled the car. Monica didn't bother to pick up her cell because she knew it was Cameron. She fully intended to give him a night in his bed alone so he would regret escorting her out of his office; and she would take the time to mull over the advice of her friend.

"Fuck stressing about something you cannot change and focus on what you can . . . like moving on if it is not moving right."

That was easier said than done.

Chapter 2
Keesha a.k.a.
"Dom" Perignon

"That's some real bullshit that you keeping my grand-baby from me."

Keesha Lands shook a cigarette out of her soft pack of Newports and lit it with her lighter. She cut her eyes over at her mother, Diane, as she took a deep inhale that was nothing like the shit she used to put into her body. Nothing at all.

She knew she was lucky to be alive. Lucky and blessed.

"So you trust Kimani around some man you just met and not me, Dom?" Diane asked, leaning against the kitchen counter in her two-bedroom apartment.

"Not some man. My father," Keesha said with emphasis, swallowing back the fresh hurt she felt that her mother played "Eenie, Meenie, Miney, Mo" with choosing a man to call her father. She went for the one with more money. Too bad that loser started to love using the drugs he was supposed to be selling. "And you know why I just met him, Diane."

Her mother—who raised her like more of a friend than anything—shifted her eyes away for a moment. Keesha had to admit she was glad for some show of guilt. Some show that the woman standing before her wasn't heartless. Some show that she gave a fuck about what she did.

Maybe the counseling is working.

"You still don't know that motherfucker," Diane spat, walking over to take the pack of Newports from Keesha's hand to ease out a cigarette. She tossed the pack in Keesha's lap and took her lit cigarette to light the tip of her own.

Keesha smirked a little and bit her bottom lip to keep from snapping at her mother. After she overdosed and went into rehab, she was freed from her abuse of heroin and weed; but the weekly counseling sessions that followed freed her from her demons. All of the shit that made getting high feel real necessary. Deaths. Lies. Betrayals. Fears. Angers. Guilt. Shame.

She thought about the release she received from writing in her journals. At first she laughed at her therapist but in time she felt like there wasn't enough ink in her pens to pour out everything she was feeling and had ever felt about her life. A love of writing was created and flourished in a place in her heart and soul where anger and hate had once dwelled.

There were times when Ms. Hardcore "I don't give a fuck" Keesha Lands would soak the words with her tears. It was a hard pill to realize and admit that you were fucked up—especially when your mother drove the car to Fuckville.

Her mother suddenly pushed up off the counter and left the kitchen to walk into her living room. Keesha's brows furrowed but she stayed seated at the kitchen table—a table that was too big and too costly for an apartment in a low-income high-rise building. But that's how her mother's mind worked; enjoying cheap rent to afford expensive things to go in it. Just ass backwards.

She shifted her dark brown eyes out the window on the

far side of the kitchen, just seeing the tips of trees and the black coil of electrical wires breaking up the blue of the sky. She took a deep breath as the urge to sit in a window-sill with her computer and write filled her.

A few months back she decided to try her hand at writing fiction. She couldn't lie—it felt good to get lost in creating a world full of characters. It was her new high. There was a quote she saw online: *"You must stay drunk on writing so reality cannot destroy you."* She thought that was the realest thing ever.

Keesha sat up straight at the faint smell of kush. The scent intensified as her mother strolled back into the kitchen. She looked over her shoulder and then shook her head slowly at the sight of her mother smoking a blunt. There was a time they smoked together; but that was before Keesha got clean. Got wise. Grew the hell up.

It was clear her mother had some catching up to do.

Keesha waved away the thick silver smoke of weed as she shook her head and let her regrets settle heavily on her shoulders. "I can't be around that," she said, rising to stand up on her heels.

Diane shrugged as she pressed her lips to the end of the blunt and inhaled. "You ODed on dope, not weed," she said as she held the smoke in her chest.

For a few long moments Keesha just stood there and watched the woman who birthed her as she extended her arm and pointed the blunt at her. Offering it to her. Offering her own daughter a one way trip back into her addiction.

And the pain of that stung like a hot blade piercing her heart.

Keesha stepped back from the blunt and held her breath to keep from even inhaling any of the smoke drifting up from the red fiery tip. She didn't want to have it in her. Affecting her. Placating her. Fucking her up. Fucking her world up.

She didn't want to love it anymore and she knew she would. She would love it more than she loved herself. *I'm out.*

Grabbing her tote she slipped it onto the crook of her arm and slid on her shades before she turned and headed out the kitchen.

"Are you coming to our session next week?" Diane asked, her voice slightly tinged with something—sarcasm, mocking, patronizing. Something.

Keesha bit her bottom lip as she stopped in the doorway and turned. "I needed the sessions because I overdosed. Because I'm an addict. Because I'm trying not to be fucked up in the head by a mother who never wanted to be a mother. A mother who is vindictive and mean as twelve hells. Unsupportive and childish—"

"You ungrateful bitch!" Diane roared, taking three large steps. She knocked over the chair Keesha had sat in to now reach her.

Keesha slid her shades up atop her short, choppy hairdo. "The limb don't fall too far from the tree," she told her calmly, their eyes locked.

So many emotions flickered in Diane's dark brown eyes before she frowned and then sneered as she deliberately raised the blunt, inhaled from it, and then blew the thick stream of smoke into Keesha's face.

She reached out and snatched the blunt from her mother's hand and reached past her to throw it into the sink of foamy dishwater. The hiss of the fire being extinguished sounded off just as Diane slapped Keesha soundly.

WHAP!

The room was quiet. Even Diane looked taken aback by her action.

Keesha's eyes flared as her cheek and heart stung with

pain. She defeated the urge to fight her own mother—to literally whip her mother's ass like she was a stranger—as the tears she fought fell quickly like they were running a race to the end of her face.

"Same shit. Different day," she said softly before she turned and walked down the short hall to the metal front door.

"Keesha. Get back here right—"

SLAM!

The shutting of the door behind her cut off the rest of her mother's words. She allowed herself one quick moment to take a deep breath and lean back against the door. But just one moment.

She didn't have any more to waste on her mother.

＊　　＊　　＊

"But you put on quite a show, really had me going . . ."

Keesha sat up straight in the bed, her heart pounding from being awakened by the sudden shrill of her "Take a Bow" ringtone. The chill of the room from the window air conditioning unit caused her bared nipples to harden. Shivering a little bit she looked down at her boyfriend, Corey, still sleeping peacefully beside her. There was just enough illumination from the streetlight outside the window to keep the small bedroom from being dark as a cave.

"Shit," Keesha swore, flinging back the covers to rush from the bed naked and cross the hardwood floors. She dug her cell phone out of her tote. "Hello," she whispered.

"Thank God you are alive."

Danielle.

Keesha rolled her eyes as she left the bedroom and walked into the small living room and dinette area of Corey's apartment. "Yes, but not asleep anymore," she stressed, frowning at the drastic shift of temperature.

Corey only had an A/C unit in his bedroom. The rest of

the apartment felt like the devil's resting place. Summers in the city were brutal. Life outside the sweet coolness of Corey's bedroom felt twice as bad.

"Well now we both can sleep since I know you are okay," Danielle said in her soft and husky voice without a hint of that unmistakable East Coast inflection in her voice.

Monica and Latoya were the friends in the group who were college educated but Cristal was the one who crossed every "t" and dotted every "i" in her pronunciation. It was like she was trying to prove that she wasn't ignorant but it all just came off like she was. It was really rare to catch her using slang—and that was way before she moved out of the hood and into that high saddity apartment building near Livingston, New Jersey.

"No, me and Corey turned in early," Keesha said, her eyes darting over to the kitchenette at the sound of something rattling under the cover of darkness. Corey's apartment was neat enough but the entire building was home to a mouse-and-roach brigade that didn't give zero fucks about the people who actually paid the rent.

"Listen, I was waiting up to talk to you about something," Danielle said.

Keesha picked up one of Corey's shoes from where he kicked them off by the sofa and then flung it like a Frisbee toward the kitchen.

THUD.

It bounced off the wall but at least the rustling stopped.

"Listen, I hate to get in your business—"

"*But,*" Keesha stressed playfully, dropping her slender nude figure on the sofa as she used a *Vibe* magazine to fan away a little of the heat.

"I'm proud of you for giving up stripping and working at Kimani's day care but it might be time to think about another job—"

Keesha's mocha shoulders squared up and her heart rhythm went askew for a second. "I know I've been late with my share of the rent, Danielle," she said, hating the wave of embarrassment she felt.

Being broke and feeling like she could never get her head above water financially was a hard pill to swallow. Kimani's father had hustled hard and by any means necessary to make sure she kept money in her pocket and the nicest clothes on their backs.

And then he was killed in a car accident. That broke her heart and her bankroll.

She stripped for a long time and the money was good but the lifestyle was a horrible choice for someone dealing with addiction and wanting to be a better mother to her child.

And so she slid off the pole after she overdosed and went into rehab.

Working as an aide at a day-care center, making just a little better than minimum wage, wasn't cutting it—especially tackling one third of the four-figure rent.

"Keesha, you still owe me part of last month's rent, the finance company called about your car note being late, and you owe Monica money that I am tired of hearing about—"

"So y'all sitting up talking 'bout me?" she asked, her anger and embarrassment coming in a heated rush that made the cheeks of her ass and her face warm.

Cristal sighed. "No, Keesha," she answered simply.

"I can't fucking tell," she snapped, jumping to her feet as the urge to smoke a cigarette nipped at her. Truth was it took setting aside every last bit of her pride to borrow money from Monica . . . especially when they just got over the fact that during her drug haze Keesha had committed the ultimate betrayal of a friend and slept with Monica's boyfriend, Rah. Her drug use and dealing—or rather not properly dealing—with the sudden death of Lex, the man she loved, led her to that short-dick, short-tempered mother-fucker. Top that off with snitching on her friend about fucking around on him, getting caught in bed with him, and then being too high to stop him from beating Monica's ass and breaking her leg. Crazy.

They were friends again but she just knew Monica had to take some pleasure in the same bitch who betrayed her now needing to borrow money from her. Keesha could admit she knew she was wrong to even ask Monica for a favor. But desperate times . . .

"You are taking this the wrong way, Keesha—"

Still naked, and not caring that she was, Keesha moved to sit in the windowsill. Corey's apartment was across the street from a deserted parking lot and there wasn't much traffic. She really didn't give a fuck either way. She needed to see more than just the four walls of his apartment be-cause it felt like they were closing in on her.

"I'll have your rent money and you can tell Monica she'll have the money I owe her too. Now you two go talk about that," she snapped, ending the call and looking over her shoulder to toss her phone onto the sofa.

"You owe somebody money?" Corey asked, strolling out of the bedroom naked.

Keesha shrugged as her eyes dipped to take in the back-and-forth sway of his dick. She glanced away as she spot-ted a roach paused on the wall like Spider-Man. She fought the urge to stretch her leg out and smash it under her foot. Having grown up in the projects of Newark, New Jersey, it wasn't the first roach she'd ever seen and she doubted if it would be the last. Still, for that motherfucker to be so bold to climb within her reach like it dared her to kill it?

"Why didn't you ask me for the money?"

Because you barely make enough to pay your own bills.

Because I relied on a man for money and he died, leaving me back at one.

Because I hate being broke, busted, and disgusted.

"I'm good, Corey," she lied.

He worked hard and put in forty to fifty hours a week. He always had her back. He was a good man. A hardworking man. She didn't want to put extra pressure on him to make up for her fucked up finances.

The old Keesha couldn't imagine being in a relationship with a man who couldn't take care of her and that's how she knew she had grown up some. And that she loved him.

Keesha looked back at him and she smiled at him, loving every bit of his dark and delicious frame. Like hers, his complexion was that deep and smooth chocolate like Hershey's Kisses. He was just a couple of inches taller than her but she felt comfort and strength in his embraces. His smile was infectious and his eyes always bright with humor.

She loved him. She really did. Her heart pounded with it.

"We'll worry about all that in the morning," Corey said, coming over to stand beside her and stroke her inner thigh. "Let's go back to bed."

Keesha tilted her head back against the window as she looked up into his face. She smiled at the heat she saw in his eyes. Licking her lips, she turned on the sill and pressed her feet and her hands to the edge as she spread her knees before him.

Corey's eyes dipped down as he took his dick into one of his hands and stroked the long length of it. He massaged her moist clit with the other. "Right here?" he asked, looking up briefly at the backdrop of the streets through the window as Keesha leaned forward to lick one of his nipples with the tip of her tongue.

"Right now."

Chapter 3
Latoya a.k.a. Moët

"*Latoya, I'm sorry but your little friends ain't on the same Christian path as you and it's time to leave them behind.*"

Those were words Latoya James wished her fiancé, Taquan, had never let leave his lips or even enter his thoughts. But he did. Hours earlier he dropped all of that weight on her shoulders as they strolled out of church after Bible study.

Humph, I'm trying to get filled up with the Lord and he disturbed my spirit with foolishness. Negro, please.

But his words were still on her mind and keeping her from sleep.

She kicked the sheet off her legs and sat up on the edge of the bed, running her slender fingers through her scalp to the trimmed ends of her shoulder-length hair. The walls of the stylishly decorated bedroom felt like they were closing in on her. She glanced at the clock.

It was almost four in the morning.

"Dammit," she swore and then waved her hands in frustration at herself for swearing.

No one ever said being saved was easy.

And Latoya should know. After years of growing up in a family with very strict religious beliefs she had learned early to play across the line separating sinning and being saved. For years she lived a double life of the good daughter for her parents and the wild child with her friends—and that was long after she was supposedly grown and should've been able to stand in the shoes of the woman she wanted to be. If anything, all of the lying and sneaking pushed her so far over the edge of sinning and away from her church upbringing that she felt lost to the woman in the mirror.

And her sins were many.

Losing her virginity in her teens and carrying on a secret affair with the minister of the church . . . *in* the church.

And that was just the beginning of it all. It was a very slippery slope when nothing mattered but what you wanted.

Lying and sneaking.

Abortions.

Secret boyfriends.

Falsely accusing the father of her child of rape.

And then selling false stories about the platinum-selling rap star to the tabloids to ensure he backed off his fight to snatch custody of their daughter away from her.

Purposefully trying to seduce Taquan to break his vow of celibacy during the first weeks of their relationship had been the act to make her check herself and fall on her knees before the altar. She had sworn in that moment to forge a closer relationship with God and to live by His word.

Latoya glanced over her shoulder to make sure her one-year-old daughter, Tiffany, was still asleep in her mahogany crib. Looking at the way her daughter pouted her heart-shaped mouth even in her sleep, brought a soft smile to her lips as she left the room and walked down the hall to the spacious living room of the apartment she shared with Danielle and Keesha.

Everything about the apartment spoke of comfort and luxury. Hardwood floors. High ceilings. Plush furnishings. Style. Substance. Completely away from any of their lives growing up in Newark.

And completely out of any of our budgets.

There was a hefty rent to go along with it. *No wonder Danielle used to run through men like they were her personal ATMs. How else could she afford the rent alone?*

Latoya felt guilty at the judgment she cast on her friend. Judgment fed by the man she loved. And too much pillow talk about her friends had fed his dislike of them. And all the pillow talk had been easy because they needed to fill the gap left by their celibacy.

But she hadn't laid out all of her own secrets to him and had no plans to do so.

Latoya grimaced as she made her way to the kitchen, opening the glass-front refrigerator to pull out a bottle of water. The coolness of the liquid felt good going down her throat as the heat of her dilemma burned her stomach. She turned and leaned back against the small granite-topped island as she looked down at her engagement ring.

Taquan was going to be her husband. The head of their family. And his role as a husband could not be denied. It was clearly written in The Word: *Wives, submit to your own husbands, as to the Lord.*

But her friends had been there through it all. Loving her. Helping to heal her. Making sure they had her back when she felt left behind by everyone and anything else. They were in the delivery room with her during her labor. Not even her parents, who chose to believe the lies of their minister over her truths about his sexual relationship with her. Her friends had never forsaken her. Never. And now she was supposed to present them her back and shun them because they weren't saved?

"Be not deceived: bad company corrupts good morals."

Taquan loved to quote that verse to her. He felt it was the backbone of his argument. She couldn't lie; it was a good one. Who could dispute the Bible? The Word? Their salvation?

Finishing her water, she quietly moved throughout the darkness of the apartment to her bedroom. Tiffany was awake and softly whispering baby talk to herself as she bent her legs to play with her chubby toes.

Latoya smiled as she walked around the bed to look down into her daughter's crib.

"Ma-Ma," she said, sounding like she missed her and was tickled pink for her return.

Latoya's heart swelled with love as she leaned over and pressed her lips against a chubby cheek. "Why are you up, Tiffy-Boo?" she asked, reaching down to quickly check if her diaper was wet.

Tiffany giggled as she reached up to lightly pat her mother's cheek. "Ma-Ma-Ma-Ma-Ma-Ma."

Brrrnnnggg . . .

Latoya was startled by the sudden ringing of her cell phone. Her heart raced and pounded as she moved back around the bed to pick it up from the nightstand. She had several missed calls and a few texts from Taquan. "No wonder my baby woke up," she said, pressing the button to answer the call. "Hey Taq—"

"Come downstairs."

Click.

Latoya frowned at her fiancé's abruptness as she tossed the phone on the bed, pulled her pale pink robe over her nightie and then moved to scoop Tiffany up into her arms. Thankfully, her little one snuggled her head against Latoya's shoulder and she knew it wouldn't be long before she was back asleep. "Thank God," she mouthed, rubbing comforting circles onto her daughter's back.

She came to the double doors of Danielle's master suite at the end of the hall. She knocked twice softly before opening the door and saying a prayer that Danielle didn't have company. Their friend was on a man sabbatical but . . .

Latoya felt relief that she was snuggled in the middle of her queen-sized bed alone.

"Someone *better* be dead."

Latoya paused on her path to Danielle's bedside at the sound of the muffled words. She was a light sleeper. Like her behind was afraid she was going to miss something while she dozed.

"Let your goddaughter sleep with you," Latoya whispered, coming to stand by the opposite side of the bed.

Danielle lifted her silk scarf-covered head from her pillow and lifted one corner of her black satin eye mask as she looked over her shoulder. "She has two other godmothers," she drawled playfully, her voice filled with sleep.

"But you're her favorite," Latoya said smoothly, already pulling back the crisp thousand-count sheets to ease her gently snoring daughter onto the bed.

"Bitch, please," Danielle said in disbelief as she rolled over onto her side on the bed and gently shooed Latoya's hands away as she pulled the sheets up to cover Tiffany's plump frame. She took over massaging circles onto Tiffany's back, sending her deeper and deeper into sleep. "You are so full of shit."

Although she knew Danielle was joking, Latoya still bristled at the use of profanity. The old Latoya who played it loose with her salvation wouldn't have cared, but the woman of God she was now had asked her friends several times to refrain from all the cussing and carrying on around her.

She bit her bottom lip to literally keep from reminding Danielle about it, especially around Tiffany. There were many times just in the last few weeks that she found herself cringing in her friends' company.

Just before she left the room, Latoya gave her daughter and Danielle one last glance over her shoulder. She moved down the hall and through the living room to leave the apartment. Her slipper-covered feet slapping against the hardwood floors echoed in the quiet of the long hall to the elevator.

Latoya's curiosity over Taquan's sudden late-night appearance was piqued. It wasn't like him to be out and about that time of the night and if he made the drive to Livingston she knew it was more than a desire to see her smiling face. These days they barely kissed heavily because they were afraid they would slip back to the days they would masturbate in front of each other.

The image of Taquan jacking off as she lay in the middle of the bed pressing a vibrator against her clit flashed. Latoya swallowed over a lump in her throat and fanned herself a bit as she forced the temptation away.

Ding.

"No sex until marriage. No sex until marriage," she repeated softly to herself as the doors to the elevator slid open. She stepped forward.

"Fuck me harder, Frank."

"Fuck back, Mindy."

Latoya moved backwards with her eyes wide and her mouth even wider at the sight of a young blond woman bent over with her dress wrapped around her waist getting furiously filled with the dick of the man standing behind her. The smell of their sex and the sounds of their moans were in the air. Their motion was steady and fast. Each thrust sent his long reddish balls and her breasts swinging back and forth. The smack of flesh echoed like claps.

Whap-whap-whap . . .

Frank was killing it and they didn't even see Latoya standing there. Shocked by them. Watching them. Turned on by them. It felt like she was at the taping of a bad porno flick.

Latoya's heart pounded . . . and so did her clit. She gasped in surprise at herself getting aroused. Frank and the nameless blonde both looked over at her but they didn't stop. Or look away. He bit his sweaty lip and pounded away harder.

Whap-whap-whap-whap-whap-whap . . .

Latoya was grateful when the elevators doors finally closed and the freaky moment came to an end. "Sweet Jesus," she sighed, finally feeling like her feet were unglued from the spot in which she stood.

Truth be told, Latoya's biggest fight with her spirituality was her celibacy. It was hard listening to the girls talk about their sexual adventures when she was clutching nothing but her Bible at night.

"Girl, Corey put it down last night."

"Cameron ate the pussy so good I passed out."

Big dick this.

Hard dick that.

Dick. Dick. Dick. Dick.

Here a dick. There a dick. Everywhere a dick dick.

Latoya sighed in frustration as she turned and fled for the stairwell, her robe fluttering out behind her like a cape as she descended the steps. Floor after floor after floor. She never stopped. Never even paused. By the time she jerked open the door to the lobby her heart was pounding so hard that she felt like it was punching to free itself from her chest.

Latoya could see through the wide glass doors that Taquan was parked outside the building. She slowed her steps and forced herself to calm down as she walked across the tiled floor, left the building, and climbed into the passenger seat of Taquan's black SUV.

His caramel handsome face instantly filled with disapproval. "You're roaming the building in your nightclothes?" he asked. "That's not appropriate, Toya."

Her eyes flittered over the sweatsuit he wore. The lights from the overhang of the apartment lit the cross dangling from the end of his gold chain.

She thought of the interlude she witnessed in the elevator and she was filled with guilt because in that moment she wished it was her getting chopped down. She missed sex. She missed masturbation to relieve the pressure of not having sex. It didn't help that she knew Taquan was blessed.

Her eyes dipped down to his crotch and she could just make out the imprint of his penis against the top of his thigh.

Here a dick. There a dick. Everywhere a dick dick.

"Father, forgive me," she mouthed quietly, shifting her eyes back up to his face.

"I've been thinking about what we talked about earlier," he began.

"Me too," she admitted.

"I realized I was asking too much of you without offering a real solution to the problem," he said, reaching over to stroke the back of her hand.

Latoya's brow wrinkled a bit in confusion.

"You live with your friends and it just doesn't make sense for you to distance yourself while you're still living under the same roof as them—"

"I'm not moving back in with my parents," she protested. "I mean, we're cool now, but I am *never*—"

"Latoya."

"I guess I could get my own place," she said, as if thinking aloud to herself.

"Marry me."

"I would have to find a place, buy furniture, be ready to take on a household of bills—"

Taquan reached up and lightly grasped her chin, turning her head towards him. "Marry. Me," he repeated with emphasis.

Latoya frowned. "We're already engaged," she said, raising her hand to show him the engagement ring on her left hand.

He shook his head as he leaned forward to taste her lips. "No, marry me now. I don't want to wait for the big wedding next year. I want you as my wife and in my life now. And then you and Tiffany can move in with me."

Latoya's eyes widened a bit and her mouth felt dry until she drew her tongue against it.

"We'll get the license and go to the courthouse after the waiting period and then we'll start our lives together," Taquan said, his eyes locked on hers.

Latoya bit her bottom lip. She let the truth of her feelings settle. *In two or three days I can be married and living with this man . . . and having all the sex I want.*

"We can still have the big ceremony later on if that's stopping you," he added.

She felt all the love she had for him as she smiled and nodded, leaning forward to cover his lips with her own before she traced the outline of his mouth with her tongue. She felt the tremble race over his body. She wanted to know what other reactions she could evoke from him. She wanted to deepen their love.

She wanted him deeply inside of her.

As they both moaned in pleasure and brought their hands up to wrap around each other's body, Latoya pushed aside the elephant in the car. Her soon-to-be husband was so serious about ending her relationship with three women she knew since high school that he just moved their wedding date up. His insistence for the ties to be cut would know no end and she still didn't know if she was prepared to do that.

Chapter 4
Danielle a.k.a. Cristal

"It's really a shame how you are letting good pussy go to waste."

Danielle Johnson shifted her slanted eyes from the message pad she was filling out to find Carolyn Ingram standing in front of her receptionist desk in the grand lobby of the offices of Lowe, Ingram, and Banks. She stiffened her back as she set down her pen and met the woman's leering gaze. Danielle felt herself cringe. "No, the shame would be your husband finding out his socialite wife is nothing more than a coke-sniffing dyke who could care less about his dick going to waste," she finally countered, not caring one bit that the woman was the wife of one of the founding partners of one of the largest law firms on the East Coast.

Months ago, Cristal had let her ambition of becoming more than just a foster kid from Newark with champagne dreams and Kool-Aid money lead her into becoming the protégé of the socialite. In time she discovered the woman's true intentions were not to groom her and introduce her to society.

Most definitely not, Danielle thought, shivering a little at the memory of Carolyn trying to finger-fuck her during a vacay in the Hamptons. She refused to remember the rest of the fuckery that went down that night and didn't care to even imagine what else occurred after she fled the estate.

Only Carolyn's fear of being outed to her wealthy and generous husband kept her from causing a stink about Danielle still working at the firm. Still, Danielle was sick of the snide comments and leers whenever they encountered one another.

Carolyn Ingram could pretty much buy anything in the world she wanted except for Danielle's pussy and she hated that.

"It's really a shame you have such a smart mouth when you're so fucking stupid," Carolyn hissed, leaning in close so that her words were low and just for Danielle's ears. "With my connections and your looks I could have made you into something."

Danielle arched a well-shaped brow.

"And we both know you want that more than anything, don't we?" Carolyn offered, the tip of her tongue darting out to touch the middle of her bottom lip lightly before disappearing again. "Little sad poor kid with no parents, raised in foster care, no education past high school but speaks proper English like you sipped from Shakespeare's cup, fucking celebrities and athletes to help pay for that lovely little apartment in Livingston."

Danielle's surprise was evident. Her anger came quickly after that. "You're stalking me?" she asked, her heart pounding.

Carolyn straightened her rail-thin frame and smoothed her hands over her bob even though a hair wasn't out of place. "Research, bitch. Just research."

The elevator doors opened behind them and Carolyn's face became distant and composed. "Please tell my husband I'm here to see him," she said, looking down her nose at Danielle from where she stood.

She picked up the phone as a trio of paralegals breezed

past her desk. She dialed the extension directly into Mr. Ingram's office. "Sir, your wife—"

Click.

A perfectly red lacquered nail ended the call.

Danielle looked up at the older woman in irritation.

"You have a face that should be on television, sweetheart," she said earnestly, her eyes glistening bright enough to put her sobriety in question.

Danielle jerked her head back when the woman raised her hand from the phone and quickly traced her jawline. "Don't put your pussy-smelling finger in my face again or I will snap your bony ass in two."

Carolyn flung her head back and just laughed.

Danielle knew right then the bitch was high. Quickly she picked up the phone and dialed Mr. Ingram's extension again. "Yes, sir. Your wife is on her way back," she said quickly, wanting the hag gone from out of her face and her life.

Click.

This time Mr. Ingram ended the call and Danielle just leaned back in her chair as she waved her hand toward the door leading to the inner offices. Carolyn just chuckled as she hitched her Birkin up onto the crook of her slender arm and walked away.

Danielle felt sweet relief flood her. She was so sick of these little interactions and interludes with the woman. Either she was tearing Danielle down with slurs or raving about her looks. Just crazy.

Bzzzzzzzz.

Rolling back in her chair she reached down to pull her cell from her purse on the floor. She checked her caller ID. She gasped in surprise as pleasure filled her. "Mohammed?" she asked herself quietly.

She hadn't talked to her ex in weeks. More than weeks. Trying to climb the social ladder on Carolyn's Hermès wings had caused major friction between Mohammed and her. Major. It weakened a bond she thought couldn't be broken after she chose her love for him over her love of the money of a wealthy man. Choosing to put some focus on herself and stepping away from their intense relationship had been the hardest and most grown-up decision she had made in all of her twenty some-odd years. Still, it didn't mean she no longer loved and missed him. And wanted him.

Even though he still worked as the handyman for the apartment building where she lived, she barely saw the sexy dreadlocked man who turned her on with his Jamaican lilt and rock-hard body.

Bzzzzzzzz.

She hit the button to send the call to voice mail and then quickly sent him a text with trembling fingers:

AT WORK. CAN'T TALK RIGHT NOW.
CALL YOU ON MY BREAK.

Danielle held the cell phone in her hand even as she answered and transferred three work calls.

Bzzzzzzzz.

A deliveryman walked up to her desk and she held up her hand with a polite smile as she opened the incoming text with her hand under her desk.

Really need 2 talk 2 U. Stop by my
house after work?

Danielle's pulse sped as she stared at the words.
Talk to me about what?
What could he want?
Should I go?

*We both have moved on and so much time has passed.
Why revisit any part of it?*

"Ma'am?"

Danielle looked up at the deliveryman, her eyes and
smile contrite. "I apologize," she said, rising on her Jimmy
Choo pointy-toe kitten heels—the same ones she saw
Michelle Obama wearing on television. She figured those
weren't a bad pair of shoes to walk in at all if her husband
succeeded in November in becoming the first African-
American president of the United States of America.

She signed for the documents, completely ignoring the
way his eyes were enjoying the fit of her sleeveless bright
red shell dress on her curves. Danielle had nothing for him
but a polite smile as she e-mailed the secretary of the attorney about his delivery.

As the receptionist for the firm, Danielle barely ever left
her desk in the front office. Although she was constantly
active, it all felt like mindless busy work. She wanted more.

Bzzzzzzzzz.

Danielle picked up her cell phone again but then sat it
facedown on her desk at the sight of Monica's office number. She immediately felt tension radiate across her shoulders and neck. She honestly didn't know how much more
she could stand.

Monica and Keesha were both tearing up her phone
bitching about the other one. Latoya had jumped up and
married Taquan yesterday without inviting anyone to their
courthouse ceremony and then announced she was moving out. Monica was ticked at her for revealing to Keesha
that they discussed the loan and Danielle wasn't particularly happy about Monica finally returning her dress . . .
complete with a torn hem.

Keesha stayed whining about money.

Latoya was steady trying to covertly change them to be more like her.

Monica kept her phone ringing with her Cameron drama—real or imagined.

And Danielle? Danielle was tired of it all.

She was the ear to listen and the shoulder to cry on in their friendships; so much so that she rarely had a chance to sing her own sad song. And it was hard to always absorb everyone else's drama and energy and never get a chance to get hers off. Somehow the one in their midst without a mother had become the mother figure.

Danielle looked down at her cell phone again and she felt one of those sad smiles filled with regret touch her lips. There was no need to answer their calls or even call them to ask what to do about meeting Mohammed later; their conversations would just turn around to their issues and she would be left again to help them maneuver and think through their problems while grappling with her own alone.

* * *

Hours later as her workday ended, Danielle was still thinking over how unsatisfied she was in her life. Her friendships. Her job. Her lack of family. Her lack of a life. Period.

Everybody had somebody they could turn to—even Keesha had her crazy, inappropriate-ass, weed-smoking mama. And that made it harder for her not to run back to Mohammed or any of the other men she used to catalog in an address book complete with their photo, financial status, and dick game rating.

No one understood, and she honestly didn't try to reveal to anyone, just how lonely she was. How lonely she had always been. How she had lived the majority of her life disappointed, hurt, and too afraid to expect and want more.

Being left behind by parents had a way of fucking someone up like that, but the years in foster care taught her how to hide it because seeing pity in the eyes of people looking at you made everything much worse.

And so her friends neglected her feelings, her life, and her own issues and Danielle hid it all well. Still, shit had been brewing inside her for a minute. A lot of shit.

She leaned back in her chair and released a heavy breath filled with a lot of that shit. Allowing herself a ten count to hold back some "cry myself a river, I'm so fucking sad" tears, Danielle took her compact from her tote to smooth her asymmetrical bob and reapply a fresh coat of sheer pink MAC gloss to her lips. Next she slid on her jet-black oversized shades and stiffened her back as she rose to her feet with her tote now in the crook of her arm.

She could have appeared to be Carolyn Ingram or any of her contemporaries as she made her way down on the elevator and out the building to her parked car. It was all a façade. Just as forged as the role of perfect wife that Carolyn played.

Behind the wheel of her car, Danielle purposefully played the music loudly as she drove. The bass reverberated in her chest. She was trying to drown out her thoughts. Her doubts. Her concerns. Her second-guessing . . .

Danielle parked her car onto the driveway behind Mohammed's battered Jeep. She eyed his house as she eased out from the car to head to the steps of his small house, nervously playing with her keys in her hand. Her body was all nerves, racing pulse, and pounding heart as she crossed the porch and knocked on the door.

There was a time I had keys to this motherfucker, she thought, taking one step back and looking around at the row of small houses and three-family apartment buildings on the quiet street.

Everything about this neighborhood screamed normalcy: working forty hours a week to live a decent life in a decent neighborhood.

"Danielle?"

She turned around and there he stood. In nothing but a pair of jeans slung low on his hips. Her ex. Mohammed Ahmed.

Danielle's eyes ate him up from the thin, black, shoulder-length dreadlocks down to his bare feet and every damn thing in between. Broad shoulders. Hard chest. Six pack abs. "I-I-I got your text," she stammered, feeling completely overwhelmed by being in his presence again.

There was a time this man—this fine man—was her everything and too much of anything wasn't good.

Mohammed nodded in understanding but he still stood there blocking her entrance into his world. "When you never responded I just assumed you said 'Fuck him' and wasn't coming."

Danielle continued playing with the keys in her hand, wishing she hadn't lost control of her body to her nerves. "I just got busy at work," she lied, taking a deliberate step forward with her eyebrow slightly arched. *Am I in or out?*

Mohammed smiled just a little at the corner of his full mouth before he stepped back and waved her inside. "You want something to drink?" he asked, his Jamaican accent light but still evident.

Danielle shook her head as she turned a full three hundred sixty degrees with her eyes, taking in the rows of boxes and covered furniture. She whirled to face him, her eyes filled with the surprise she felt. "You're moving?" she asked, pointing behind her to the boxes.

Mohammed nodded and licked his bottom lip as he slid his hands into the front pockets of his jeans. "My mom is not well and I'm going back to Jamaica," he said, shifting his eyes up from the floor to fix them on her.

Danielle swung her eyes away from his as she locked her knees and fought not to show him her bitter disappointment. "I hope it's nothing too serious with your mother," she said, barely able to get the words past the tightness she felt in her throat.

The end of a relationship was always easier to swallow for the one who leaves the relationship over the one who gets left. In her heart there had been some assurance because Mohammed was there, easy to find, easy to contact . . . when *she* chose to have him back in her life. He was leaving and snatching away her option to take him back.

"She broke her hip and is having surgery," Mohammed said, taking a few steps forward toward her.

Danielle nodded and turned away from the sight of him. "She is going to need help around the house as she recovers," she said softly, her eyes shifting about the small living room as she fought not to let her emotions show.

"Yeah," he agreed.

"When are you leaving?" she asked, nibbling at her bottom lip.

"In the morning."

Danielle whirled to face him. Her heart clenched. Her eyes widened. *Tomorrow!* "She . . . uh . . . must be happy you're—"

The rest of her words were swallowed by Mohammed's lips. Danielle's eyes widened and she paused for just a hot second before she returned his kisses and brought her hands up to tangle in his dreads. She moaned in sweet pleasure even as her tears of loss welled up in her eyes.

"Don't cry," he whispered against her lips in between heated kisses.

Danielle shook her head even as she let it tilt back to expose the smooth skin of her neck to his mouth. "I'm not."

"Not yet," he said, sucking the spot just under her chin as his hands moved from deeply gripping her hips to massaging her ass.

She shivered as he licked a sultry circle at the base of her throat as he roughly jerked her dress up around her waist. "Shouldn't you ask first?" she whispered hotly, her heart pounding as she freed his dreads to reach down in between them to undo his belt and the button of his pants.

"Do I need to?" Mohammed asked in return, leaning back to look her in the eye as his jeans fell down around his ankles.

Danielle panted as that crazy energy between them pulsed heavily and surrounded them like a cocoon. She licked the sudden dryness from her lips and freed his dick from the flap of his boxers. "Do I?" she countered boldly, tightening her hold on his hard inches.

"Hell no," Mohammed said darkly. He wrapped one strong arm around her waist and took three large steps to roughly back her body against a wall before tearing her lace panties away with one tight tug. Danielle gasped in anticipation and locked her legs behind his strong back just as he worked the thick tip of his warm and hard dick inside her.

Mohammed's body went still as he fought for control at the tight and moist feel of her surrounding his shaft. "Shit," he swore, dropping his head to her heaving chest as she winded her fingers into his dreads.

Danielle kissed his temple and deeply inhaled the scent of the coconut oil he used on his scalp. Love for him swelled inside of her. Lust for him intensified at the feel of his hard dick pulsing against her walls. "Fuck me," she begged in a ragged whisper.

And he did. And well.

Each stroke of his dick felt like a jolt of life. Not even

the pressure of his body lightly slamming her body against the wall with each thrust broke through the sex daze.

Thump. Thump. Thump.

Fuck it.

In that moment Danielle didn't give a shit about anything else. "Fuck me," she demanded again, her voice sharp like a commander dictating to his troops.

And he delivered hard, forceful thrust after thrust.

Danielle cried out and tugged his locks with her fists, sharply jerking his head back to suck his neck.

Thump. Thump. Thump.

His neck was slightly salty from the sweat of his work. Danielle felt the valley of her breasts and her inner thighs dampen from the sweat of her pleasure. Their hearts raced and pounded. Their sex was wild. Frantic. Frenetic. They both could almost see the white hot chemistry they created.

Thump. Thump. Thump. Thump. Thump. Thump.

Danielle tugged harder on his hair and tightened her ankles against his back as she felt the explosion in her core build with a feverish pace. "Don't go, Mohammed," she whispered, pressing her upper back against the wall to brace herself as she fucked him back with a steady back-and-forth churn of her hips. "Please don't leave me."

He twisted his head to free his locks from her hands and looked forward to lock his eyes on her as he continued the onslaught. Continued to fuck her. Continued to bury himself inside of her like he wanted to be lost in each rhythmic spasm of her pussy walls against his dick. "I have to," he said, his voice filled with his regrets. His eyes tortured with the pain he knew he caused her.

As Danielle rode wave after wave of her release as she came, she let her tears flow even as she cried out roughly and got lost in the pleasure while grappling with her pain.

It was a true emotional roller coaster and Danielle wasn't quite sure that she wasn't about to cross the line into madness.

Mohammed's dick hardened as he roared with his own nut. He continued to thrust upward inside of her, slickly coating her walls with his release. "Aaaah," he cried out against her shoulder as his face twisted and his hard buttocks clenched and unclenched with each plunge.

Danielle was breathing so hard the muscles against her ribs ached. As she came down off her dick high she opened her eyes and spotted her torn panties on the floor. And then her eyes shifted to take in all of the damn boxes. Tomorrow Mohammed would be gone and she would be left behind with only a memory of him and this last encounter.

Danielle lightly knocked the back of her head against the wall as she arched her back. Regret filled her and her soul just couldn't take another emotion being added. She pushed her hands against Mohammed's shoulders and shook her head back and forth, fighting to get the hell away before she really laid everything she was feeling out in front of him.

"Danielle?" he said, freeing his dick as he stepped back and allowed her body to slide down the wall until she stood up on her heels.

"Good-bye, Mohammed," she said, blinking rapidly as she moved past him quickly to reach the door.

"Wait, Danielle," he called out.

She glanced over her shoulder just in time to see him stumble from his shorts around his ankle. He fell to his knees, his dick flopping back and forth like one of those inflatable Sky Guys outside of a car lot. For a half sec, she considered going back to help him but changed her mind as a quick vision of his sexy ass living it up—without her—in Jamaica in less than twenty-four hours filled her mind.

Ignoring the sticky wetness coating the crack of her ass,

Danielle raced out the house and to her car, leaving behind her torn panties and broken heart. Mohammed had just rushed out onto the porch as she reversed down his driveway and sped away up the street.

The familiar smell of their sex filled her nostrils and Danielle rolled her eyes. She hadn't laid eyes on the man in weeks and she gave up her panties like a whore selling pussy for a penny. Pussy topped brains again.

"Don't go, Mohammed. Please don't leave me."

Danielle gasped in horror at the memory of her pleading. Insult just trampled all over injury. She slammed on her brakes in the middle of the street and let her head drop to the steering wheel.

I begged him not to leave me, she thought, lifting her head and looking at the reflection of her eyes in the rearview mirror.

Insecurity was hard to look at and so she shifted her eyes away.

And the very last thing Danielle Johnson wanted to be was insecure. Needy. Desperate.

She wanted more.

"With my connections and your looks I could have made you into something."

Danielle's eyes shifted back to the rearview mirror as Carolyn's voice echoed in her ear like a tiny well-dressed minion pushing devilment. She could just picture the woman propped on her shoulder in a form-fitting red Versace dress and six-inch heels—red-bottom Christian Louboutins of course.

Danielle didn't know how long she sat in the middle of the street with her thoughts racing. She didn't move her car even as the minimal traffic on the quiet street was forced to drive around her. She had a lot of shit on her mind.

Her needy friends.

Her thankless job.

Her invisible parents.

Her pathetic childhood.

Her shady past.

"I need more," she admitted to herself.

She reachd down to the floor of the passenger seat to grab her tote. She dug out her cell phone. Mohammed had called a dozen times. He was leaving and there wasn't a damn thing he could do to help her get her life off pause.

With one breath and hopes that she didn't live to regret it, Danielle dialed a number she knew by heart. It rang twice.

"Well, well. Lookey, lookey," the female voice said smugly into the phone, sounding like a more refined Sheneneh from the 1990s sitcom *Martin*.

Rolling her eyes, Danielle stiffened her spine against the driver's seat.

"With my connections and your looks I could have made you into something."

"Carolyn, we need to talk," she said, tucking the phone between her ear and shoulder before she accelerated her car and finally sped off toward home.

Fast Forward Five Years . . .

"The secret of two is God's secret,
the secret of three is everybody's secret."

—Proverb

Chapter 5
Monica (née Alizé)

Present Day

"Come on, baby girl, let's make this money, yo."

Monica smoothed her hands over her form-fitting pencil skirt as she coolly settled back in her leather executive chair and eyed her client with a demeanor that completely spoke of her belief that he was not to be taken seriously. And over fifty percent of the time, she was completely serious about her life and everything in it.

The television sitcom star who wanted to become a hip-hop icon was a caricature. The slang that sounded forced. The diamond jewelry that seemed borrowed. The tattoos that were random as hell. Kelson Hunt a.k.a. K-Hunta was on the back of a speedy bullet headed to obscurity.

It wasn't her job to tell him to use both hands to grab hold of his life. She was hired to manage his money, not his career.

No, Monica did not take him seriously at all.

She didn't bother to hide it. She didn't care to.

In the three years since she established and became the CEO of Winters Investment Services, Monica had steadily climbed the ladder to success. Her boutique agency included a small but very exclusive roster of celebrity clients who respected her and her ability to make the wealthy even wealthier.

And she had only just begun.

Monica rose to her feet and extended her hand. "It was good meeting with you, Mr. Hunt," she began with a polite smile that was meant to be a subtle nudge that it was time for him to leave.

She didn't miss how his eyes lingered on the way the rich satin of her blouse clung to her breasts. Monica cleared her throat as she removed her red-framed spectacles and held them in her hand.

"Just call me K-Hunta," he said, rising to his full six-foot-five-inch frame.

Uh, no, sir. I will not. "Yes, so, I'll be touch with more information on your portfolio. I think it's wise of you to let your money make money," she said, coming around her large glass desk to guide him by his elbow to the door.

"Usain said you're straight, so we're all good," K-Hunta said, his chains lightly hitting against each other as he finally walked out the door to his entourage scattered about her waiting room.

Monica never talked business in the company of hangers-on. An attorney or business manager? Fine. The fellas you grew up with from the block? Nada.

"Talk to you soon," she said to him even as she gave her young secretary, Jamal, a hard stare for openly turning up his nose at the loud and boisterous crew filling the outer office.

He instantly flipped his frown up.

Monica glanced at her Cartier watch as she closed her office door and turned to make her way back to her desk. The blunt edges of her waist-length weave brushed lightly back and forth against her shirt as she moved. She raked her navy-painted nails through the bone-straight hair that was parted down the middle before picking up the phone headset as she plopped down into her seat.

Knock-knock.

Her finger paused over the phone. "Come in," she called out, looking down at the keypad as she dialed.

Her face filled with confusion at the sight of K-Hunta's manager, Usain Hands, poking his head into her office. Monica forced a smile. "What's up, Usain?" she said, still holding the phone. "I didn't know you were here."

He stepped inside, looking suave in a pinstriped suit and paisley tie with plenty of diamonds to prove to the world he was successful as an entertainment manager. "Just wanted to thank you for doing me that favor and seeing Kelson," he said, his eyes hidden behind dark shades.

Monica wondered if he slept in them because she had yet to see the man without them. Hanging up the line, she nodded. "No problem. Hopefully he'll take the advice I give him so we can set him for life after entertainment, you know," she said, really anxious to finish her call.

Usain laughed as he twisted his watches and bracelets on his wrist. "You make it seem like he has a shelf life."

Monica leaned back in her chair and shrugged a bit. "Just being realistic, Usain," she offered lightly. "But you never know, right?"

He nodded. "Right," he said, coming forward to extend his hand. "How about joining me at the Hip-Hop Awards next week?"

Monica slid her hand into his even as she let her surprise fill her face. She took in his handsome face and clean-cut style with a bit of edge but there was nothing about Usain that piqued Monica's interest and she had never picked up the vibe that she sparked his. "Business or pleasure, Usain?" she asked, having gained even more boldness in her late twenties than she dared to ever have before.

Success had bred confidence.

He smiled, highlighting his looks. "Business for me . . . pleasure for Kelson," he admitted. "He asked me to ask you along."

Monica frowned at visions of an armored SUV filled with more weed smoke than LA fog and more profanity than a hundred street-lit books combined. And she wanted K-Hunta even less than she could fake a desire for his manager. "I politely decline both," she said, easing down into her seat.

Usain laughed as he nodded in understanding. "You can't blame the brotha for trying," he said.

"No, not at all," she agreed, already dismissing him and lifting up the phone handset again to finally make the call he interrupted. "Be safe."

"You too."

The sound of the door closing echoed as Monica closed her eyes and leaned back in her chair as she listened to the phone line ringing in her ears. She swiveled and looked out at the expanse of towering buildings across the street from her two-room office suite on the sixth floor of the Seventh Avenue building in the heart of Manhattan.

Not bad at all, she thought, swiveling again in her chair and leaning forward to replace the handset as the call went to voice mail.

She beamed a little as she looked around at her stylishly decorated office, but it was her degrees framed on the wall above her low-slung bookcases that made her smile widen. Those degrees, her internships during college and grad school, her diligence to fulfill her dreams plus one hell of a lucky hookup from a classmate led to a black girl from a so-called broken home in Newark, New Jersey, owning her own business and making six figures at it.

And she wasn't done yet. She had just begun to scratch at her bucket list.

She leaned forward again in her chair and pressed the intercom button. "Jamal, I think we're done for the day. See you Monday," Monica said, lightly massaging her chin with her free hand.

"Should I call for your car?"

Monica nodded. That's what she loved about the young man who recently graduated from New York University. He had plenty of initiative and drive. He was hungry for success and looked for ways to make Monica's life easier. "Yes, thank you."

She hadn't quite figured out if he was gay or not and she completely didn't give a fuck either way. Her interest in him was completely above his neck and not below his waist.

"See you Monday, Ms. Winters."

She rose to her feet as she picked up her briefcase and slid a few files into it before grabbing her purse. By the time she made it out of her office, Jamal was long gone with his desk left tidy and the light of the outer office already dimmed for the night. She locked up and walked down the tiled hall to the elevator shared with the two other office suites on the floor.

"Time for the weekend," she said softly as she pressed the button to summon the elevator.

As she stepped between the opening doors a soft smile touched her glossy lips. There was a time when an upcoming Friday night meant something more than lounging on the couch with a glass of wine and files to review. High heels, short skirts, and the club with her friends were a long way from that.

But that was a long time ago.

The heels were still high but the friends she hadn't spoken to in close to five years and the club were off her to-do list. Surprisingly, she didn't miss either that much. Her priorities had changed.

Bzzzzzzzzz . . .

As the elevator landed she reached in her purse for her iPhone. "Hey, mama," she said, after checking the caller ID.

"This your daddy, LadyBug."

Monica pinched the bridge of her nose as she walked across the lobby. "And does your girlfriend Andrea know you're laid up on your ex-wife's phone?" she asked, waving at the security guards at the front desk open before strutting through the glass door the doorman held for her.

"Andrea and I are not together."

Monica paused and almost collided with a dog walker and his five clients on a leash. Her driver was standing outside her blacked out Yukon Denali waiting to help her slide into the back. Monica ignored him as she turned her back. "Did she get tired of you dipping back to swim in my mama's goodies?" she said, stretching her eyes with vaguely contained sarcasm.

"First off, I was swimming in your mama's goodies long before you came out of them," he said, his voice amused. "Secondly, whatever is going on between me and your mama is none-ya. Third, and most importantly, I'm your father and you need to find your mind and your respect because you obviously lost both."

And just like that Monica felt properly chastised and put in her place without her father raising his voice or changing his dismeanor one bit. "I apologize, Daddy," she said, turning on her five-inch crocodile heels to finally make her way to her SUV. "You know what I went through with Mama all those years after you two got divorced. She can't take it if it all goes wrong again . . . and neither can I."

Monica slid onto the butter-soft leather of the rear seat, dumping her briefcase and purse beside her as she kicked off her heels. "Matter of fact, Daddy, I can't even handle this now. So, with all due respect to the man who made me and raised me . . . I'll holler at you two lovebirds later."

She took a deep, encouraging breath and ended the call.
Beep.

"Headed home, Ms. Winters?"

She nodded at her driver, Sampson, even as she closed
her eyes and let her head fall back against the headrest.
Soon the soft sounds of Ledisi filled the vehicle and Monica felt her shoulders relax. Sampson knew her well. Somehow in the year since he was hired as her driver he was
able to sense her frame of mind and played music to suit it.
The only time he didn't mess with the music? If she was
mad as hell and not in the mood. Then the twenty-minute
ride home was as silent as death.

Monica let herself stay in that relaxed zone until she
heard Sampson climb from his driver's seat and close his
door. "Home sweet home," she mouthed, opening her eyes
and looking out the window at the upscale high-rise building on New York's Upper East Side.

It was a long way from Newark, New Jersey's central
ward.

"A long ass way," she muttered, before entering the
building.

Even though it had been over a year since she first
pressed stilettos to the marble floor, her breath was still
taken away by the grandness. She wondered if she would
ever get used to it. Just accept that this was her life now.
This was her reality. And it was a reality that topped every
one of her childhood dreams.

I made it.

"Good evening, Mr. Steele."

Monica stiffened in surprise before she turned and
smiled at Cameron walking into the lobby with the confidence to fool anyone into thinking he owned it. *Cor-
rection, we made it,* she thought, her heart pounding like it
had been years since she had seen the man she loved, instead of just that morning.

He walked right up to her with his eyes missing not one detail about her before he used one strong arm to sweep her body up against his to dance her in a small circle right there in the middle of the lobby. He kissed her neck and hummed some tune she couldn't recognize as she brought her hands up around his neck and enjoyed the movement of their bodies.

This was their home. Well, the lobby of their home. Theirs alone. Both names on the mortgage. Together.

"People are staring at us," she whispered up to him as she eyed their neighbors.

Cameron chuckled and began to move them toward the elevator. "Let's not be the dancing Negroes in the lobby then," he said with a chuckle.

"No, let's not."

He dipped her with one arm and reached for the button to summon the elevator with the other. "Love," he said, smiling down at her.

Monica's eyes sparkled but not as bright as the light his words exploded inside her chest. "More love," she replied, as were their custom.

The elevator arrived. People got off and a few more got on along with Cameron and Monica. They snuggled close together with his head resting atop her head as she leaned forward into his chest. Lost in each other.

And she did love him. For his love as her man. For his intensity as her lover. For his power as the chief financial operating officer of Braun, Weber. For his security. His understanding. His humor. His humility.

As soon as they stepped off the elevator onto their floor, he slapped her ass soundly and then massaged it before scooping her up into his arms to carry her down the tiled hall to the door to their two-story condominium. She reached down and pressed her thumb to the pad to unlock the door.

"Are you ready to make a baby?" he spoke against her neck.

Monica froze as he carried her over the threshold. "Say what now?"

Cameron pressed his lips to her cheek before sitting her down on her feet. He pulled his iPhone from the inner pocket of his tailored blazer and then used his thumb to swipe across the screen several times. He handed it to her.

Monica's heart was beating fast as she looked down at the calendar reminder he titled: Baby Making. And then she remembered. Last year when Cameron last brought up having children she begged off for a year. A year ago to the date. *Leave it up to this Negro to set a motherfucking reminder.*

Not once during the year had they broached the subject of children. Not once. But he had just been lying in wait. Like a predator on her uterus.

Monica visualized gaining eighty pounds, her nose spreading, ankles swelling, and her neck darkening. Morning sickness. Constant peeing. And labor? She fought not to shiver at the thought of that. *Fuck to the no.*

She cut her eyes over at him and his eyes were leveled on her. She smiled and rose up on her toes to press a kiss to the corner of his mouth. "Not this week, baby. Aunt Flo came to visit this afternoon," she lied.

"Damn," Cameron swore in disappointment.

She pressed another kiss to his mouth before she dropped down to her knees and bit her bottom lip. "Let me get some of that pressure off," she said softly, unzipping his pants.

He smiled, spread his legs wide and thrust his hips toward her playfully. "Do what you do," he said.

"And do so well," she teased, the sound of his zipper being undone echoing in the air.

Monica licked her lips before she pulled his dick free

and licked him. Stroking the length of him until it hardened in her hands. The faint scent of him, his sweat, and his soap surrounded her as she took all of him into her mouth. He hissed in pleasure and tightened his fingers in her hair as he flung his head back and slightly pumped his hips.

"Hmmmmmmm," she moaned, enjoying the stroke of his dick against her tongue.

"Mo," he moaned.

She sucked him harder, closing her eyes as her cheeks caved with each deep pull. She could taste the slight drizzle of pre-cum coating the tip. His balls lightly rocked against her chin with each back and forth motion of his hips. His buttocks were tight as his thighs quivered from the pleasure she gave.

Usually, Monica would blow him until he was close to a nut and then jack him the rest of the way home, but not this time. This time she listened to him gasp harshly and then cried out as his release filled her mouth. She sucked harder.

It was the very least she could do for him because she had absolutely no plans of getting pregnant. Ever.

Chapter 6
Keesha (née Dom)

Keesha licked her lips as she lit a cigarette and eyed the frame holding the covers of her two books. It was poster sized and hung in the center of the far wall of her office. She smirked a bit at the urge she felt to set fire to it. *Burn, motherfucker, burn.*

She had poured her heart and soul into that first book. It was fed by her misery. She thought writing it would release her demons and instead she had to draw upon them to write the second book centered on a crazy stripper named Lick Me who was battered and bruised emotionally and physically.

The first book had been a release and she poured her all into it.

The second book had seemed like a torture that drained her of her all.

And now the third? Keesha was still on empty.

She twisted her bottom lip to the left and exhaled the cigarette smoke in a smooth stream upward as she cut her eyes to the screen of her laptop. The blinking cursor on the blank screen mocked her. *You ain't a real writer, bitch.*

Knock-knock-knock.

She rolled her eyes heavenward and ignored whomever was at the door. Outside that solid wood was a party she regretted throwing in the first place. Her agent and editor were on her to turn in her proposal for a third book. No proposal. No new book deal. No hefty advance. No money.

And she had been one of the lucky ones to score a good agent who negotiated a hefty six-figure advance and then sold the movie rights to her book for another good amount. There was no promise of the rights actually being picked up by a great production company to make the film, but the money and the extra press about the deal had been nice. And had led to the push for a new book in the series.

But the words would not come.

No story would develop.

"Shit," Keesha swore, stubbing her cigarette out in the ashtray.

Knock-knock-knock-knock—

"WHAT THE FUCK DO YOU WANT?" she screamed at the top of her voice, picking up the same ashtray, about to fling it at the closed door. Her frustrations made her dizzy. Unsure.

The door opened a crack and the head of her preteen daughter, Kimani, peeped in. "Ma, you busy?" she asked.

Keesha sat the ashtray back down and shook her head, causing her chin-length asymmetrical bob to swish back and forth. "What is it, Ki?" she asked, forcing herself to calm down as she used her hands to sweep up the ashes and cigarette butts now littering the top of her desk.

"Uhmm, Diane just got here and she got pissed to see Pops. They're arguing," she said, picking up one of Keesha's advance review copies of her second book, *Lick Me 2.*

Keesha felt a twitch above her left eye like she was about to stroke the hell out. Standing up she came around the wooden desk and took the book from her daughter's hand. "I knew I shouldn't have invited her," she mumbled, her flip-flops slapping against the hardwood floors as they made their way down the stairs of the townhouse and to the open patio doors leading to the backyard.

Her mother and her father were nose to nose but only her mother's hands were flailing in the air.

"You fucking sperm donor!" Diane yelled.

"I would've been more than a sperm donor if you didn't lie on another motherfucker about being Keesha's father!" William shot back.

"Great idea to bring the whole family together. You know Diane stay trippin'," Kimani said, running off in her sundress to reclaim her seat by Keesha's little sister, Hiasha. Keesha didn't have time to once again contemplate that both her father and she had children the same age. She had to put a kibosh on the drama unfolding between her parents . . . who hadn't seen each other since a pregnant Diane decided to kick the mailman to the curb in favor of a money-making drug-dealing future drug addict.

Keesha eyed the partygoers. Some openly stared. Others tried to pretend the drama was not unfolding in front of them. She saw a couple pack a plate and head for the gate leading to the front of the house where cars were parked.

"You just going to stand there?"

Keesha stiffened and then looked over her shoulder at Corey carrying a tray of raw hamburgers out to the grill. His dark complexion looked delicious in the navy shirt he wore with white shorts. She shook her head. "This your house too. You could break up Holyfield and Tyson," she told him, her Newark accent still in place even though they had moved to the suburbs of South Orange, New Jersey.

Corey made a face before he kissed her cheek and moved past her. "And risk Diane flipping out on me? Naw," he said before heading out the patio doors.

Keesha eyed him head right past the confusion and to the grill.

See, I got to handle this bullshit.

"You and your silly bitch better give me fifty feet before both y'all corny asses get slam dunked in that pool."

Keesha felt like she could drown herself as her mother turned her verbal onslaught onto her stepmother. *Why did I invite this bitch?*

Her eyes flittered about the faces of her neighbors and friends. Their eyes were filled with confusion, anger, indignation, and disgust. They had never experienced Diane or probably anyone like her.

Keesha thought of the only people in her life who would have expected this and warned her against even inviting her mother to her home. Her party. Her life.

But those friends were out of her life and had been for a long time. Toward the end there had been arguments and petty shit that led to silence about shit she couldn't even remember. Shit she didn't even care about anymore.

Keesha's eyes widened and she took a few steps back as she watched Corey go over to her mother and attempt to get her to sit her silly self down in her bright red strapless jumpsuit. Keesha's eyes shot over to Corey's side of the family. They were some Newark brawlers too. If Diane said something too shady all hell just might break loose.

Keesha knew she should go out there and say something. Do something. But she couldn't. She just couldn't deal.

That familiar itch nipped at her. Not as strong as it did years ago, but still there. Still identifiable. Still needing to be scratched.

Once a junkie, always a junkie.

Keesha pushed away the urge, wanting her sobriety more than she wanted to use drugs to forget the fuckery unfolding before her.

Thankfully Corey said something to make Diane shoot her father and his wife one last glare before she turned and walked over to where Corey's cousin, Shawn, was serving up the liquor. The DJ turned up the soulful eighties music and the party soon resumed. The show was over . . . for now.

Keesha wasn't crazy. Her mother was still the talk of the party and still getting the long side-eyes and judgmental twists of the lips. And as soon as she stepped her ass out there all the talk, looks, and lip-twisting would turn on her. *Fuck this shit all the way from here to there.*

Keesha turned, determined to head back up to her office to try and get some words on her computer.

"Oh no you don't."

She closed her eyes at the feel of Corey's hand, the sound of his chastising voice, and the annoyance of his intrusion. Placing a fake grin on her face, Keesha turned to him just outside the spacious kitchen of their home.

"Come on, baby. It's straight," he said, placing kisses along her jaw as his hands massaged her upper arms. "Come on out and enjoy the set."

His words, his touch, and his support caused her shoulders to relax as she stepped forward to press her face into his neck. She took a deep inhale of his spicy cologne before kissing his neck. Her lips tingled a bit from his salty sweat and she almost felt the chemistry they used to share. The undeniable thrill of loving the hell out of someone.

Almost but not quite.

It wasn't as good as the blinding white of love and not as horrible as the darkness that leads to a couple never speaking again. Keesha and Corey were in that gray zone of not wanting to be there but not wanting to let go, either. And to her that gray zone was much worse.

"Just let me write a little bit more and I'll be back done," she lied easily, already easing away from him.

He pulled her back and held her chin with his hand to force her eyes to meet his. "If you'd fuck me more than you fucked that keyboard we'd be okay," he said.

Anger and a smart retort about that keyboard fronting the majority of their bills came in a rush, but Keesha swallowed it down and reached for humor instead. "You jealous of a keyboard?" she teased.

Corey eyed her thick and curvy figure in the racerback maxi dress she wore. "These days I'm jealous of the seat of your panties for getting to be so close to the pussy."

Keesha saw the desire he had for her in his eyes. She was thirty pounds heavier than when they met and although the pounds were packed in all the right places, he never once complained. Never once. Stepping back close to him she pressed her lips to his mouth a dozen different times before she sucked his bottom lip softly.

"Shit, I'm about to say fuck this party," he moaned into her open mouth, his hands coming down to massage the flesh of her buttocks.

"I'm about to say fuck me," she whispered, tilting her head back with a sigh filled with the sudden pulse of her clit as she felt his hard dick press against her stomach.

"Yo, cuz, this grill firing up."

They both looked at Corey's cousin Shawn standing in the doorway of the open patio doors.

"I don't want to burn down the neighborhood," Corey told her with one last firm swat to her ass. "Later?"

Keesha nodded in agreement, watching as he turned to follow his cousin out the doors and over to the grill. She moved over into the kitchen and washed her hands at the sink, looking out through the slats of the plantation blinds at the backyard.

She closed her eyes and took a deep audible breath.

The feel of warm masculine hands on her hips didn't surprise her at all. She hissed in pleasure and leaned back against his chest as his fingers eased inside the top of her dress to massage her breasts and nipples. "God, that feels good," Keesha whispered up into the air, pressing her ass up against his hard dick as she worked her hips back and forth.

He sucked at the back of her neck as he rushed to work her dress up around her waist. His fingers trembled as he pulled her black cotton thong to the side. "You think I was gone let that ninja get *my* pussy?" he asked.

She shook her head no as she felt the thick and heavy weight of his dick being rubbed up and down the crevice of her buttocks.

"You want this dick?" he asked thickly.

"Yes," she said.

His hand to the back of her neck roughly guided her to bend down over the sink. She rose up on her toes and arched her back as the moist tip of his dick probed her pussy from behind. "Hurry up," she gasped.

Behind her he bent his legs to a squat and worked his hips back and forth to fill her inch by inch with his dick. "Aww shit," he gasped, reaching on either side of her body to grip the edge of the counter as he fucked her from behind with fast and furious pumps intensified by their betrayal.

Keesha opened her eyes and lifted her head to look out the window at Corey flipping ribs on the grill. And they remained locked on him even as she bit her lip with each forceful thrust. Even as she felt her climax build and cried out as forceful spasms racked her core, she kept her eyes locked on him.

Her lover's finger moved up to massage her nipples as his body stiffened. "Get this nut."

Keesha reached behind him to grab the side of his clenched ass as she worked her hips, drawing all of his release from him until their thighs were wet. "Damn," she gasped, her heart pounding and her steps unsteady as she backed him off of her and let her dress fall back down around her ankles.

She heard the zip of his jeans as she left the kitchen. "Go back outside. I'll be out in a little bit," she said over her shoulder, sparing Corey's cousin Shawn one last look before she dashed up the stairs and into the master bedroom.

She rushed through a douche and a quick ho bath at the sink, not wanting Corey to wonder why she took a shower in the middle of their barbecue. Not wanting Corey to know that she stopped fucking him because she was fucking someone else. Not wanting Corey to know that she betrayed him with a man he considered as close as a blood brother.

After pulling on a fresh pair of underwear, Keesha went back down the stairs and finally joined the party. She ignored Shawn's look of satisfaction as she walked over to Corey and took his drink from his hand to taste.

What the fuck have I got myself into?

Chapter 7
Danielle (née Cristal)

"Thank you again for joining my cohost Danielle Johnson and I during our first week. We'll see you Monday night for a new edition of *The A-List*."

"Good night everyone," Danielle said, looking into the camera with her million-dollar smile and easy-breezy stance that was anything but.

"We're clear," someone yelled out in the studio.

The smile faded and Danielle playfully pinched the hand of her cohost, Kent Yarborough, as her assistant made her way over to her. "Have a good one," she said.

He starting loosening his leather tie and reached up to muss his slicked back blond hair until it stood up in funky spikes. "You too," he said with a wink.

They shared a little look as they both stood still while their mic packs were removed. Danielle wondered if he too was fighting the urge to hug her. This was huge for both of them. Major league. They both had just begun as the co-anchors of the nightly entertainment show after a nationwide eight-month search. He had been a current events reporter on a small station out of Little Rock and she had been working at a local cable station in New York. Danielle had to fight not to twerk her ass because she was so happy about the new gig. Today marked the end of the first full week on camera but in the months since she first snagged the job she had already done one-on-one interviews with Tom Cruise and Denzel Washington, tried on three racks of clothes and dozens of shoes for the show wardrobe, and did the red carpet for the movie premiere of a new, sexy Michael Ealy flick.

This was a long way from her days on WNYP, a twenty-four-hour local cable station out of New York. A long way.

"What else do I have to get done today, Ming?" Danielle asked her assistant, accepting her cell phone from the young woman as they strode out of the studio and toward the elevators.

"That's actually it for today. You've gotten some more flowers and welcome gifts that I left in your office. Also, invites came in for dinner parties that you'll need to go through and decide which ones to attend. Lastly, I wanted to show you I updated both your website and your Wikipedia page," she said, handing over her iPad.

"I'll check it on my computer upstairs . . . in my office," Danielle said with satisfaction. Her mind was stuck on *". . . you'll need to go through and decide which ones to attend."*

She bit back a smile, completely amazed at her life.

It was everything she ever dreamt of and more. *Well, almost everything . . .*

They rode the elevator upstairs in silence and Danielle pulled out and unlocked her cell phone and quickly updated her Twitter and Facebook accounts:

> Just wrapped up my first week of taping #TheAList. Still feel like I'm floating on clouds. #blessed.

In just the days since her announcement as one of the new co-anchors her follower counts had almost tripled.

"Do you want to order lunch or are you leaving for the day?" Ming asked, her thumb poised and ready over the touch screen of her phone.

Danielle stepped off the elevator onto the fifth floor, which housed the wardrobe and makeup department. She kept the doors from closing by holding her hand out to fool the sensors. "You go on up ahead of me and order me some tempura. Please," she added, not wanting to come off with a bad attitude.

"No problem."

Danielle removed her hand and smiled as the doors closed her part-time assistant off from her. She walked down the narrow hall to the oversized room housing the wardrobe for all of the female correspondents for the network. She smiled and spoke to anyone who crossed her path.

Danielle had gone through too much to make it this far and she was determined not to mess it up with a bad attitude. "Thanks again, Justin," she said to the slender-hipped stylist.

He and his team of four wardrobe assistants were cataloging the racks of clothing. "You're welcome," he said, his short and spiky hair dyed a deep shade of purple. It perfectly matched his own quirky style that was a mix of '80s punk and some futuristic vibe that scared the shit out of Danielle when they were first introduced. "We got in some really cute dresses for the Teen Choice Awards but we can worry about all of that Monday."

"Perfect," she said, walking over to one of the small dressing rooms designated just for her use.

Danielle rushed out of the bright yellow-and-white striped sleeveless dress she wore. She left it over the back of the makeup chair and sat the pair of five-inch straw-and-gold stilettos in the seat. Her bold pieces of gold jewelry were next. All of it was designer and expensive and not hers.

But Danielle was used to nice things of her own. She had always worked—and took on wealthy sponsors—to make sure she could purchase the very best. That was back when material things mattered over love. BM and then AB (Before Mohammed and After the Breakup with Mohammed). He was the defining point in her personal history.

She paused for a moment and got *so* lost in the memory of him. He had never moved back from Jamaica and she had never accepted his calls . . . or e-mails . . . or texts. The last time against the wall had been the last time. . . .

Danielle's eyes glazed over and she bit her lip at the memory before pushing it away. Mohammed was her past. Her career was her future. She wanted more for her life and she went after it.

Her eyes locked on her reflection in the mirror.

She quickly got dressed in the linen pencil skirt and silk tank she wore that morning with her five-inch cork heels. Being sure to grab her phone she left the dressing room. Her steps paused as she looked at the rack holding nearly a dozen garment bags. She made her way toward it, feeling more boldness to explore since the long and wide room without walls was now empty.

"Amazing," she whispered, reaching out to touch each of the garment bags and trace her manicured finger over each of the designer names. "Thank you God for my blessings."

Danielle wasn't religious. She wasn't even that spiritual. But in that moment she closed her eyes and released a long stream of air that was a tactic to beat off the emotions that flooded her. The past that continued to shadow her.

Being poor, without parents, and shuttled from foster home to foster home with a few trips to group homes in between was a lot for any child to bear. A lot. It had a way of stripping a child of hopes and dreams.

For the first time ever she believed dreams were possible.

But it still hurt she had absolutely no one to share it with. No one.

Stiffening her back and swallowing a sigh she left the wardrobe room and made her way back to the elevators. She was glad to make it back to her office on the floor housing the offices for the various correspondents of the shows produced by Network New. Around the perimeter were the small offices with windows for the TV personalities and in the center clustered in cubicles were the non-production personnel.

Ming was on the phone in her cubicle right across from Danielle's corner office—which was the same size as the rest of the offices, but with an additional window. Danielle loved it like it was more than that.

"Your lunch is on your desk," Ming told her, covering the mouthpiece of the handset.

"Thank you," she mouthed before walking into her office.

She closed the door and leaned back against it, her eyes taking in the beauty of Los Angeles. Everything about it was so different from the East Coast but she was learning to like it and once she truly learned to maneuver the congested traffic she would love it.

Kicking off her shoes she sat down in the chair before her desk, and pushed into the corner directly under each of the windows on both walls. She tucked her bare feet underneath her as she clutched the edge of her desk and rolled the chair forward to grab a disinfecting hand wipe from the tube on the corner of her desk to cleanse her hands. Her stomach growled at the thought of her food.

Knock-knock.

"Come in, Ming," she called before she filled her mouth with a bite of chicken tempura that was sinful.

The door opened but the beautiful and sizable floral arrangement Ming carried completely covered everything but her lower body. Danielle's mouth opened in surprise and pleasure as she moved aside her lunch to make room for her to sit it on her desk.

"I did a squat to pick it up to protect my back," Ming said dryly, pushing her spectacles up on her nose with her index finger.

Danielle laughed as she dug the tiny envelope out from the colorful variety of roses, lilies, orchids, and sunflowers. She pulled the card out and her eyes went from curious and pleased to hesitant. As she leaned to take in the sweet scent of the flowers her thumb moved back and forth softly over the slashing signature of Omari Knight.

> Missing your face around the building.
> TV does you no justice.
> Call me — O.

She thought of the handsome man she met earlier that year in the elevator of the apartment she kept in New Jersey. He was a computer software engineer and way sexier than the sound of his career choice. Still, no matter how bangable, Danielle was not looking for what he was looking for, which was a relationship. She didn't have the time for it.

The daily phone calls.

The checking in.

The mind games.

The expectations.

The disappointments.

And on top of that, long distance drama as well?

"No, hell no," she said, leaning forward to drop the envelope and card in her wire trash can.

Still as she ate her lunch her eyes kept drifting back to the arrangement. *He really is one fine motherfucker and he always . . . always smells so damn good.*

Danielle cut her eyes down at the card and envelope sitting propped against the inside wall of the can. She used her tongue to pull a piece of meat from in between her teeth as she wiped her fingers on a napkin. While arching a well-shaped brow she reached down and picked up the card, sitting it on the edge of her desk. And then in the corner pocket of the blotter on her desk. And then down into the side pocket of her tote sitting on the floor.

She loosened her hair from the chignon and ran her fingers through it with one hand as she pulled up her website on the touch screen all-in-one computer.

She did a little dance at the Network New logo at the bottom of the screen as she read over her updated bio. She also checked her updated Wikipedia page. Both accurately reflected her meteoric rise in the industry.

Well, almost . . .

Although it mentioned that she pursued her associate's degree in journalism while working full-time at WNYP for four years and how she auditioned and snagged the anchor position, there was a lot between the lines and behind the scenes that she would never divulge . . . and never forget.

The friends she stepped away from to focus on herself.

The many hours upon hours she put in to being the very best in her job, going above and beyond, to dispel that she was just the girl with the pretty face and the connections.

She squeezed her eyes shut and visibly shivered in disgust.

"With my connections and your looks I could have made you into something."

Although the words were once spoken by the wife of one of her ex-employers it felt more like the spider drawing in the fly. A tempting trap.

"Carolyn, we need to talk."

Danielle had crawled right onto the spider's web.

Fuck the devil. She signed, sealed, and delivered her soul to Carolyn Ingram in exchange for an on-air position at the cable station owned by one of her business associates.

Every moment she spent covering local entertainment stories, and working along with people with more education and experience, she wondered if they all knew just how she snagged the position. And if they didn't, she knew. And that was enough.

She had wanted to prove herself and it was her idea alone to pursue the journalism degree and to put in more time and effort than anyone else. She was trying to outrun her ties to Carolyn.

Securing *The A-List* had been some declaration for herself that this time she fought hard and worked hard to actually feel like she earned the position on her own.

Again Danielle shivered and forced her past back where it belonged: not darkening her present or slowing down her future. She just prayed it stayed that way. She hated waiting for the other shoe to drop.

Danielle scratched at her neck, feeling her anxiety rise. She needed something to relieve her stress and help her cap off one helluva good week. Champagne just wasn't going to do it.

But she knew just what—or rather who—could.

I wonder if his number has changed. . . .

She picked up her cell phone from her desk and unlocked the screen with a swipe of her thumb.

I wonder if his dick game has changed. . . .

She paused for just another second more before she dialed the number she was ashamed to admit she knew by heart. *Hell with it.*

"I thought you would have changed your number since you hit the big time."

Danielle smiled a little. "I would have thought you forgot all about me among the masses," she countered, leaning back and kicking up her bare feet to prop up on her desk.

"You're hard to forget."

"I'm not paying for you to blow air up my ass."

"You could."

Danielle laughed. "You know what I mean."

"Yes . . . but I don't know why you called."

"Business first, huh?"

"Always."

That didn't bother Danielle in the least. There was no confusion about their "relationship." He sold dick and on occasion she bought it. Win-win.

"I need you to catch the first flight out to LA," she said, sitting up in her chair to navigate her computer to an airline website.

"For the weekend?"

Danielle frowned. "No. Just one night," she admitted. She was looking to be fucked well, not to play house for the weekend and sightsee LA. Never that.

"Just in and out?"

Danielle pushed her hair behind her ear. "Of town? Yes. Of me? No."

"You know how I do."

Danielle licked her lips and let that one slide. "I can book your flight right now."

"No, I'll book it and you reimburse me. You would need to know my real name to book a flight."

Danielle stood up and knocked her shoes upright with her feet before she stepped into them. "Oh, yes, I forgot. You're just Pleasure to all us tricks, right?" she teased.

"We'll see what you think when I slide my dick in you."

It was by no means love, companionship, or even meaningful in any way. But it was enough to make her shiver in anticipation as she tossed her cell phone and keys into her tote before hitching it up in the crook of her arm. "Just make it worth my dime."

"Your many, many, many dimes."

Beep.

Danielle ended the call on that note. She gave her floral arrangement one last long look before she cut the light out in her office and left it to go and prepare for the dick she was flying in.

Chapter 8
Latoya (née Moët)

"Let the church say . . ."

"Amen," the entire congregation sang in unison.

Latoya lowered the right hand she held up during the benediction. She smiled up at her husband standing proud in the pulpit of the United Love Church of Christ. She kept her eyes on him as he shook the hands of the other ministers in the pulpit before one of the ushers helped him to remove his robe as everyone in the church looked on.

Taquan straightened his silver and blue tie and smoothed his hands over the front of his gray suit as he came down the few stairs to make his way over to where she sat in the front pew to the right of the pulpit. He pressed a kiss to her brow and then bent a bit to kiss the cheek of their six-month-old son, Taquan Jr. Lastly, he picked Tiffany up and sat her up on his hip. Together they made their way up the empty aisle as the ushers kept any of the churchgoers from flooding the aisle. They exited the massive double doors of the church and came down the stairs to stand at the foot of the brick steps.

It was a routine they had down pat. They could all do it in their sleep.

"Smile, Latoya," Taquan said low in his throat to her as the first of the worshippers began to descend the stairs.

Latoya put on her perfect First Lady smile as they shook

the hands and shared a few words with his flock. She was there physically but her mind was elsewhere. She was on autopilot. Said the right things. Kept her composure. Played the perfect role.

Just the way Taquan wanted.

Just the way the Reverend Taquan Sanders wanted it.

What did Latoya want? She didn't know for sure and Taquan didn't care. And that left her in one helluva rut.

"You know how to deliver the word, Rev."

Latoya shifted the baby in her arms as she looked over at her husband smiling broadly as a tall and round man shook his hand vigorously. She had a vision of her husband turning his hand over and presenting his ring to be kissed. She snorted in derision.

Taquan and the man both glanced at her.

Latoya gave them her hallelujah smile as she lifted the baby up onto her shoulder and soothingly rubbed his back.

"Sister Sanders, the baby is getting so big."

Latoya shifted her eyes down to Reeba Nunzio, the president of the Women's Ministries. The woman was barely five feet in height and wide like she enjoyed good food all the time. Latoya could barely stand her. If the woman put as much time into praying as she did burning up phone lines with gossip she'd be the next Mother Teresa. "Yes, he surely is," Latoya finally answered her and then eased her free hand past the woman to shake the hand of the next person in line.

And she shook hand after hand and gave smile after smile as she felt her calves cramping from standing up. She checked and was glad to see the line of parishioners was finally dwindling. *Thank God for* that.

It wasn't that she didn't want to spare any of her time on the churchgoers; she just had so much on her plate. Her life was so much more than just sitting and looking pretty on Sundays. She was busier now than she was working for

DYFS. It was no joke being a full-time mother, wife, and First Lady to an ambitious minister.

And Taquan was very ambitious. So much so that his eyes were locked on his goal and completely missing the unhappiness he was causing in their marriage. In her.

"We need to get the kids home for a nap," she said, reaching up to wipe a fine beading of sweat from her daughter's forehead as she slept on Taquan's shoulder.

"We can put them down on the sofa in my office," he said as they turned and walked back up the stairs and into the church. "I have a meeting with the deacon board."

Latoya felt her jaw clench. "Taquan, we came early because you had a church board meeting. I still have to finish dinner, prepare my speech for the awards banquet tomorrow, clean the house—"

He stopped in the middle of the aisle and looked down at her. "Latoya, you know I am trying to get everyone to support getting a loan for the renovation of the church," he said.

"Yes, I know but what I don't know is why you even want to double the size of the church anyway," she said, her eyes widening in frustration. "You're already stretched with the church at *this* capacity."

Taquan's frame stiffened. "And it's up to you to put a limit on the Lord's work."

"I think the Lord's work can be done in a megachurch or in a lot," she snapped, as she used her free hand to shake Tiffany lightly. "Come on baby wake up."

"I'll carry her to the car for you," Taquan said, turning and striding away from her back down the aisle.

Latoya looked around at the large church that could easily seat a thousand people or better. And although it didn't matter to her the church was beautiful. White walls. Stained glass windows with Biblical figures. Deep oxblood carpets. Pews that were a dark mahogany.

Why isn't this enough for him?

Taquan had received his calling four years ago and attended divinity school. Initially Latoya had felt it was a blessing to be married to a minister. She felt like they could really do God's work, but once he was appointed as the minister of United Love his work became more about growing the church than growing within the church. Everything he did was not for the glory and grace of God but for impressing someone else or garnering support for something else he planned. All of it was to make himself more powerful.

Everything else, including their marriage and even his relationship with the children, was falling to the wayside.

With one last look around Latoya turned and headed out the church. Taquan was already buckling Tiffany into her booster seat in their white Denali. She walked around to the other side of the car and placed the baby in his car seat in the second row.

They looked up at each other briefly as they worked.

Just as quickly they looked away.

"I'll come back and get you when you're done," she said softly, her eyes on a smiling Taquan Jr. She genuinely smiled down at him in return, feeling her heart swell with motherly love.

"It shouldn't be any more than a couple of hours at the most."

Latoya nodded as she stepped back and closed the door. She gave herself a few deep, calming breaths before coming around to slide into the driver's seat. She didn't particularly care for driving the SUV, especially in a skirt almost to her ankles and heels almost to the sky, but she didn't have a choice since they all drove together.

Taquan came over and closed the driver's side door. Latoya lowered the window as she turned the key in the ignition. "No kiss, huh?" he asked.

She turned and looked at him, a smile begrudgingly spreading across her face. They always shared a kiss whenever they separated. Always. Even if they were mad enough at each other to spit, they still shared that kiss. Be it on the lips or cheek it was a moment to demonstrate their love that they never let pass.

Latoya closed her eyes and puckered her lips as she leaned out the window.

"Reverend Sanders!" someone called out.

Latoya waited for the touch of her husband's lips. And when the moment never arrived she opened one eye to see her husband hustling over to the church steps where the members of the deacon board all stood. "No, this nigga didn't," she muttered in surprise.

But he absolutely did.

Latoya fought the urge to flip the whole crew of them a forceful bird as she raised the window and reversed out of the reserved parking place. She checked her rearview mirror and Taquan entered the church without sparing a glance. *Or thought.*

And there on the edge of every other emotion was anger. It was stewing slow and long, but there. She felt it like a second skin. Swallowed it like water. Embraced it like a long lost friend. Like three long lost friends that she turned her back on for *him*. Danielle, Keesha, and Monica were three of the most important people in her life but the day after they were married she packed up her things, gathered her daughter in her arms, and moved in with Taquan. No phone calls. No visits. No catching up. Nothing.

And as her happiness dwindled, her anger over that grew until it had a pulse of its own.

During the entire twenty-minute drive to the home the church provided for their use, Latoya dwelled somewhere inside the triangle of anger, hurt, and emptiness. Each of the emotions took their blows. She was just grateful that

Taquan Jr. was a pleasant baby who only cried for a Pampers change, out of hunger, or from a certain positioning during sleep. And Tiffany slept peacefully.

She would absolutely freak if she had to deal with her emotions, traffic, a crying baby, and a talkative child. She would absolutely freak. Like hit the brakes in the middle of the road and snatch every single piece of hair from her body. Just freak.

"Never would have made it . . ."

Latoya pulled to a stop at the next red light and reached in her console for her cell phone. She always left it in the car during the church services. Checking the caller ID she shook her head. "No. No. No," she said, letting the phone slide back down onto the console as she accelerated forward.

She loved her parents and they had come through the roughest of times over the last ten years with the war between their strict religious beliefs and her desires to be anything but religious. Like seriously rough, but they were in a better place and they were so eating up the fact that their daughter was a minister's wife, but at times they were still overbearing. Still pushing her more toward their way of loving God than her own.

"Your skirt is too short."

"Are you having a glass of wine with dinner?"

"Those are some . . . high heels."

"Is that any way for a minister's wife to act?"

Latoya shook her head as she made the turn onto the paved driveway of their modest two-story brick home. It was a nice, family-oriented neighborhood in Hartford, Connecticut, just a few blocks from the school and a park. To Latoya the house was the best of the perks the church offered.

She climbed from the car and opened the rear door. "Come on and wake up, Tiffany," she said, gently nudging. She hated to do it but she had to because there was no way she could carry both of the kids in her arms.

"Surprise!"

Latoya froze as she was bending over to unlock Tiffany's seat belt.

Tiffany lifted up in the booster seat and turned to look out the rear window. "It's Grandma . . . and Grandpa," she said with excitement, all of her sleep completely gone.

Latoya wished she could feel the same way. She undid the seat belt and Tiffany climbed down and pushed past her to go running toward her grandfather. The other rear door opened and her mother spared her a quick glance before she cooed at Taquan Jr. as she freed him from his car seat.

As always, Lou Mae's naturally waist-length hair was twisted up into a bun at the nape of her neck and her face was completely free of makeup. She wore a beige T-shirt and long jean skirt that shadowed the tops of her flat shoes. Latoya's mother could make Michelle Duggar look like a sexpot—and that's what she wanted from her three daughters as well.

"How are you, Mama?" Latoya asked, stepping back to close the door.

"Better now," Mrs. James said, her Alabama accent still in place. She pressed her face into the baby's neck.

"So y'all were just in the neighborhood . . . from Newark?" she asked.

"We need an invite to see our family?" she countered.

Latoya let her be. The summer sun beamed down on them brightly and Latoya shaded her eyes with her hands as she looked at her father walking up to her with Tiffany's hand firmly in his. She felt a pang of regret that he had never been that demonstrative with her or her younger sisters. When they were growing up Deacon James had nothing but condemnation and Bible verses for them.

"Hi Daddy," she said, not knowing if she should hug him or kiss him or just nod.

Latoya wondered if the awkwardness between them would ever thin.

"Is that what you wore to church?" he asked, frowning a bit over the rim of his glasses.

Latoya ignored the question and moved past him to hug each of her sisters. Latasha was eighteen and Latrece was about to turn seventeen. They reminded her so much of herself at that age, looking like mini-Mamas with their gloss-free lips and severe ponytails. Spending time with them was the only bright spot of this family hijacking— uh, visit.

They weren't going to say much in front of their parents and Latoya knew she would have to get them alone to really get the scoop on how they were doing. She turned and moved back to the SUV to retrieve her purse from the car, then unlocked the front door. She froze as she took in the unkempt living room. Tiffany's and Taquan's toys were everywhere. The laundry she had yet to fold was in a hamper by the suede sofa. The dishes from the breakfast they ate were in front of the television set. And no, there was no down-home Sunday dinner waiting to be eaten.

Latoya's shoulders slumped lower than Eeyore's from *Winnie-the-Pooh*. She opened the door wide and waved them in. "Excuse the house—"

"Lord, *truly* have mercy," Mrs. James sighed.

Her father clucked his tongue in disapproval.

Taquan Jr. reached for Latoya.

Tiffany went straight to the sixty-inch flat screen and turned on her favorite DVD of *The Powerpuff Girls*.

"Excuse me," Latoya said, holding up her hand and turning to head down the hall to the guest bathroom off the den.

Her parents were so critical and Latoya knew she had

just given them a plateful to digest and spit back out at her. The last thing she needed was a surprise visit from her parents. She had to get her mind right if she was going to put up with their mess.

Latoya opened her purse and pulled out a can of Altoids. She popped the square tin open and shook one into her hand. She tossed it back into her mouth and drank water from the faucet before rising and settling her eyes on her reflection in the oval mirror over the sink.

"Just to take off the edge," she told herself.

Two or three put her to sleep. One or two put her at ease.

If they were really Altoids and not OxyContin pills there really wouldn't be a problem.

Chapter 9
Monica

One Month Later

Over the rim of her flute Monica surveyed the crowd mingling and conversing with one another in the living room of the condo. It was a nice mix of business colleagues and friends. Everyone seemed to be enjoying themselves, including Monica. She loved it when a plan came together.

The catered dinner had been served and leisurely enjoyed with lots of lively banter among everyone at the table. The perfect wines accompanied each course. Their house manager, Halston, had selected the perfect staff who knew how to appear and disappear as needed to make their guests feel comfortable.

She raked her fingers through the long lengths of her waist-length hair as she eyed Cameron across the room talking to several men. Like them he was in a hand-tailored suit but in her eyes the men could not compete with the way his clothes hung off his athletic frame. Cameron looked like a man of power and wealth. He looked like the alpha male. The big dog. Top motherfucking gun.

She pressed her thighs together as she felt her pussy wake up. *Not now kitty-kat. Not now.*

Monica strolled over toward Cameron. She smiled at the gentlemen before leaning in a bit to lightly touch his chest beneath his silk shirt as she whispered in his ear, "I need my pussy ate the same way you licked the spoon during dessert."

Cameron tensed as he turned his head and looked down at her. She tilted her face up and gave him a soft expression meant to show him just how playfully sexy she felt. Their mouths were less than six inches apart. "I can take care of that."

She licked her lips and patted his chest. "I look forward to it," she said softly before strolling away, knowing his eyes were on her in the bright red body-hugging dress she wore.

She knew that the years of being a dancer had her body right and tight and even though she had given up what once was her one true love she still made sure to stay in shape. She blinked hard and lost her step as she flashed back to the day her ex, Rah, stomped on her leg and broke her thighbone in half. As if catching him in bed with Dom had not been enough, the bastard beat her ass.

She pushed the thought away, pleased that his psychotic dope-sniffing ass was still in jail for what he did to her. It had been over six or seven years and the time had dulled the pain and anger, but she was nowhere near forgetting and doubted she ever would be.

"Monica, girl, this night was everything."

She turned to find Hopper Cruz standing behind her looking party ready in a red linen suit with white leather shoes. Hopper was a fashion blogger who was well respected for his fashion sense and style. She made sure he was invited to add a little bit of intelligent humor to the crowd.

"Thank you, Hopper. I had a good time that I needed after working so hard to set up my business," she said, taking another sip of her Bollinger champagne.

He touched his flute to hers. "Make money, money.

Make money, money," Hopper sang low enough for just the two.

"That's the name of the game," she said, her eyes landing on her newest client, Kelson Hunt a.k.a. K-Hunta.

She was dying to ask him if their lighting was so intense that he needed the shades on . . . in the house . . . at ten at night. She was surprised to see him minus the entourage and dressed in a suit. She wondered if he was more Kelson than K-Hunta that night.

"He is really headed on a one-way train to Nowhereville in OneHitWonderland," Hopper said.

The man was also an incorrigible gossip.

Monica bit back a smile. "Not my job, Hopper," she said. "But I am going to help him live well after he gets there though."

"Please do," he stressed, with another touch of his flute to hers.

"I love you, Hopper," she said, giving in to a laugh.

"You're going to love me even more as you watch me scoot my fine ass over to your guest bathroom to catch Jasmine coming out after her fifth trip in there tonight," he said, his eyes piercing the door. "She's gone sniff her fucking nose off."

And he was gone, fast walking just as he promised, to lean against the wall outside the guest bathroom, as he waited for Jasmine Lee, a well-known publicist, to exit.

"Any chance you'll let a man spoil you?"

Monica turned and eyed Kelson standing at her shoulder. She briefly wondered when he double backed around the room to sneak up on her. *Like a silent fart just appearing out of nowhere and offending.* "As a matter of fact I let a man—my man—do that every day," she said smugly.

Kelson eyed her from head to toe, his eyes lingering on the deep plunge of her dress front. "Lucky man," he said.

Monica bit back a smart-ass Brick City-style retort.

"Thank you," she said politely before turning her attention back to Hopper just as he pretended to accidentally bump into Jasmine, knocking her sequined clutch onto the floor.

"Let me help you get that," Hopper said with a meaningful glance at Monica as he twisted his mouth like *Bitch, please*.

Jasmine pushed Hopper back and bent down to scoop up her own purse. "Thanks anyway, Hopper," she said, hurrying away from him to reclaim her spot by her husband's side.

From across the room Hopper swiped at his long aquiline nose with his finger and then sniffed. Monica just shook her head at him.

"I just want you to know the offer is on the table."

She didn't even look at him. "I didn't know you were still there, Kelson," she said. She was lying. She knew and she hoped ignoring his ass would send him on his way. Monica was regretting her decision to welcome him to her business dinner with an invite. *His first and motherfucking last*.

"When it comes to a chance to have you, I want you to know I'm not going anywhere," he said, before strolling away like a modern-day Superfly or some shit.

Monica rolled her eyes and resolved to place a call to his manager, Usain, first thing Monday morning to get his client straight that the only service she was offering up was financial advice and not pussy. If he couldn't get that then he could get the million dollars he gave her to invest and haul ass.

Monica stiffened as a hand touched the small of her back. "Look, motherfucker," she whispered harshly. The rest of her words died in her throat at the sight of Cameron standing behind her. "Sorry."

"You okay?" he asked.

"I didn't know it was you touching me," she said, stopping one of the uniformed servers to set her empty champagne flute on the tray he carried.

Cameron kissed her brow. "It's good to know that's how you would check a fool for trying," he said, his voice deep.

She turned and brought her hands up his back. "This pussy is all yours," she assured him.

"All mine?"

"Except when I need it to pee," she quipped.

Cameron laughed. "Come on, let's wind this up," he said, reaching down for her hand to take in his as he led her across the expansive, stylishly decorated room to the foyer.

The effects of the champagne and the success of the dinner party had Monica in a great mood. She really enjoyed the life she and Cameron had built together. She really couldn't imagine anything they could do to make it better.

"Sleepy?" Cameron asked after they closed their front door behind the last of their guests.

"Happy," she told him.

" 'Night, Halston," they said in unison as they made their way through the living room, leaving their house manager to supervise the cleanup.

When they arose in the morning all signs of the dinner party would be gone.

"Good night, Mr. Steele. Ms. Winters," he said.

They walked down the hall leading to the staircase that winded up to the second floor where the bedrooms were located. "Sure would be good to hear you called Mrs. Steele," Cameron said, his hand massaging her bottom as they climbed the stairs.

"I thought having one Mrs. Steele floating around New York was plenty," she said.

"You mean my mother?"

Monica side-eyed him as they reached the top level and stepped into an area in the center of the bedrooms that was big enough to make into a room of its own. "Not funny, motherfucker."

"I haven't laid eyes on that *Ms*. Steele since our divorce five years ago."

They walked down the hall to their master bedroom suite. "I should have married you," he said, loosening the knot of his tie.

"Yes, but you didn't," she reminded him, being sure to say it in a tone to let him know she was being playful. She picked up the remote and turned on the television on the wall as she kicked off her heels.

"Yes, but I want to now," he said, reaching out to grab her by the waist and fall back on the middle of the king-sized bed with her. "I'm ready to marry you and have babies running around this big motherfucking apartment."

His eyes were on her intently as he lay above her, cushioning her body into the bed. She made sure not to frown. This was an old-ass argument and she was in too good of a mood for the baby debate. Again. *Damn*.

"*Welcome to . . . The A-List.*"

Monica lifted her head up and looked over Cameron's broad shoulder at the flat screen on the wall across from their bed. She eyed Danielle looking fierce and fabulous standing next to her cohost.

The sight of her transported her back to the days Danielle ended their friendship.

At first she had been angry and resentful of Danielle pulling away from their friendship. Then she got over it and kept moving. Seasons change and friends don't always remain. Obviously what they built up over the years wasn't as important to Danielle as it was to her.

Monica twisted her head to the left as Cameron began pressing kisses to her collarbone.

"Stay tuned for my exclusive interview with Salma Hayek up after the break."

Five years.

Monica remembered the summer day the four of them grabbed their men and rented a room at this nice hotel in New York just to enjoy the pool. They had all answered the question about where they thought they would be in five years.

The answers were fuzzy to her now but she knew no one guessed that they all would no longer be friends.

"Monica."

She shifted her eyes back up to his.

"Fuck what's on that television," he said in clipped tones, his face tense. "I want a family."

She picked up the remote from where she dropped it on the bed and turned the TV off. She licked the sudden dryness from her lips. "I do too . . . one day," she admitted. "But not now, Cameron. No."

His face filled with disbelief before he rolled off her and jumped to his feet. "No?" he snapped. "To marrying me? To having my baby? To building a stronger life with me? Huh, Monica? No to what?"

"I have so many plans for my business . . . for *my* life, Cameron," she told him, shifting to rise from the bed and walk over to him.

"*Your* life? So what the fuck are *we* doing?" he roared, the veins in his throat stretched as he threw his hands up in the air.

"We are helping each other go for our dreams," she snapped. "And whether you believe it or not my career is just as important to me as yours is to you."

Cameron let out a laugh that was brimming with sarcasm. "I hardly think juggling seven clients requires so much attention that you can't be a mother as well."

Monica balled her hand into a fist to keep from slapping the shit out of him. His derision of her business was clear. She didn't like the taste of it. Not at all. His words hurt her. "Fuck you, Cameron," she said in a low voice that carried even more weight than his roar. "I am sorry that I am not Serena, some lifeless, useless, asinine-ass woman who wanted nothing more than to be Mrs. Cameron Steele and pop out a brood of fucking children for you. I am *so* sorry that I wear shoes around this motherfucker and stay my 'educated, career-driven, want-to-succeed-on-my-own' ass out the fucking kitchen," she spat, her eyes blazing.

Cameron shook his head before he hung it to his chest with his hands in the pocket of his slacks. "And I'm sorry that your priorities are fucked up," he said, swiping his finger across the tip of his nose before he turned and strode over to the door leading to the bathroom. He paused at the entrance but didn't turn around. "I hope it's worth it."

He disappeared into the bathroom.

Monica punched and kicked at the air with frustration like she was having a hood fight. She ran across the room and tried the doorknob. It was locked. She lightly dropped her head onto the door. "It is worth it. It's worth it to me," she yelled.

That first jolt of spray from the shower echoed.

Monica closed her eyes. "It's worth it to me," she whispered, turning to press her back to the door as her chest heaved.

Bzzz . . . Bzzz . . . Bzzz . . .

Her eyes shifted over to the wooden box on the end of the dresser where they both charged all of their electrical devices. She could see it was her glittered-covered iPhone that lit up. Pushing up off the door she massaged her face as she made her way across the black tile of their bedroom. She unplugged her iPhone and walked out into the hall as she checked it.

A text message.

She opened it and then frowned in confusion. "I'm watching you, Monica," she read aloud. She checked the phone number the message came from and didn't recognize it.

How did they get my cell number?

"Watching me do what?" she asked herself. "Please. What the fuck ever."

Shrugging she turned to head back into the bedroom but stopped at the threshold. She made her way toward one of the guest bedrooms instead, locking the door securely behind her before she lay across the fully made bed and pressed her face into one of the pillows. She didn't care that her makeup and her tears would run together and stain the five-hundred-dollar sheets.

GIRL TALK

The three women sat so closely together that the black of their garments and their wide-brimmed hats seemed to run together. One tightly held the hand of the woman to her right and then she held the hand of the woman to her right as well. They were on the last pew in the back of the church. The sounds of mourning for their friend surrounded them even over the crescendo of the organ and the words of the minister giving the eulogy.

"Gone too soon," the minister said, reaching down to pick up his monogrammed handkerchief to pat at the sweat beading on his bald head and upper lip. "It is always difficult to see someone in the prime of their lives go on to our Heavenly Father. We believe death is only for the old. We believe and hope that every baby born into this world will live a full life until they are old. But see our plan is not always God's plan and . . . and we have to accept and to believe that He knows best."

"Amen, preacher," a woman called out.

"And so you cry because you miss them. You cry because you think of everything they will never get to experience. You cry because you are mourning them. But you rejoice in knowing that your loved one is with God and there is no better place to be than in the sweet embrace and presence of our Heavenly Father."

Their grips of their hands tightened. Their shoulders sank just a bit more. Their hearts ached. Their souls were weary.

"I wish it was that easy," one whispered.

The other two barely heard her and they leaned in closer.

"I promise you that we will get through this," the other said, locking her eyes on the other two one at a time.

The last nodded as if she believed that. But she didn't. None of them did.

Chapter 10
Keesha

Keesha rolled over onto her back and opened her eyes. She allowed herself a long stretch, enjoying the feel of the crisp cotton against her body. She glanced at the time displayed on the digital cable box. It was almost two in the afternoon. Her days of getting up at seven to mess with a nine-to-five were over two years ago. *The good life.*

She cleared her throat and reached over onto the nightstand for the remote, turning on the TV before she finally rolled up out of bed. Her feet got tangled up in the clothing littering the floor. "Shit," she swore, kicking a platform sandal out of her path to the bathroom.

Keesha looked over her shoulder at the bedroom door and Corey walked into the room. "You off early?" she said.

Corey made a face. "I was off today."

"And you let me lay up in bed all alone?" she asked, continuing on to the bathroom to run the shower. She pulled the oversized T-shirt she wore over her head, careful not to disrupt the satin scarf holding her hair in place.

He mumbled something.

She stuck her head out the door. "Huh?"

Corey paused in searching through his wallet to look up at her. "Hell, you ain't fucking. Why would I lay up in bed next to pussy I got to beg to sniff?"

Keesha made sure her facial expression didn't change and her eyes didn't shift, revealing her guilt. "Whatever, Corey," she said, turning away from him. "And we need to hire a maid."

"No the hell we don't."

Keesha stepped back out of the bathroom, the steam from the shower swirling out around her naked body. "Yes we do. I don't have time to keep the house up."

"It's a townhouse, Keesha, not a mini-mansion," Corey said, turning to leave.

"It's five times bigger than that roach trap your ass was living in," she snapped.

Corey turned. "And before you *thought* you became the next Terry McMillan that roach trap was all your ass was used to, too."

Keesha waved her hand at him dismissively. "So I ain't supposed to want better?"

"Yeah but don't forget where you came from."

Keesha sucked her teeth. "We're getting the maid," she told him, turning to walk back into the bathroom.

Corey appeared in the doorway. "We can't afford that."

She glanced at him over her shoulder. "No, *you* can't," she said before she stepped inside the shower and closed the glass door in his face.

He slammed the bathroom door on his way out.

Money—or rather *her* money—was the biggest cause of arguments between them. And Keesha couldn't understand what his problem was. She grew up in the projects, stripped to raise her child, and fought back from a drug addiction. Now was the time to live and live well. Why not spend it and enjoy?

Corey had been fully behind Keesha's dreams of writing her book. He purchased her a computer, encouraged her to finish the book, and even kicked ideas around with her.

It was Corey who made her take getting her book published seriously. He made her believe in herself. And that made her hustle harder. For herself, her daughter, and for him.

All of the happiness they shared the day she got a call from a New York agent offering to represent her disappeared a long time ago. *Happy don't live in this bitch anymore.*

Keesha finished her shower and dressed in yoga pants and a tank, prepared to finally start her day. She grabbed the wallet she kept her cigarettes in. As she left their bedroom she eyed the closed door to her office. She really needed to get in at least twenty pages that day if she was going to meet her new extended deadline. "After I eat something," she said, continuing on down the stairs and into the kitchen.

At the sound of girlish giggles she looked out the window. Kimani and a couple of the girls from the neighborhood were playing in the inground pool.

Keesha made herself a sandwich and took it with her outside to lie on one of the patio chairs. She waved at her daughter and her friends, hoping they stayed in the pool. She was not in the mood to hear nary nothing about whatever little boys they were crushing on.

Not when she needed to figure out the big fight scene at the end of her book. Keesha felt like she wanted to do something with her lead character, Lick Me. She wanted to give her readers an ending that left them with their mouths opened. Something that would shock them.

"Hey, Keesha."

She leaned up and looked over her shoulder. She smiled as their neighbor Jeremiah came down the steps of the deck to sit down in the patio chaise beside her. He moved into the townhouse four or five months ago and Keesha had instantly clicked with the man. "How'd you get in?"

she asked, sitting up to pull a cigarette and her rhinestone-covered lighter from its case.

"Corey let me in on his way out," he said, reaching over to take half of her sandwich.

Keesha frowned. *Where the fuck he going?*

"When did you get back?" she asked him even as she reached over to where Kimani had the cordless phone sitting. She dialed Corey's cell phone number so quickly that the beeps seemed to run together.

"I just got in yesterday. I would have come over but I had to get over that long flight from Hawaii," Jeremiah said.

Corey never answered. The call went to his voice mail and Keesha hung up at the sound of the automated message. "Next time you and your boo take me with you," she said, sounding as distracted as her thoughts.

Is Corey fucking around on me?

She tried calling Corey's number twice more and neither time did he answer.

"Marcus won't mind," Jeremiah said, leaning over to lightly tap and free the ashes from her forgotten cigarette.

"Huh?" Keesha asked, turning her head to look at him.

"I said Marcus won't mind," Jeremiah repeated. "He loves your books."

Keesha smiled even though her nerves were shot. "You'll have to bring him over to meet me one day," she said.

She blinked to remove an image of Corey's dark and naked body sweating as he grinded between the legs of some faceless whore.

"I will. He still isn't willing to admit to anyone he's gay." Jeremiah looked over at the girls in the pool.

"So he's manly like you?" Keesha asked, putting out her cigarette butt on the concrete and reaching for another one.

Jeremiah eyed her.

Keesha waved her hand dismissively. "I mean none of that finger-snapping, lip-smacking, honey boo-boo shit," she said.

Jeremiah still eyed her and cocked his head to the side.

"Hell, you don't look gay." She threw her hands up in the air. "You're not flaming—"

"You're going to need a ladder and a prayer to get out the hole you're digging," he said, before finally smiling.

Keesha realized he had been joking with her. "Ooh fuck you," she said.

"No thank you."

Brrrnnnggg . . .

Keesha snatched up the cordless phone, thinking it was Corey calling her back. "Where you at?" she asked.

"So you finally answering your phone?"

Keesha held the phone away from her head and gave herself a five count at the sound of her mother's voice.

"Something wrong, Keesha?" Jeremiah asked.

Taking a deep breath she looked down at the phone with her thumb poised above the button to send Diane back out of her life. After the way her mother acted a complete fool at the cookout, Keesha had decided that she had enough of her. Diane was on the no-call/no-answer list at the Lands-Miller household.

She heard Jeremiah's concern but didn't answer him as she finally pressed the phone to her ear. "What do you want, Diane?"

"So you just forgot you got a mama again?"

"What do you want, Diane?" she repeated.

The line went quiet.

Keesha knew what was coming next.

"I'm on the list to be evicted and I need to borrow money to catch up my rent."

I knew it.

"They gonna put my shit on the curb next week, Keesha."

She pulled her knees to her chest. "Diane, I don't have—"

"Or I could just put my shit in storage and move in with you."

"Fuck no!" She knocked her hand against the armrest, causing the fiery end of her ashes to break off and drop onto her thigh. She yelped as it burned a hole into her pants and then singed her skin.

"Ain't this 'bout a bitch," she snapped, wetting her thumb and pressing it to the burn.

"Did you call me a bitch, bitch?" Diane asked.

"What's wrong, Keesha?" Kimani called from the pool.

"You call your mama by her first name?" one of the kids asked.

"Your mother's fine," Jeremiah called over to Kimani.

"Look, Diane, I can't keep bailing you out. I got my own bills," Keesha said into the phone.

The line stayed quiet.

Keesha dropped her head into her hands. *I'm so tired of her shit.*

They both knew she would catch up on the rent because they both knew that Keesha had no plans of moving her mother into her home. She would never inflict Diane's ratchetness on the neighborhood. Never.

"How much?"

"Eight hundred and eighty."

Keesha's eyes got big. "Your rent is under a hundred. When the last time you paid your shit?"

"And you're talking to your mother?" Jeremiah asked.

Keesha waved her hand at him.

"I kicked Doc to the curb, lost my job at the Dollar Store, and my unemployment ran out," Diane explained.

Keesha squeezed one eye shut and arched the brow over

the other as she fought not to lose it. "I'll take the money straight to the office tomorrow. I have to go."

Click.

And Diane was gone. No thank you. Nothing.

Keesha dropped the phone. "Crazy bitch," she mumbled.

"That was . . . different," Jeremiah said.

Keesha lit yet another cigarette as she laughed a little. "That's one word for it," she said. "So are dysfunctional, debilitating, and damaged."

Jeremiah remained quiet.

"I think my mother is crazy. Like seriously, needs-to-be-on-a-pill type crazy," Keesha admitted, looking off into the trees and garden surrounding the edges of the backyard.

"I remember the scene at the cookout," Jeremiah said. "You should get her some help."

"Been there, done that," she said, her voice sad and tired. "I used to get high and I, uh . . . overdosed. I had to go to therapy and my mama issues came up."

Again Jeremiah stayed quiet.

"My mama taught me how to smoke weed and how men were only good for money. When I told her I wanted to strip she gave me that bullshit line from *The Player's Club*."

" 'Make the money, don't let it make you.' "

Keesha nodded as she took a deep inhale of her cigarette, enjoying the feel of the smoke against her tongue. She went on to tell him she started therapy while in rehab. Her therapist had suggested inviting Diane to a session. In the beginning their relationship had improved. Diane started acting less like a friend and more like a mother. Her mouth had become less reckless and she had seemed genuine in asking Keesha to forgive her for playing Russian roulette with the choice of her father.

"That shit lasted all of two or three months," Keesha said with another release of a long stream of smoke. "Diane told the therapist to lick every bit of black off her ass before she left the session and never returned."

Jeremiah looked apologetic. "That's . . ."

"Different," they said in unison.

Brrrnnnggg . . .

Keesha picked up the phone but this time she checked the caller ID. "Where are you?" she asked Corey, standing up to walk out of earshot. "How you just gone up and leave without saying anything?"

"Let you tell it, you don't need me around there."

Something in his tone filled her with guilt. "When will you be back?" she asked.

"Whenever I get the fuck back."

Click.

Keesha raised her brows in surprise. *Humph.*

Jeremiah stood up. "You cool? I have to get to work."

He worked nights as a security guard.

"I'm good. Be sure to bring the photos of your trip next time you come over," she said.

He waved to the girls in the pool and disappeared through the opening in the wooden fence separating their properties.

She tapped the phone against her chin as that image of Corey and another woman sexing each other flashed again. Turning the phone over she dialed Shawn's cell number.

"Whaddup."

"You," she said, feeling some of her stress release. A side dick was a welcome distraction.

Chapter 11
Danielle

"Ms. Johnson . . . Ms. Johnson. We're here."

Danielle lightly smacked her lips as she opened her eyes and sat up. When her vision focused she looked into the smiling face of her driver. "Thank you," she said, smoothing her hand over her slicked-back ponytail before she picked her tote up from the floor of the limousine.

She stepped out onto the sidewalk in front of The Top. It felt good to lay eyes on the building. It felt like home and for a former foster kid that was huge.

"Thank you," she told the driver again, a burly man with flaming red hair and startling green eyes. She passed him a tip.

"Good night, ma'am," he said, sounding more Kentucky than Jersey.

Danielle entered the building with a yawn. It was just after nine but she felt exhausted. First her flight from Los Angeles and then the ride from New York to New Jersey.

She was in town to attend a movie premiere and had her own junior suite at the Hotel Gansevoort in New York, but she had wanted to check on her apartment. For the rest of the weekend her day would be filled with preparations for the premiere. Hair. Makeup. Wardrobe. Going over the facts the producers provided to make sure she asked the best questions on the carpet. Reading up on the details of the movie.

"You're late."

Danielle looked over to her left at the sound of the deep voice. Pleasure sat in one of the leather club chairs surrounding a low-slung wooden table. He was dressed in black track pants, a snug-fitting tee with a baseball cap over his thin dreads. Just like he was every time she saw him. She decided to meet him at her apartment and not at the hotel where the rest of the *A-List* staff were staying. Her business was her business. Especially sex for pay. "My dime, my time."

He smiled and he rose to his full height. "Tick-tock."

They walked together to the elevator. Danielle was relatively tall for a woman at five foot eight, but a tall and well-built man like Pleasure made her feel delicate and small. "I thought you weren't coming," she said, as they stepped into the elevator like two strangers.

"Last-minute cancellation."

She cut her eyes up at him. "You're a busy man."

Pleasure cut his eyes down at her. "Business is good."

"I bet it is," she said.

He chuckled.

"I'm curious," she said, turning to lean against the rear wall of the elevator and look up at him. "Ever fell for one of us?"

He looked down at her briefly before turning his head back to look out toward the closed elevator doors. "Almost."

"Free dick and all?"

A broad smile spread across his handsome chocolate face. "Free dick and all."

"Does she know?" Danielle asked as the elevator stopped on her floor.

He shook his head.

"Still . . . seeing her?"

"She no longer needed my services."

They walked to her door.

"Did that bother you?" she asked.

"Nope, because I made sure she wouldn't want my services anymore."

Danielle nodded in understanding. "You set her free."

He didn't say anything else. That was fine because Danielle was done with her questions. Whatever fatigue she felt had already began to dissipate when she laid eyes on him. Whatever fatigue was left after completely vanished as she turned on the lights inside her apartment.

Pleasure dropped the athletic duffel bag he held and instantly picked her up into his arms. "Bedroom," he said.

Danielle pointed to the hall as she splayed her fingers against his strong shoulder and used one foot to kick off the shoe of the other. They dropped with resonating thuds as he carried her across the living room and down the hall to the room at the end.

He set her down on her bare feet and then sat on the foot of her bed, pulling her body between his thighs. And she stood as he slowly undressed her of the sheer blouse and pencil skirt she wore. Next were her lace bikinis and demi-bra. With each layer of clothing he removed and let drop to the floor he pressed kisses to her skin.

And when she stood before him naked and exposed, he rose and lifted his arms high above his head for her to undress him. She did; repaying him in kind with heated and moist kisses to his skin as she exposed every inch of the hard contours of his body.

They fell on the bed together and he used his body to press her down into the softness before rising to his knees. His dick was hard and curving from his body like a strong upper arm as he began to massage her body from head to toe.

Danielle lay back and gave in to the pleasure.

He was worth every cent and she needed it. He knew how to take his time and miss not one spot on a woman's body. His focus—his aim—was to please. His name suited him well.

Danielle hollered out as he slid the first few inches of dick into her from behind, his hands twisted in her hair, pulling her head backward as he delivered delicious thrust after thrust.

"You need this dick, don't you?" he asked, his voice deeper than his thrust—and that was no small feat.

"Yes," Danielle cried out, feeling his sweat drip from his body onto her buttocks.

"Tell me," he ordered, his voice steady but determined.

"I need that dick," she whispered, her voice tired from the exertion of being fucked well.

"I'm fucking the shit out of you, ain't I?" he asked, sucking his thumb before he gently worked it into her ass.

"Yes," she moaned, biting her bottom lip.

"What's my name?"

"Pleasure, motherfucker."

He chuckled and slapped her fleshy and full ass. *WHAP.* "What's my motherfucking name?" he asked with a deep, hard thrust that caused the soft hairs surrounding his dick to press against her pussy from behind.

"Pleasure," she cried out.

"And what do I give?"

Danielle bit her bottom lip as she grabbed a pillow and pressed her face into it. "Pleasure," she mumbled into the sweet coolness.

Ding-dong.

Danielle lifted her head from the pillow.

Pleasure kept plowing away behind her. Thumb still in ass. Dick steadily filling her as he bent over her to massage her nipples the way he knew she loved.

She got lost in him again as he pulled his condom-covered dick out of her just long enough to slap it soundly against her ass, slide it up and down the length of her open core before he slid back in her in one hard thrust. "Shit," she swore, as he moved to squat behind her with his hands pressed into her shoulders as he delivered tiny thrusts that were just as lethal as anything in his sex arsenal.

Ding-dong.

Danielle lifted her head from the sweat-soaked pillow again.

"You want to get that door or get this dick?" he asked, patient as ever.

Danielle's heart was pounding. "Let me see who it is," she said.

Pleasure gave both of her ass cheeks a light tap before he pulled his dick out of her and lay down on the bed.

She climbed off the bed and grabbed a silky housecoat from the door of her walk-in closet, pulling it on as she left the bedroom. She raked her fingers through the lost curls of her hair, crossing the living room and looking out the peephole of the door. She dropped back down onto her bare feet at the sight of Omari standing there.

No one even knew she was in town.

She looked over her shoulder toward her bedroom and then back at the door before she finally opened it. "Hi, Omari," she said, hiding her body behind the door. "I was in bed."

He smiled at her, looking handsome and dapper in a linen suit with rich brown leather accessories and a crisp white shirt. "I just happened to be pulling into the parking garage when I saw the limo dropping you off. I thought I would stop by and welcome you back to town."

Danielle smiled at him genuinely. The man was fine. His style of dress fashionable. And his persistence endearing. But she was not looking for a relationship.

She turned the deadbolt lock on her door and then stepped out into the hallway, letting the door close behind her. She crossed her arms over her chest to keep her nipples from pressing against the thin silk. "Omari, listen, I have to be honest with you. I'm really focused on my career and I am not looking for a relationship right now. I just can't be distracted from my goals. I don't multitask very well and right now it's all about my career."

He leaned against the wall and looked down at her. "I'm a busy man myself so I can understand and the fact that you are so driven makes your fine ass even more attractive to me," he said, pressing a hand to his chest.

Danielle looked down at her bare feet and her nude-colored toenails. There was something about the man that gave her that thrill.

He reached out and lightly touched her chin to lift her face up. "Listen, you're in LA and I'm here, so let's just take it easy. Chill. Enjoy dinner when we're in each other's town. Nothing major. Grown folks shit."

Her face tingled where his hand touched her chin. "Nothing major," she stressed with a meaningful look.

He chuckled deep in his chest before he lowered his head and lightly pressed his lips to hers. Curious, it was Danielle who reached up to grab the sides of his face and deepen the kiss. It was slow and deliberate. Warm and tasteful. Simply electrifying. She moaned as his hands came down to her waist to pull her body close to his as he gently sucked the tip of her tongue. She felt her clit come alive again.

And then she remembered Pleasure waiting for her in bed.

With regret she ended the kiss. "I don't have to be in New York until three so I'll call that number you gave me in the morning."

Omari nodded and turned to stroll with pure swagger

to the elevators. He gave her one last look before stepping into the elevator. "In the morning?" he said, pointing at her with a smile.

Danielle just nodded and gave him a wave before she turned and entered her apartment, removing the deadbolt lock before she closed it securely. She grabbed enough hundred dollar bills to pay his fee and then slipped the robe from her body to walk back to the bedroom naked.

Pleasure was lying in the middle of the bed stroking his snakelike dick back to life as he put on a new condom. Danielle sat the money on the nightstand and climbed onto the bed, straddling him. She leaned down to sway her hard nipples against his mouth. Pleasure moaned as he tilted his chin up to capture one in his mouth and swirled his tongue against the chocolate bud.

Her horniness was intensified by the pure chemistry she experienced with Omari at the door. Pleasure was hell in bed and had a dick that should be licensed but they both were clear that it was just sex and so there was no chemistry. They would never make love. They fucked each other. Simple and plain.

She swatted his hands away and sat up to guide his dick inside her as she took the lead of what could be their last session. If Omari was even half as good as Pleasure and willing then she saw no need to pay for dick.

Danielle played with Pleasure's nipples as she circled her hips against him, sending the hard shaft of his dick in slick movements against her clit.

Danielle wanted to cum and she was going for it.

My dime, my time.

But Pleasure was used to being in control and so he dug his fingers into the flesh of her hips and rocked his hips back and forth on the bed, intensifying each thrust.

"Ah," Danielle cried, leaning back and covering her

eyes with her forearm as she felt an explosive nut brewing in her.

Pleasure moved quickly and grabbed Danielle around the waist, his dick still buried deep within her, and turned her onto her back. He lifted one of her legs over his shoulder and twisted his body at an angle as he continued to clench and unclench his hard buttocks with every stroke of his dick against her walls.

Danielle's head hung off the bed and she didn't give a damn. Pleasure pressed his thumb against her clit and quickened his pumps. She cried out as tiny explosions went off inside her until one big continuous spasm of white-hot release coated his dick.

He turned his head and sucked at a spot on her calf, his eyes tightly closed as his body tensed with the first fiery jolt of his cum. It was a struggle to ignore the sensitivity of his tip as he fought to continue plunging his dick inside of her again and again until they both were spent.

"Whoo," Danielle sighed, feeling out of breath as her heart pounded fast and hard.

Pleasure fell back onto the bed and used his strong grip to pull her up more so that her head no longer dangled like a test dummy. "I don't know who was at the door but thank them for me," he said, his hand splayed across his chest as it rose and fell with his labored breathing.

Danielle curled up onto her side as she felt sleep coming on strong. "You can catch a nap for a couple of hours if you need to," she said, her voice slightly muffled by the pillows her face was sunk into.

Pleasure chuckled as he sat up in bed. "Oh this some eat-and-run type shit," he teased, walking over to the bathroom with the condom still clinging onto his dick.

Moments later she heard the toilet flush.

And that was all she heard as she gave in to the rest her body needed.

*   *   *

When Danielle awakened early that next morning, Pleasure was gone. That was fine by her. They both got what they wanted last night.

She hopped from the bed, still naked, and pulled off all the covers, making a mental note to drop the duvet cover at the dry cleaner and to place her linens in the wash. Both had to be sweat soaked and stained with . . . fluids.

She laughed at that as she entered the bathroom. When she emerged twenty minutes later the steam of the shower escaped with her. She had a plush pink towel around her body and another around her freshly shampooed hair.

Danielle was looking forward to grabbing something to eat with Omari before she headed back into the city, but first she just wanted to decompress and enjoy being home for the first time in a long time.

"Welcome home," she told herself as she stood at the entrance to the living room and enjoyed the sunlight beaming through the bay windows.

For one second she allowed herself to remember the fun times she had in her home once Latoya moved in with Tiffany and Keesha moved in with Kimani. But somehow the fun times turned into stressful times as she took over the mother role. That shit had become tiring and she felt more of herself disappear as their lives took precedence.

She grabbed her iPad from her tote on the couch and walked into the kitchen to put on a kettle of water to make tea. The only food in her fridge was eggs left over during her last weekend trip home. She worked on frying a couple of those. It would be enough to hold her until she made plans with Omari.

Once her food and drink was ready she sat at the counter and turned on her iPad. She read through all her favorite gossip blogs, swiped through a couple of the digital magazines to which she subscribed, and checked Twitter to see what was trending. Last, she checked her e-mails and then her text messages.

Her eyes skimmed the list for the sender and the subject line. She opened messages according to priority and business trumped everything else. Danielle paused. Her eyes shifted up the list and widened a little bit as she re-read, "I know your secrets, Danielle."

Her heart pumped as she opened the text. "The hell?" she whispered, looking at the taunt, in caps, repeated more times than she cared to count.

I KNOW YOUR SECRETS, DANIELLE.
I KNOW YOUR SECRETS, DANIELLE.
I KNOW YOUR SECRETS, DANIELLE.

Over and over and over again.

She sat back from the iPad as she frowned. Being in the public eye she knew she was open to all types of people of various levels of competency. And it was sent to the e-mail address on the network's website. But still . . .

She couldn't lie and say the shit didn't rattle her, especially since she had secrets she damn sure didn't want revealed.

Chapter 12
Latoya

"I love you, Mama."

Latoya made a sappy face as she looked at her daughter's face via Skype on her laptop. "I love you, too," she said, wishing she could see more than just the blank wall behind her daughter's head. She did know they were at his house in Short Hills, New Jersey, and she didn't doubt that his mother, Janice, was on the premises helping him to take care of his little girl.

Tiffany was halfway through spending two weeks with her father, Lavitius Drooms, better known as the platinum-selling rap artist Bones. It had been a couple of years since his last big hit but his hefty child support check came monthly like a menstrual cycle and he was constantly on the road touring. She couldn't lie that he always made time for Tiffany even though he still hated every bit of her mother's guts.

Latoya couldn't blame the man. She did falsely accuse him of rape to prevent her parents from knowing she was having sex. That was just childish, weak, and completely reckless of her. A moment Latoya was not at all proud of.

"Grandma is making me pink pancakes for breakfast," she said, all smiles and dimples and missing teeth.

"Ooh that sounds good," Latoya told her, shifting on

her seat on the side of the bed. "I sure wish I had me some pink pancakes."

"I'll tell Grandma to send you some."

Lord, don't. If there was anyone who hated her worse than Bones it was his mother. Thank the Lord they all were able to hide their true feelings for each other and put Tiffany first.

"A'ight Tiff, tell your moms you'll call her tonight."

Latoya heard Bones's deep and gravelly voice clearly even though he didn't step in front of the camera.

"Daddy said—"

"I hear him, baby. You have fun today and you make sure to be just as good a girl as you always are," Latoya said. "Kisses."

Tiffany leaned forward and pressed her lips to the computer.

"I felt that. That's a good one, baby," she said before she leaned forward and did the same. "You get it?"

Tiffany nodded. "Got it."

"Good."

"Kiss my baby brother too," Tiffany said, waving just before the connection ended.

She shook her head. *If Bones ever finds out the stunt I pulled to make sure I won our custody battle all those years ago . . .*

Was there an emotion greater than hate?

"I did what I had to do," she said, rising to move across the room to check her appearance in the mirror one last time.

She took some solace in the knowledge that the money she made selling false stories about him to the gossip mags was safely tucked in a trust account for their daughter. Latoya never touched one penny of it. In fact, she made sure that she banked whatever money was left over from the child support after purchasing things Tiffany needed.

Latoya smoothed her hand over the base of her pixie cut beneath the wide-brimmed hat she wore tilted to the side. She then made sure the skirt of her dark purple suit was not too high above her knee. She loved the cut of the suit and the way it framed a curvy shape she hardly got to show. Having Taquan Jr. and nearing thirty had added a fullness to Latoya's shape that she liked—and that her husband liked as well when he had time to remember that they both still liked sex.

The bedroom door opened.

Speak of the devil slayer. She smiled as Taquan eyed her from her head to her feet in the four-inch neutral pumps she wore. She spun for him. "You like, Rev?" she asked, walking over to taste his lips.

He brought his hand up to rub the small of her back and then patted it like a father did to reassure a child. Latoya leaned back. "What?" she asked, instantly annoyed.

"Baby, I think it's beautiful. Matter of fact that suit makes me want to make another baby," he began.

"But?" she added, stepping away from him.

Taquan moved past her to pick his watch up from the dresser. He focused on putting it on as he said, "I don't think the church board would approve—"

Latoya threw her hands up in the air. "Well God forbid the church board doesn't give my clothes a stamp of approval. A bunch of uptight fools with their old behinds looking like they worked the Underground dang-on Railroad."

"Latoya."

"Latoya, hell," she said her voice filled with warning. "I'm not changing."

He reached for her but she swiped his hands away. "I

draw the line with *your* bosses telling me what to wear and to say and how high to jump. Enough is enough."

"I never thought the devil would try to block my path to serve my God in the greatest capacity possible through my wife," Taquan said, the lines in his handsome face showing his disapproval.

His words left her speechless. He just accused her of being a minion of the devil.

She started to argue her point but she pressed her lips closed instead, feeling her anger and hurt sharply. The feelings were so familiar to her these days. She turned from him, unable to lay eyes on him after such an accusation when he knew how much religion meant to her.

"I'll understand if you feel like you need to find a less judgmental church to worship at," he said.

"Now perhaps the devil is using you to block my path to serve our God in the greatest capacity possible," she gave his words back to him in a low voice.

Taquan snorted and tugged on his monogrammed sleeves with a jerking motion. "Your parents are ready to leave," he said.

Latoya said nothing to him and he stood there in the doorway, just as silent, as if he was waiting on her to say something. *Well wait on . . .*

A few moments more and he left the bedroom.

Latoya fought the urge to take another pill. She fought and won. For now. She was pretty sure the one she popped just an hour ago was completely responsible for the mini-tirade she just released on her husband.

Her parents and sisters were spending the weekend with them so that they could attend church together. As much as Latoya loved worshipping the Lord she had never been so happy to see a Sunday because they were leaving to head back to Newark right after Sunday dinner.

She looked in the mirror and made a face as she threw up a deuce sign, wishing she had the nerve to chuck it up in her parents' faces. She left her bedroom, still in her "devil in a purple suit" outfit. She was about to head down the stairs when she spotted her baby sister, Latrece, walking out of the bedroom she was sharing with their middle sister.

"All ready?" she asked, still amazed that the sixteen-year-old was now just as tall as she was.

"Ready to get away from them? Hell yes."

That took Latoya aback. "I meant are you ready to leave for church but . . . uhm . . . okay . . ."

"I put Vaseline on my lips this morning and Mama made me take it off. Vaseline, Toy. Vas-E-Line," she stressed. "I am so sick of them and they got Latasha just as whacked in the head as they are."

And then Latoya saw it. Her baby sister had that same fire and defiance she had. It was the same rebelliousness that made her so determined not to follow their rules that she made some of the worst decisions of her life. She was one First Lady with a past that would have sent her straight to hell if she had not asked the Lord for forgiveness.

Abortions. False accusations of rape. Sleeping with a minister.

Latoya wanted none of that for her sisters. "Maybe—and let me think about it and talk to Taquan first—but maybe I'll ask Mama and Daddy if you can live with us?"

Latrece's eyes got big and she almost jumped up high enough to scale Latoya. "Please think about it. Pleeeease."

"We'll see," she said, grabbing her hand and leading her down the stairs where the rest of the family was already climbing into the vehicles.

Latoya continued her silence with Taquan during the short ride to the church. She was very deep into her emotions. She looked down at her diamond-studded wedding band and felt like some of the love and commitment it symbolized was beginning to fade. As soon as they pulled up to the church, she felt a pang of hurt over Taquan's words to her that morning.

Even as he unbuckled their squirming son, Taquan and Latoya said nothing to each other. They waited on her parents and sisters to walk the short distance from their parking spot and entered the church together.

Latoya smiled and warmly hugged the tall usher already positioned in the vestibule with programs in his gloved hands. "Hey, Brother Deel. You're back on the usher board. Haven't seen you in a while," she said as everyone continued inside the church.

He smiled. "I'm back. My mother was sick and it was taking up a lot of my time the last few weeks but she feels much better," he said.

"Good."

"How you been?" he asked, reaching to squeeze her hand quickly but comfortingly.

Marion Deel was such a spiritual warrior. From the moment he joined their church Latoya had spotted a goodness about the man. He always had a positive way of looking at things and she couldn't remember him saying a negative word. She had been drawn to his light. Nothing sexual. Just as someone whose focus was doing good deeds in honor of the Lord and nothing else.

There were many Sundays after church while Taquan was in meetings or working in his office that Latoya actually sought out Marion for his advice. It just felt good to unburden herself to someone.

"I'm okay," she said, giving him a smile and a quick squeeze of his hand before she continued into the nearly empty sanctuary and took her seat on the front pew where her family waited.

Latoya reached in her purse and opened her Altoids

can. She quickly counted the pills inside. Less than a dozen. The last bottle she went through was from a year ago when Taquan had his tooth pulled and didn't even bother taking any of the pain pills prescribed. *That ain't gonna work,* she thought, pulling one out of the can with her index finger to slide into her mouth. *I need more.*

She snapped the can shut and literally chewed on the pill before she swallowed it to make it dissolve faster. She winced at the bitter taste that she was getting used to.

"What's that?" her father asked, sitting beside her with Tiffany standing up in front of him playing with his cufflinks.

"Peppermint," she lied.

Tiffany's head came up. "I want one," she said, holding out her hand.

"Yeah me too," her father added.

Latoya felt alarmed. "That was the last one," she said, focusing her eyes forward as Sister Nunzio took her spot behind the microphone at the front of the church to do the welcome and read any church announcements.

By the time they were done with morning devotional, Latoya felt like her head couldn't stay up straight and her mouth was dry. She gripped the armrest of the pew as her neck and cleavage dampened with sweat.

"You okay?" her father whispered in her ear.

Latoya nodded and licked her lips, squinting as the rear door of the pulpit opened and Taquan entered in his flowing white robe. His image blurred as he took his seat while the choir sang Mary Mary's version of "Wade in the Water."

I'm tripping, she thought, covering her mouth as a giggle bubbled up in her.

"*Wade in the water . . .*"

She stood up and walked up the aisle, trying to get to

the ladies' bathroom in the vestibule. She stopped as her head spun and she squeezed her eyes shut.

"*Don't you know that God's gonna trouble the water . . .*"

"Are you okay, Sister Sanders?"

Latoya squinted and her vision cleared up just enough to see Marion coming down the aisle toward her. She licked her lips again and took one step forward just before her body went slack and she collapsed onto the carpet.

She felt the heat of bodies surrounding her. The feel of hands on her.

Even through her fuzzy state she knew she had to get up. *They can't know I'm high.*

The church music stopped and the choir's voices faded to an end.

"She caught the Holy Ghost," someone said clearly amongst the many voices surrounding her.

Latoya closed her eyes as she heard her parents' voices asking her if she was okay. *Do something! If I just get up now they will take me to the hospital. No, no, no!*

She rolled over onto her back and began speaking in tongues, hoping she didn't sound too much like the "Mama-say mama-sah-ma-ma-coo-sah" chant from Michael Jackson's "Wanna Be Startin' Somethin'."

Those surrounding her began to cry out and pray. In the distance someone else cried out as if they too had caught the Spirit.

The church broke into "The Presence of the Lord Is Here."

Latoya knew she was dead wrong for the charade. *Forgive me, Lord.*

Chapter 13
Monica

Two Months Later

Monica looked across the long expanse of their black glass dining room table at Cameron's empty seat. His table setting, coffee cup, and the traditional newspaper he preferred to the digital editions sat waiting for him. But he would not appear.

Just like he hadn't in the month since he was forced to resign as the CFO of Braun, Weber.

They usually had breakfast together, discussed their days, and listened to the CBS morning show via the house's surround system as they exchanged ideas over all of the latest finance news—hers via her iPad and his via his papers.

Her eyes fell on the stack of folded papers. A dying tradition. She was beginning to suspect her man felt the same way about his career.

Halston stepped into the dining room, dressed in his navy slacks and vest with a crisp white shirt, carrying a coffeepot.

"Did he at least get breakfast in his office this morning?" she asked him as he refilled her cup.

"No, ma'am."

They had just barely gotten back into the groove of

their lives when that particular piece of funky shit hit the
fan.

Monica nodded even as she felt her disappointment
sting. She took another sip of her coffee—already light
and sweet the way she liked it—and dropped her napkin
atop her breakfast of an egg-white omelet with spinach and
feta cheese. She uncrossed her legs and rose to make her
way across the room to where their matching offices sat.

When Cameron first called to let her know that he had
been forced to resign from Braun, Weber she knew there
would be some adjusting to it all. Cameron had risen
through the ranks of the company off his own achieve-
ments to be appointed as chief financial officer. For the
board to appoint a new chief executive officer with whom
Cameron clashed over his more aggressive, hands-on ap-
proach was difficult enough. For the man to make a power
play to have Cameron ousted—with the board's majority
approval—had to be disheartening and was completely
fucked up.

Still, Monica had no clue that the man who once served
as her mentor in the industry would let the power play rattle him. In the beginning days after the press release an-
nouncing the "amicable parting of ways," she honestly
believed Cameron would dust it off and glide right into
another position with a rival company or firm.

It didn't *quite* go down like that.

Monica looked through the glass of the ebony French
doors at him still in his pajamas looking out the window
at the New York landscape. She knocked lightly on the
glass twice before opening the door and entering. Everything about the black walls and the ebony floorboards
spoke of the power and confidence of Cameron.

"Morning, Cam," she said, coming around his oversized desk to lean against the wall and look down at him.
The smooth brown of his skin was darkened by the

shadow of a beard. He had lost weight and his cheekbones were a bit more prominent.

He spared her a brief glance before shifting his dark eyes back out the window.

"I miss you at breakfast, you know," she said lightly, reaching out to stroke his chin. "That was our thing. Our ritual."

He grabbed her hand and pressed his lips against her palm. "I know," he said. "Just trying to process everything and make some plans."

She nodded and hitched the charcoal skirt of her dress up to her waist and straddled his hips. She brought his hands around to cup her full bottom. She smiled when his fingers massaged circles into the soft flesh.

"Where are your panties?" he asked, running his hands up her ass until he felt the lace of her thong. "Oh."

Monica laughed.

He lifted his face and lightly bit her chin.

Monica sniffed the air. "You brushed your teeth?" she joked.

Cameron bit down a little harder.

Monica sighed at their lighthearted mood. In that moment she was almost able to forget Cameron's drama *and* the drama of her own that she was facing alone. The text messages taunting that someone was watching her came with more frequency and intensity. Each time the e-mail address was different but the message the same.

And she was sick of it and whoever the unfunny motherfucker was trying to play in her life.

"Until my black ass finds a new job we can do this as our new morning ritual," Cameron said softly against her flesh exposed in the vee of her dress.

"You know there's an open invite to join Winters Investment Services," she said, letting her head fall back until the ends of her hair tickled her ass.

"Yeah right," Cameron balked.

Monica froze and jerked her head up as she leaned back to eye him. "Uhm . . . excuse me?" she asked.

"What?" Cameron asked, looking completely lost.

"I'm serious," she said.

Cameron's face filled with disbelief. "No thanks, baby," he said.

The hell?

Monica politely rose up on her heels and then climbed off his lap. "I know my little boutique firm cannot compare to the seven figures you made in salary and bonuses," she began, smoothing her skirt back down over her hips and legs. "But there is some sense of security that my fall will be of no one's making but my own. See I can't be forced out. I *own* my shit."

"Monica," he said, reaching out for her hand.

She jerked away. "I have a business dinner so I'll be home late. Don't wait up," she said over her shoulder as she strolled out of his office.

"Monica, I didn't mean it that—"

She slammed the office door on the rest of his words. *BAM!*

* * *

Monica turned away from the elevator just as it closed. When she turned to walk back to her office the smile was gone. She had just finished a lengthy meeting with a prospective client but in that moment her growling stomach was her focus. "Jamal, could you please order me some lunch?" she asked him as soon as she walked into her office suite.

He nodded. "What do you feel like, boss?" he asked her, sliding on glasses to look through the folder of take-out menus they kept stashed.

"Honestly?" she said, her hand against her flat stomach. "I want some down-home, greasy, gonna-cause-gas, need-a-Pespi-to-make-you-belch-while-you-eating, line-up-the-Ex-Lax-afterward soul food."

He smiled. "I know a place but they don't deliver. I'll have to go get it," he said, already rising to his feet behind his desk.

"Sounds like a plan," she said, going in her office to take a crisp hundred dollar bill from her wallet. She came back in the outer office and handed it to him. "I want something smothered, some greens—collards, and mac and cheese. The works. I'm just blowing the calories today."

"Got you," he said, tucking the money in the pocket of his fitted vest before he left.

She walked back into her office and took her seat behind her desk, tucking her hair behind her ears as she studied the finances of a comedian who was looking to downsize in preparation for his formal retirement from touring at her suggestion. She tapped her pen against the desk as she studied his list of monthly bills. "A'ight now," she said at the monthly bill to a doctor well known for his work in correcting erectile dysfunction.

There was nothing else that revealed more about a person than their financial statements.

"Hey beautiful, you have e-mail."

"Shit," Monica swore. She meant to put the phone on silent. She reached for her iPhone with her left hand, even as she continued perusing the reports and making notes with her right. She swiped the screen with her thumb and looked down at the incoming message.

U CAN DRESS A NEWARK HOOD RAT BITCH UP AND PUT HER IN A MANHATTAN LIFESTYLE BUT ITS STILL JUST A NEWARK HOOD RAT BITCH PLAYING DRESS UP

Monica's heart seized for a few precious seconds. She dropped the phone and sat back in her chair to eye it like it bit her to the white meat. This was the first harassing e-mail she had received. "First text. Now e-mails. What's next, fucking Skype?" she snapped, hating how anxious she instantly felt.

Was this the same fool or a new one?

"Hey beautiful. You have e-mail."

She rolled her eyes and slammed her hand against the desk. She hated this shit. She reached for the iPhone.

NICE DRESS BITCH.

As the image of her in the same outfit she was wearing began to fill the screen, Monica felt real fear for the first time since the harassment began months ago. There was no denying the photo was snapped that morning and either they were less than five feet from her or had one helluva zoom on their camera.

"What the fuck?" she said, jumping up out of her chair to look out the window down at the street.

Her eyes moved swiftly, taking in every spot someone could have been to take the picture. The lobby of the office building next door or across the street. It could have been taken when she left the house that morning.

"Or downstairs," she said. She turned and raced out of her office and across the outer office to lock the door.

"Jamal's ass just gonna have to knock," she said, moving back into her office and leaving the door wide open.

*   *   *

Monica checked her diamond watch as she let her driver, Sampson, help her down from the Denali. "Thank ya, thank ya," she said, turning back to grab her Céline bag.

"Yes, ma'am."

Monica paused and turned to look over her shoulder at the man. Sampson had been her driver for a year. He would definitely be in a position to "watch her." She was sure there were plenty of conversations he overheard that he could use to make her life uncomfortable. But there honestly wasn't a blessed reason she could think of why he or anyone else might hold a grudge against her.

Chill, Mo.

She'd already side-eyed the doorman at both her residence and her business, her assistant, business associates, the delivery guy, a random man who stared at her too long, and now her driver. *This bullshit got me fucked all the way up.*

She turned and made her way inside the restaurant. "I'm Monica Winters and—"

The maître d' instantly nodded. "Your party is waiting for you. Right this way," he said.

Monica followed him through the upscale soul food restaurant to a large table in the corner where Kelson, Usain, and a beautiful redhead were sipping on drinks. "Hello, everybody, I'm sorry I'm late," she said, remaining standing as she shook everyone's hand.

"This is my date, Veronica," Usain said.

"Nice to meet you," Monica said, but her eyes went back to Kelson. Gone were the shades and tacky diamond jewelry. He wore a lightweight cargo jacket with a crisp white V-necked T-shirt and a bold brown leather watch. Urban casual. She liked it and it looked more authentic on him. She started to tell him so but decided to mind her own.

"It's good to see you again, Monica," Kelson said.

She nodded and looked away from him, realizing that she was staring at just how nicely his greenish brown eyes looked against his deep caramel complexion. Without all of the fuckery in place she could see why so many women enjoyed seeing him on the television screen every week. The rap career? That K-Hunta bullshit? Negro please. She still wasn't buying it.

"Kelson told me how the first quarterly reports of his investments were looking and we both thought we should have a congratulatory dinner for him getting his finances in order under your guidance," Usain said, motioning for the waitress with a flick of his fingers.

She instantly appeared with a bottle of champagne and four flutes. She filled each one halfway with a flourish.

"I see big things in store for you, Monica," Usain added.

"I hear that," she said with a smile as they all touched glasses lightly.

She sipped the champagne and nodded in approval. "Okay, this is good," she said, her voice echoing inside the flute.

"Only the best," Usain said.

Monica shifted her eyes to him over the rim of her glass and was surprised to find his eyes already resting on her intently. She shifted them to Kelson and his eyes rested on her as well. Kelson she expected, but Usain? She took another deep sip and shifted her eyes back just in time to see the pale redhead give Usain a hard stare.

So she saw it too?

Monica focused on reviewing her leather-bound menu because sitting at a table with two fine men who were both giving off that "Damn, you fine" vibe could definitely go to a girl's head.

Chapter 14
Keesha

"**I** think it's time we tell Corey about us."

Keesha lifted her head from Shawn's sweaty chest and looked at him like he had completely lost his entire mind and a part of someone else's. "And why would I do that?" she asked, sitting up and reaching for her pack of cigarettes.

"I love you and I'm tired of sharing your pussy," Shawn said, reaching over to stroke one of her exposed nipples.

This motherfucker.

Keesha climbed from the bed naked and moved across the guest bedroom away from him. "Listen, Shawn, I care about you too—"

"Care about me?" he balked, sitting up in bed.

"But I love Corey and you know you don't want to hurt him," she said.

He flung back the covers and hopped to his feet, his now-limp dick flailing like a broken arm. "So I ain't nothing to you but a fuck?" he asked.

Yes, motherfucker.

"No," she lied. "But I'm not ready to give up on Corey and I thought when you first started coming at me like that, I made it clear that regardless of what went on with the pussy that my heart belonged to him. Right?"

"Shit changed for me, Keesha," Shawn said, bending over to look through the tangled bedcovers for his boxers.

Not for me.

She fought the urge to take her foot and press it right in the crack of his dark ass. "Listen, let me think about some things. You caught me off guard, you know. I didn't know you felt that way," she said, releasing a thick stream of smoke.

Shawn jerked on his boxers before he looked down at her with his hurt feelings written all over his face.

I shouldn't have swallowed on this Negro.

Keesha stood before him and wrapped her arms around his neck, careful not to burn him. She kissed both sides of his mouth. "Just give me a little time, okay?" she asked him, her voice soft.

Shawn nodded and captured her lips for a kiss as he hugged her back. "I better head out of here before Corey gets home," he said, moving from her to finish getting dressed.

Bounce, nigga, bounce.

She left the guest bedroom and walked across to their master bedroom to retrieve her kimono-style housecoat. She glanced at the bed she shared every night with Corey. There were many things she was dead wrong for but she refused to sex his cousin in his bed. There was a line even she wouldn't cross.

By the time she made it back across the hall, Shawn was dressed and pulling on his Jordans. She rushed to replace the covers on the bed and then opened the two windows wide to let the room air out. She made sure there was nothing incriminating left in the room and then politely led him out.

The day was over, Kimani was with Keesha's little sister and the rest of her father's family. Corey was at work. She and Shawn had enjoyed a day of floating around playing house.

That what's got this fool all the way gone.

"Call me, Keesha," Shawn said, digging his fingers into her ass as she opened the door.

"Oh . . . ooh . . . oh . . . okay."

Keesha and Shawn both jumped back at the sight of her neighbor Jeremiah standing on the porch holding a box and looking directly at Shawn's hand on Keesha's ass.

Shawn jerked it away. "So yeah, uhm, thanks cuz," he said, before he squeezed past Jeremiah's tall frame and jogged down the stairs to his Impala parked in the drive behind Keesha's Benz.

Jeremiah turned to watch Shawn back down the drive and then zoom up the quiet street. "Keesha, I don't mean to get in your business—"

"Good idea," she told him.

"But you know this is the makings of a *First 48* episode or some shit," he said.

Keesha leaned against the door and looked up at him. "It's not what you think," she said weakly.

Jeremiah opened his mouth and then closed it. "Just be careful."

"What's in the box?" she asked.

"I wanted to see if you could sign these books for Marcus's bookclub meeting this weekend," Jeremiah said. "He wants to surprise everyone."

"Just leave them and I'll walk over and let you know when they're ready," she said, pointing to a spot by the door.

Keesha wanted to shower before Corey got home.

Jeremiah set the box where she told him. "You know I'm headed out to work and I'll probably stay over Marcus's house tonight. So I'll walk over tomorrow some time. No rush," he said.

"Okay. See you tomorrow." Keesha stepped forward, pushing the door closed with her.

She shook her head as she jogged back up the stairs. If that had been her dope-sniffing—or even weed-smoking—days, she would've burst out laughing at the whole scene.

Brrrnnnggg . . . Brrrnnnggg . . . Brrrnnnggg . . . Beeeep.

Keesha paused at the door to her office as she waited to hear the message being left on her answering machine.

"Hi, Keesha. This is Madge. Give me a call as soon as you can. I have news on the proposal you sent Bianca on the third book and—"

She flew into the room and snatched up the cordless phone. "Hello Madge," she said, forcing herself to breathe normally as she folded her figure into the chair behind her desk. "What's the good news?"

"Well, it's not exactly good . . ."

Damn. Keesha squeezed her eyelids with the tips of her fingers. She really needed that next big advance and soon.

"They want you to work on this proposal. They are not happy with it as is."

Keesha remained quiet.

"Are you still there?" her agent asked.

"Yes I'm here."

"So I'm going to e-mail you the things she pointed out about the storyline," Madge said. "And I'm going to be honest with you, Keesha, you really need to hit it out of the park with this. The numbers for the second book nowhere near match the first one."

"Are they going to drop me?" she asked, clearing her throat after her words came out in a squeak.

"No, they just want the tightest story possible," Madge said. "Let me send the e-mail, you take a look at it, mull it over for a couple of days and then let's talk."

Yes, just call, fuck up my day and hang up so I can mull it over.

"Okay. All right. Thanks, Madge."

Keesha dropped the phone back on its base as she turned on her computer. She was anxious to see the notes on her proposal. As she pulled up her e-mail account, she hit play on the machine to play the rest of the messages—mainly because she wanted the indicator light to stop blinking.

"This is Keesha Lands. Leave me a message."

Beeep.

"I have two hundred new e-mails. Shit," she swore. It had been several months or more since she even checked her e-mail, Facebook, or Twitter accounts. She usually got Internet happy in the weeks leading up to a new book release and for about a month after.

The e-mail from Madge had not arrived yet.

"Hello I am Frank with Yarborough Recovery Systems and I am trying to reach Keesha Lands on a very important matter. Please call me back at 888-555-1212."

Beeep.

"Fuck your important matter, Frank," she muttered, her eyes scanning the e-mails. The majority were from readers of her books.

"Hello, this is Dr. Vogle's office. Please give us a call back."

Beeep.

"The hell is this shit?" Keesha asked, her eyes squinting as she took in a series of e-mails from someone named YOUR DIRTY SECRETS with the subject line: "Is this spam?"

Beeep ... Beeep ... Beeep ...

She waved her hand dismissively at the e-mail and picked up the phone to dial her doctor's office. She had to take a physical last week for her and Corey's insurance policy.

"Vogle Medical Center."

"Hi this is Keesha Lands. Someone left a message for me to call."

"Hold please."

She refreshed her e-mail's inbox as she waited. The e-mail from her agent had finally arrived and she opened it.

"Ms. Lands, Dr. Vogle would like for you to come back in for additional tests. Can you make a four o'clock appointment today?"

"Is something wrong?" she asked.

"He's not in the office at the moment, he just noted your chart."

"Uhm . . . I'm on my way," she said, standing up to make her way across the hall to their bedroom.

"See you at four."

Keesha dropped the phone on the bed and turned to look in the mirror over the dresser. *What's wrong with me?*

*　　*　　*

When Keesha walked back through the door of their townhouse, Corey was home and the smell of food was thick in the air. She closed her eyes and released a heavy breath before she made her way into the kitchen.

He looked over his shoulder from a pot he was stirring in. "Hey. Where you been? I called your phone."

"I had to mail some stuff off at the post office," she lied, sitting her tote bag on the counter along with her keys.

"I made spaghetti," he said.

Keesha nodded, hating that her actions would lead to him being hurt. She turned from him when tears welled up in her eyes. She blinked them back rapidly.

Corey was a good man. He paid his fair share of the bills. Helped her raise her daughter. Had patience about her crazy mother. Cooked meals. Supported her. Supported them.

I fucked up.

"Did you hear about the new book yet?"

Keesha turned back to him. "They didn't like it. I have to work on it and turn it in again," she said.

"You'll work it out," he said, coming over to rub her lower back.

"I don't have no choice with all these bills," she admitted. "If that new deal doesn't come through . . ."

Corey stiffened. "Look I don't want to argue about money. I just wanna eat dinner. Chill. Watch a movie. Just not tonight, Keesha," he said, moving back to the stove to turn off the pot of pasta.

"That's not how I meant it, Corey."

He glanced over at her as he dumped the pasta and the water through a drainer sitting in the sink. "What's wrong?" he asked.

I fucked up. I fucked up.

He wiped his hands with a dish towel and came back over to her. "Look if you worried about money if—and that's if—the book deal doesn't come through we'll make it. If I have to get a second job we'll be straight."

Guilt damn near swallowed her as she stepped forward and rested her head on his chest. "You mean that too, don't you, Corey?"

"Have I ever let you down?"

She shook her head. No he hadn't. Ever. *I'm the one that ain't shit.*

"You hungry?" he asked, moving back to the stove. " 'Cause I'm starving."

"I'm pregnant," she said, her eyes locked on his strong back.

"I had a crazy day at work, baby," he said.

"I'm pregnant," she repeated, raising her hand to press again her stomach.

Corey turned. "What'd you say?"

She smiled through all of the emotions jumping her like a hood beatdown. "I'm pregnant."

Corey raced back over to her and dropped down to press his hands to her belly. "A baby. We're gonna have a baby?" he asked.

Keesha stroked the back of his head and nodded. In what should have been the happiest moment of the world she felt karma bite her in the ass like a rabid dog. The sins of the mother do often visit the child and here she was, a victim of her mother picking the wrong man of two to be her father. And now Keesha didn't know if she had done the same.

Shawn or Corey could be the father and Keesha had absolutely no idea which one would hear "You are the father" on a *Maury Povich* episode. But the better man was Corey. She wanted Corey. She loved Corey.

Smiling through her tears and swallowing a lump of guilt and her own hypocrisy, she said, "Yes, we're having a baby."

Chapter 15
Danielle

"You okay?"

Danielle looked up at Omari sitting on the small sofa against the wall of her dressing room. She nodded as she reached behind her to massage the small of her back. "I think all of the standing in those five-inch heels is wrecking my back muscles," she told him with a grimace as another spasm radiated across her back.

"Let me see if I can help that," he said, rising in his navy linen pants and white tee with matching navy and white spectator shoes. "I shouldn't have laid this dick on you so hard last night."

Danielle arched a brow as she eyed him. "Or maybe I injured my back working so hard riding that dick down 'til it deflated," she shot back.

"You did do that," he agreed. "Hell of a job."

She kept her eyes on the man as he came over to press his fingers against the small of her back. She moaned in pleasure at the small circles he made. "That's nice. That's real nice," she said, imitating Bernie Mac.

Omari chuckled. "This little vacay was nice. Thank you for showing me LA," he said, his hands still working magic on her back.

"I just wish I wasn't so tired and cranky," she told him,

folding her arms across the top of her desk and then settling her head on top of her arms.

"It's all right baby," he assured her. "I'm just happy to
finally get to see you face to face."

Danielle fell silent and just enjoyed him putting in work
on her back.

This was the first weekend Omari flew out to Los
Angeles to spend with her, although she had been back to
New Jersey one weekend during her downtime. She had to
admit that she liked the laid-back nature of their "friendship." Omari lived up to his word and was never clingy or
asking too much of her. Most nights they talked a little on
the phone. Some nights they didn't. There were no missed
calls on her phone while she was taping or doing spots. He
completely understood that she had a life and a career of
her own—grown-woman shit.

And the dick was nice. Real nice.

She spun in her chair and walked over to the door to
lock it.

Click.

She turned and walked back over to him, running her
hands down the front of his thighs and then around to
grip his firm buttocks before she sucked his bottom lip
into her mouth with a soft moan.

Omari followed her lead and brought his hands up to
grip the back of her thigh beneath the full skirt of her burnt-
orange dress. "You smell so good," he told her, nuzzling
his face against her neck before pressing his lips there.

Danielle shivered. "That's my new body wash," she
whispered as she closed her eyes and tilted her head back.

He slid her delicate panties to the side and stroked his
finger against her bare pussy lips. Danielle widened her
stance in her six-inch heels. He slid one thick finger and

then another inside her and then plucked her swelling clit with his thumb.

She hissed in pleasure, her fingers digging deep into flesh where they rested on his shoulders. "I absolutely love fucking you," she whispered into the rising heat in the air as she raised one leg to wrap around his waist.

"You do?" he asked throatily, looking down into her face as he slid his fingers in and out of her slowly.

Danielle nodded as she worked her hips in motion to his fingers planted inside of her. Her entire body felt alive. Sexy. Vibrant. Electrified. He made her feel like she tingled everywhere with all the hairs left on her body standing on end.

Pure chemistry.

Omari brought his free hand up to her nape and pulled her head forward to kiss her. First softly and then deeply. His tongue tasted of the juice he had been drinking.

She wondered if all his juices were as sweet.

Danielle lowered her leg and stepped back just enough to free his fingers from her pussy. Omari slid his fingers into her mouth. She reached down to stroke his hard dick as she kissed him, sucking both his tongue and his fingers in a mini-ménage.

"Damn," Omari swore.

"Oh that ain't nothing," she whispered against his open mouth as she pulled the front of his pants away from his dick and jerked his zipper down.

"Shit," he swore.

Danielle dropped to her knees and freed his dick to take the thick and warm tip into her mouth. She sucked as much of the length of him as she could into her mouth, being sure to stroke his thickness with her tongue.

"Danielle," he moaned, biting his bottom lip as he tilted his head to the side to look down at her.

She let her spit drizzle against his tip before she freed his dick from her mouth and stroked the length of him swiftly as she bent her head to flicker the tip of her tongue against his balls.

Omari cried out and roughly fell back against the book-stands on the wall. Shit fell over and onto the floor.

Fuck it.

Danielle moved back to lizard-lick his tip as she continued to work her wrist and jack him.

"Girl you hell," he said, his voice nearly a high-pitch soprano as he dug his fingers into her hair and made a fist. "Don't make me move to LA."

Her soft laughter tickled his dick as she continued her onslaught, causing the sucking noises to echo inside the small office.

"You gone make this bitch cum," he said, sounding somewhere between excitement and regret.

She gave his dick one last lick, suck, and kiss before rising to her feet and sitting on the edge of her sofa. "Oh no. You got work to do before you leave LA this morning," she told him, opening her legs wide and using one finger to pull the now-moist seat of her panties to the side.

Omari rushed to snatch his wallet from his pocket.

Danielle watched as he eventually unrolled a condom onto the length of his hard dick. She used her free hand to lightly pat her plump lips and then spread them to give her clit air.

Omari dropped to his knees and slid his dick inside her until it was buried. He leaned forward to suck at her mouth as he worked his hips, sending the length of him against her walls.

"Thank you for coming to LA," she whispered against his lips, already feeling a fast and furious nut about to explode.

"You're more than welcome," he said.

Moments later they both clenched tightly at each other as white-hot spasms sent them free-falling through one hot climax after the next.

*　*　*

Hours later, long after she made sure Omari was securely on his flight back to New Jersey, Danielle was in her dressing room getting her makeup done in preparation for doing a live edition of *The A-List*. Everyone was on alert, excited and nervous about the first-time try at going live.

Her back was acting up and she was seriously considering requesting to wear flats but she knew her stylist would have twelve fits if she ruined his ensemble by not wearing the feather-covered Louboutins sitting and waiting for her by the door.

Danielle fanned herself. She didn't know if it was the bright lights surrounding the mirror of the dressing room or the cluster fuck of more than three people being inside the small room at one time, but she was hot. "Can I get some water, please?" she asked, her eyes closed as the makeup artist finished her eye shadow.

Bzzzzzz . . .

Her cell phone vibrated in her hand but Danielle waited until the makeup artist moved onto her lips before she checked it. An e-mail. She felt her body go tense. The last thing she needed before going on air live was another taunt.

The e-mails from her unknown tormenter proclaiming to know her secrets and threatening to expose them had continued. They increased in frequency so much that she was almost afraid to answer her e-mail. So far there had been nothing but the dumb-ass e-mails but Danielle was aggravated. She thought about reporting it to the police but what would she say—"Excuse me, very busy officers, someone is e-mailing the shit out of me?"

This is some childish shit.

And she was beginning to be very clear about the identity of the overgrown adolescent.

"Can I have a quick minute everyone?" Danielle asked suddenly. "Please."

As soon as they filed out of the room she checked the e-mail. Sure enough. Same-old same-old.

I KNOW YOUR SECRETS.
I KNOW YOUR SECRETS.
I KNOW YOUR SECRETS.

Danielle already knew there was no reason to respond. Anytime she tried over the last few weeks the e-mail always bounced back.

"I know your secrets," she mumbled. "I just bet you do."

She used her thumb to quickly make a call.

The phone rang three times and she started to end it just before a voice filled the line.

"If it isn't the star *I* made. How are you dear? Are you calling to say thank you?"

Danielle hated the very sound of Carolyn Ingram's voice. "I believe I have thanked you enough, Carolyn," she said, forcing civility into her tone.

Carolyn laughed in her deep, throaty voice. "Yes it was adequate. Definitely not everything I dreamt it would be."

"Listen, stop sending the e-mails, Carolyn. We had a deal."

"E-mails," Carolyn balked. "What e-mails?"

"You know damn well—"

"Hold on one sec, dear."

Danielle rolled her eyes.

"Candy, sweetie, your tongue is far too wet. I want you to eat the pussy, not drown it."

Danielle gagged at the imagery of Carolyn's withered old body being nude.

"Okay, I'm back. Now what's this about e-mails?"

"Just stop threatening me about my secrets," Danielle snapped.

The door opened. She turned in the chair to eye her assistant, Ming. "They want you on the floor in five minutes. They really need to get in here and finish getting you dressed," she said, looking apologetic.

"I have no reason to contact you about anything. I got everything I wanted that night," Carolyn was saying.

Danielle held up her finger for just one minute. Ming left her alone with a nod.

"If I knew you would cum so fast I would have made a deal for more than one lick of that pussy of yours," Carolyn said with a mocking laugh. "But no worries. A deal is a deal. I got you the job at WNYU and you let me finally eat that good pussy."

Danielle felt her shame spread across her body because it was true.

"Did you want a refresher?" Carolyn asked and then smacked her lips loudly before she released a shrill laugh.

Danielle ended the call, jumping up to her feet quickly to walk over to the door. But before she could make two solid steps she felt a sharp pain at the base of her head. She reached for the wall as she got dizzy. She cried out as she felt her body go slack. Seconds later she hit the floor.

In the moments just before she felt herself slipping into unconsciousness she heard Ming enter the room and then call out for help.

*   *   *

Danielle lay back in the hospital bed. "Two steps forward and three steps back," she said, looking down at the IV in her arm.

Even after two days in the hospital she still felt weak and tired. Plenty of well-wishers had sent flowers and her room was full but there was no one sitting at her bedside. No one to make her smile through the disappointment. No one to tell that the only thing the parents she never met gave her was a genetic disorder that could one day lead into her having dialysis and/or end-stage renal failure. Death.

Polycystic kidney disease.

Danielle could hardly pronounce her newly discovered disease that made such a late appearance in her life.

A tear raced down her face.

The doctors said all the niceties about how regular checkups and medicine to manage her symptoms meant she could resume her life. It all sounded good but she couldn't keep her eyes off the end of the line. Death.

Another tear raced to find the other.

She hated being alone with it all.

Her relationship with Omari was far too casual to burden him. And although she could almost see Monica, Keesha, and Latoya here at her bedside she couldn't bring herself to call them. How could she use them up for love and companionship when she turned her back on them to focus on herself?

"Two steps forward, three fucking steps back," she said with a tinge of bitterness, wishing she had the strength to even punch at the air.

Danielle had set the rules of her life and now felt she just had to live by them.

Chapter 16
Latoya

Latoya arched her back as her husband dipped his head to lick at her nipples as she sat atop his thighs, his hard dick planted deeply within her. She grabbed the headboard on either side of his bald head as she rocked her hips back and forth, sending his dick in and out of her with a sweet groove.

His hands gripped her ass and she cried out as he slammed her down harder on his dick while he thrust his own hips in unison with hers. "Give me this pussy," he said with a near ferocious growl as he sucked wildly at one nipple and then the other. "Good pussy-having bitch, you."

Latoya tucked her feet under his legs and rode him harder as she felt her nut coming on strong. "Who's the best?" she gasped.

Taquan grunted.

"Say my name," she demanded, jerking her titties free of his mouth as she sat up straight and looked down at him. She slapped him soundly. WHAP. "Say. My. Name."

Taquan blinked hard and shook his head as if to clear it. "Latoya . . ."

She slapped his other cheek.

WHAP.

"I'm cumming . . . I'm cumming . . ."

"I'm cumming. You better get this nut."

"Latoya."

Her eyes opened just as she felt the explosion going off inside her. Her body was still tingling and alive. Her core felt extra moist.

Taquan looked down at her from his side of the bed, his Bible open in his lap.

That had to be real. Right? she thought, fighting the urge to press her hand down between her legs as she felt herself throb with life.

"Where are you coming to, baby?" he asked.

Latoya looked around the room. The sun was just beginning to rise. She was in her nightgown and nowhere near naked. Taquan nor she would never use the foul—but titillating—language like "good pussy-having bitch."

It was most definitely a dream. A wet one. But a dream nonetheless.

Taquan used the piece of ribbon attached to the Bible to mark his page before he closed it. "I'm glad you're up. I wanted to talk to you about something before I headed to the bank to see about the loan today."

Latoya sat up in bed, leaning back against the pillow.

"You know I finally got the church on board to grow the church and if that loan goes through today there's going to be even more pressure on me—on us—to make sure that we keep their support. A church doesn't double or triple in size overnight."

More rules. More obligations. More restrictions.

Latoya just waited to hear the next phase of his plan for world domination via his beloved megachurch.

"I want to adopt Tiffany," he said.

Latoya was confused and she knew it showed on her face. "Tiifany's father isn't dead," she said simply.

"I know but he has a jacked-up hip-hop image for smoking weed, making all that women-hating music with every other line filled with cussing," Taquan said as he sat his Bible on the nightstand. "I feel we need to distance ourselves from him."

"Well we—as in you and I—are distant from him. So distant we don't speak to him. But I will never keep Tiffany from her father and as a man, a father, and a minister I can't believe you would even suggest that," she said, climbing from the bed to look at him. Her face was beyond incredulous. "Really, Taquan? Really?"

"I see her more than he does," he balked, jumping up from the bed as well.

"Because she lives with us not because you're the better man."

He looked offended. "And I'm not?"

She shook her head. "Of course you are but it's not about that and you should know that."

"You still want that fool or something?" Taquan asked.

She eyed him in disbelief. "You really are a mess, *Reverend*," she finished with mocking emphasis.

"Judge not, Latoya," he shot back at her in a hard voice.

"Oh, so you can judge Bones, but I can't judge you?"

Taquan threw his hands up in exasperation, before he placed his hands on the low-slung rim of his sleep pants. His chest was bare and the hair on his abdomen perfectly dwindled down to what she knew to be a skillful penis that he only released once a week. Tops.

She shook her head to stay focused. "Look, if he ever does anything to risk Tiffany's health and well-being when she is in his care then we'll look at revising the custody agreement. But only then. Okay?" she asked, softening her tone at the end because like Keyshia Cole she just wanted it to be over.

He shrugged and waved his hands like "forget it."

She said nothing else as he grabbed up his clothing and strode into the bathroom to prepare to start his day.

Latoya eyed the closed bathroom door and waited for the sound of the shower before she crossed the room to get her purse from the top of the armoire. She quickly went in her can and popped some pills before replacing her purse and climbing back into the bed to wait for the effect to take hold.

* * *

"Latoya . . . Latoya. Wake up."

She smacked her lips and fought hard to raise her head from the pillow. She fought and she lost. She opened her eyes and the bright light of the bedside lamp caused her to wince and squeeze them back shut.

"Latoya, you in the bed and these kids are here?" Taquan asked, his voice filled with reprimand.

"You wake now, Mama?" Tiffany asked.

Latoya fought her limbs, feeling like dead weight, and sat up on the edge of the bed, rubbing her eyes before she opened them. Her line of vision rested right on Taquan Jr. sitting in the middle of his playpen with his legs open wide to help him sit up. She could tell from the massive swelling of his Pampers that he was wet. Very wet.

Sometime around noon she had taken more pills and she absolutely did not remember falling asleep. She was trying to make the kids lunch, preparing her speech for the Women's Night during the annual conference, coming up with ideas for a church fund-raiser, trying to clean the house, making appointments for Tiffany to get her shoes in preparation to start school next week, needing to finish up her school shopping. . . .

The list went on and on.

Top that with her sister and parents getting into it and she getting thrown in the middle when Latasha let them know the offer was on the table for her to live with Latoya. Sweet baby Jesus. That was a two-hour conversation and berating from both her parents on children *of all ages* honoring and respecting their parents. *I told her fast behind to wait and let me mention it.*

Add on a nearly sexless marriage, an ambitious husband, a judgmental church board, and missing her career working for DYFUS. Latoya didn't know any other way to make it through her day.

She stood up and stumbled to her left, holding her hands out in front of herself to keep from falling. "I think it's something I ate," she lied to her husband as he continued to watch her. She sat back down on the bed. "I just dozed off for a few minutes."

"Tiffany said she's been trying to wake you all day," Taquan said, coming to sit down on the edge of the unmade bed beside her.

Latoya shifted her eyes to her daughter as her husband checked her neck and forehead for signs of fever. She smiled at her and was rewarded with Tiffany coming over to sit her favorite pink elephant in her lap. "You can hold Bungee until you feel better, Mama," she said.

"Thank you, baby," she said softly.

"Well the kids are all right. Praise God for that," Taquan said, bending to press a kiss to her forehead.

Latoya successfully rose to her feet. "Let me get myself together and I'll make dinner, baby," she said, running her hands over her unkempt hair and tasting the residue of her pills and sleep in her mouth.

"Actually, I have good news and I thought we would go out to dinner to celebrate," Taquan said, taking the baby out of his playpen and laying him on the bed to change his diaper.

"They approved the loan," she said, moving into the bathroom at a snail's pace to brush her teeth.

"Not just that, baby."

That was bad enough, she thought, rinsing the toothpaste from her mouth before she stood up. She jumped back at the sight of herself in the mirror. Darkness under her eyes. Sleep drool crusted to the corner of her mouth. Her short-cropped hair standing up in every porcupine-like direction on her head.

Taquan came to stand in the doorway with the baby blowing bubbles as he held him in a sitting position in his arms. "The renovations to the church won't start until the first of the year but in the meantime a producer contacted me about televising the service on a local cable channel every week."

Latoya forced herself to smile as she stepped forward to kiss his cheeks and then his lips. She leaned back to look up at him as he wrapped one strong arm around her waist. She had to admit it was the first time in a long time that she had seen the man she loved so genuinely happy.

She understood he had dreams and she believed in those dreams, but along the way their connection to God was diminishing . . . and he couldn't see it.

His wife was addicted to pain pills . . . and he couldn't see it.

She needed him . . . and he couldn't see it.

Ambition had him blinded.

She kissed him again and again, wishing he could feel her desperation in the pressure of her lips. She didn't have the strength or the guts to cry out for help. And unfortunately she had far too much practice with leading a double life.

"Congratulations, love," she told him as the baby reached out for her.

"Oh no little man. You're going with me so your mama can get back pretty," Taquan told their son.

Latoya eyed him. "Get back pretty?"

Taquan nodded somberly.

"Your behind, Reverend Sanders," she said, turning to fill the bathtub.

Taquan reached out to soundly slap her bottom.

Latoya whirled with a gasp, her hands rubbing her cheek.

"You better be glad these kids are awake because I would get in that tub and teach you some manners," he said, before leaving the bathroom and softly closing the door behind him.

Latoya smiled, thinking of her wet dream that morning. She could actually use some alone time with her husband the man and not just her husband the minister. They had a fabulous sex life but their activities at the church and raising two children left them both so tired at night that they seemed to be snoring before their heads hit the pillows.

Maybe we could make the time.

Latoya moved to stand back in front of the mirror over the pedestal sink. "Maybe we have to make the time," she spoke to her reflection.

And she knew one thing was tying her up.

I slept all day and basically left my children in the home unsupervised.

She left the bedroom and grabbed her purse from where it sat on the top of the armoire. Thank God she had enough sense to keep it out of Tiffany's easy reach. She walked back into the bathroom and closed the door, locking it. Her fingers trembled as she took the Altoids can out of her purse. It looked just as beaten, battered, and worn as she felt.

Tiffany could have very well gone in her purse and taken the pills thinking they were candy while she lay in a drug stupor.

Hell no. I gots to do better.

She opened the lid to the commode. Then she lifted the lid of the Altoids can. Twenty OxyContin pills sat there figuratively calling her name.

"Help me Father God," she prayed. "Help me."

God helps those who help themselves.

Latoya took a deep breath and turned the can over. The pills hit the water like heavy rain. *Plop-plop-plop-plop-plop . . .*

She slammed the lid down and swirled her body around to plop down on it.

"God helps those who help themselves. God helps those who help themselves," she said, almost like a chant.

And she needed the affirmation because there was a sick and twisted piece of her that wanted to open that lid and stick her head in the toilet to lick at the water that dissolved the pills.

Danielle rocked and clutched her purse to her chest. "Father God, I'm calling on you. This ain't our first rodeo. Please help me help myself, Lord. Please," she prayed reverently.

With one last deep, steadying breath she reached behind her with her right elbow and flushed the toilet.

God, please.

Chapter 17
Monica

One Month Later

*K*nock-knock.

Monica knew she shouldn't be there. She knew she should have declined his request. She even knew she had time to turn and run.

But she didn't.

She was curious about the invite.

She shivered as the October night became chillier. She started to turn up the heat but remembered the building's owners weren't required to supply any until the fifteenth. That was next week.

Dressed in a black lace skirt and leather blazer, Monica rose from behind her desk and opened the door to her office. He stood there looking very handsome in a black leather jacket and dark denims. She stepped back and waved him in, but he didn't move past her. Instead he wrapped one of his arms around her waist and pulled her body close to his.

She brought her hands up to grasp at his upper arms. "Excuse me?" she snapped.

He turned her body and pushed her up against the wall, pressing a line of hot kisses to her neck and then down to the exposed vee of her blazer. "If you didn't want this you wouldn't have agreed to leave the party and meet me here," he said, unbuttoning the blazer and jerking it open to expose her full breasts barely held by the sheer bra she wore. He lowered his body to suck at one plump nipple while his hand gently rolled the other between his fingers.

Monica closed her eyes and arched her back with a moan.

There was something so deliciously sneaky about it. So deliciously wrong.

He jerked her skirt up around her waist.

Monica pressed her back to the wall and thrust her hips forward to help him. She shivered as he shifted her panties down over her hips until they fell to the floor around her ankles and the top of her leather booties.

He pressed the side of his face to the soft swell of her hairless pussy, inhaling her scent deeply as he grazed his chin, cheeks, and mouth against it. "I told you I was going to eat this pussy good, didn't I?" he asked her, looking up at her as he raised one of her quivering thighs onto his shoulder.

The lace of her bra rubbed against her throbbing nipples and she brought her hands up to tease them as he released his tongue and took the first lick of her pussy with a deep moan. Monica banged her foot against his back as he sucked at her clit. "I told you I was the king of eating pussy."

She opened her eyes and looked down at the man with his head buried between her legs. "What the fuck am I doing?"

"Getting your pussy ate."

She pushed at his head until his mouth freed her clit. She shifted so quickly to move off the wall that her panties around her ankles tripped her up. She fell face first to the hardwood floors. Ass exposed.

He slapped her on the ass and chuckled as he helped her to her feet.

Monica snatched away from him and fought to free her panties and jerk her skirt back down. "This was a mistake. Too much champagne," she said, trying to find reasons that she could believe her damn self.

She thought she had left all of her ratchetness behind years ago in her early twenties. Her days of single-handedly juggling dicks were over.

"Right," he said in disbelief, walking around her office and studying the photos on her bookcase.

Monica frowned and walked over to remove the photo of her and Cameron that he picked up. "Listen, I have to get home. Again I'm sorry if I led you on. Blame it on the alcohol," she said, moving to the door to hold it open.

"Jamie Foxx don't believe that shit," he said smugly. "You been eye-fucking me all night."

"I believe it was you and your client eyeing me," she said.

Usain turned and smiled at her. "You got a kick out of two men wanting you. Both throwing off those sex vibes. Both waiting like dogs to see who you would pick to . . . bone."

He was right.

There had been a listening party at the 40/40 Club. She hadn't been that surprised to see Usain or Kelson there. They all floated in the same circles. But she had been surprised when both were so attentive to her all night. Both elaborating on their desire to see just what she hid between her thighs and under the pencil skirts she loved to wear so much. Those drinks had made her lose her damn mind 'til she was caught up in the hype and finally let Usain suck on an ice cube as he proclaimed to be the best pussy eater ever born, just wiping all of her good sense away.

She couldn't believe she actually sat in a club deciding between Kelson or Usain. Usain or Kelson. She completely forgot all about Cameron.

He tapped his hard dick lying down the upper part of his thigh before he unzipped his pants and fought to free it through the hole. "You want this dick," he said.

Monica shifted her eyes up. "You're drunk too. Be sure to use a car service. We'll all laugh about this crazy shit when we see each other again. Sober. And less horny," she said.

He put the beast away and walked over to her. "Maybe you're right. I am feeling nice," he said, stepping over the threshold. He turned. "But I still can taste your pussy on my tongue."

Monica watched him until he left the outer office and made his way to the elevator. Her cab was waiting downstairs with the meter running. Sampson was still at the 40/40 Club waiting for her wherever drivers waited as the employers enjoyed their night. He didn't need to know her every move.

Cameron paid his salary and his loyalties could lie with him.

After waiting long enough for Usain to disappear she left the office. As soon as she was in the backseat of the cab, she called Cameron. The liquor and champagne were making her sleepy and she yawned as he answered his phone. "You still up?" she asked.

"Yeah, just waiting on you to get in safe."

"I'm on my way," she said, slumping back against the vinyl, pleather, plastic, what-the-hell-ever of the seat. All she knew was it stuck to the back of her thighs. "I am walking out the club as we speak."

The cab driver eyed her in the rearview mirror.

"Love you."

She opened her mouth but the words wouldn't come. "Me too," she said instead.

Monica knew that she still loved Cameron but seeing how he was handling his layoff was making her reevaluate the traits about him that she loved. The traits she wondered if he still possessed.

She had no idea who the couch-loving, CNN-watching, cookie-eating, I-live-in-my-silk-pajamas man was anymore. He was a shadow of the former powerful businessman he used to be. And a part of his appeal to her was his power and position in their industry.

It hadn't been that long since the layoff but she knew if he continued on the same path she wasn't sure if she could walk it with him . . . and she damn sure didn't want to have a baby with that man either.

The driver pulled to a red light and Monica shifted her eyes to him as he began searching through the junk on his front seat. Curious to make sure he wasn't getting a gun or some shit, she leaned forward and looked through the Plexiglass just as he picked up his cell phone.

Oh.

She leaned back against her seat but just as quickly she leaned up again and looked down at the seat. Her eyes completely bugged at the book lying there. "Keesha Lands," she read in complete shock.

The driver pulled off at the green light.

Monica rapped her knuckles on the glass twice. "Excuse me, could you hold that book up please?" she asked, fighting the urge to press her face against the glass to get a better look. She didn't though. It probably was an oversized petri dish for germs.

"Well, I'll be damned," she said, looking at her ex-friend's name in print. It had to be Keesha. Or was it another Keesha Lands, best-seller of what had to be street lit from the half-naked girl on the cover?

The driver kept his eyes on the road as he reached over to feel for the book and then held it up, pressing it against the glass and even turning on the overhead light. "It's pretty good. My daughter wants to read it but I told her to let me check it out first."

"Can I buy that book from you?" she asked, digging into her purse cash.

"Naw, this is my daughter's book. I couldn't do that," he said, shaking his head as he continued to drive.

Monica pressed a hundred dollar bill onto the glass as soon as he stopped at another red light.

"She'll be the fuck all right," he said, hopping out of the car to open the passenger door and quickly swap the book for the money.

Monica turned the book over and there was Keesha's photo near her bio on the back.

The driver pulled up to the 40/40 Club and Monica dug out another twenty to pay him for the fare before she climbed from the car, pushing the book down into her tote as she went to stand by the valet parking stand. She called for Sampson to pick her up, but her mind was focused on getting home, taking a shower, and hoping to sober up enough to read the book.

"That bitch actually wrote a book," she said, still amazed.

She was the wife of a CFO who was laid off but still a wealthy man. Danielle was on TV. Keesha was an author.

I wonder what Latoya's churchy ass is up to?

Is she still married to Taquan?

Oh, and little Tiffany is . . . let's see . . . she should be six.

And Kimani is . . . eleven or twelve or so?

She smiled as she remembered some of the crazy stunts Diane used to pull that would embarrass Keesha so much. *Now that bitch is out there.*

"Ms. Winters. Are you ready?"

She turned her head to find the Denali double-parked and Sampson holding an umbrella to shield a sudden light rain. "I'm sorry. My mind wandered. I'm ready, thank you," she said, lightly holding his arm for support as he led her to the rear of the SUV.

"Early night," he said.

"Yes and still too late," she said with a yawn.

Soon the mellow sounds of Curtis Mayfield began to play.

That's my Sampson, she thought as she let her head drift to the side. She didn't bother to sleep, though. He would be dropping her home before she could get into a deep enough sleep to matter.

And not fifteen minutes later the Denali pulled to a stop before her apartment building. The doorman immediately stepped out with his own umbrella and headed toward the vehicle. "No need to get wet, Sampson. The doorman is right here. See you tomorrow," she said, letting the man help her from the car.

"There's a delivery waiting for you at the desk," he said, stepping back to hold the door to the building open for her.

"They could have taken it up to the apartment," Monica said as she watched him go around the tall desk and sit a box on top of it.

"No, ma'am. It was specified that it be given directly to you. We didn't even mention the delivery to Mr. Steele."

Monica eyed it. It was a bright red box with a huge gold bow. "Did you see the person who delivered it?" she asked, picking it up.

"Just a regular delivery service," he said, moving around the desk to go and open the door for one of her many neighbors.

Monica carried the lightweight box to one of the seats

before the lit fireplace in the elaborately decorated area. She set her purse on the seat beside her and then set the box on the table. It had been a minute since she received one of the ridiculous e-mails and whoever got a kick out of wasting her time had never bothered contacting her via any other method. Except the text the one time.

She pulled the card from under the bow. She almost dropped it as she read the words.

CANDY IS SWEET, REVENGE IS SWEETER.

Monica dropped the card onto her lap and removed the bow and the lid from the box. It was a box of Godiva chocolates but taped to the wax paper was another card. She opened it and the chorus to Babyface's song "Never Keeping Secrets" played loudly.

"So I'm never keeping secrets, and I'm never telling lies . . ."

Monica read the printed words.

I'm bored with you. Meet me at the Elizabeth Ballroom of the Hilton at Newark Airport at eight o'clock. Friday. Show up or I have another package to send Cameron.

Babyface's voice singing that hook continued to repeat itself. Monica slammed the annoying card shut. She picked the package up as she rose to her feet. As soon as she was near enough to the flickering flames she tossed everything into the fireplace and then stood there and watched the fire consume it.

Chapter 18
Keesha

Keesha sat quietly in the chair in front of her agent's unkempt desk. Madge was a tall and thin woman with a fuzzy bob that was more white than any other color her hair used to be. She looked at Keesha with concern over the rim of her red-framed glasses. She reached in the top drawer of her dresser and pulled out a pack of cigarettes and a fifth of Johnnie Walker Black Label. "Did you drive?" she asked as she stood up to grab two paper coffee cups.

Keesha shook her head as she bit her bottom lip and looked out the window at another brick building. It was definitely a room without a view. "So what does this all mean? How do I pay my bills? Am I supposed to just give up writing and go get a job? Like—and excuse my language—what the fuck am I supposed to do, Madge?" she asked, shifting her eyes back to her agent and the cup of brown liquor she handed her.

Keesha took it and even got it close enough to her mouth to get high off the fumes before she remembered she was now four months' pregnant. She didn't bother to explain all of that. She just set the cup on the edge of the desk in a random clean spot.

"Your editor was willing to offer you a deal—"

Keesha sat up on the edge of her chair. "For a third of

the original deal? Then I only get half up front with a deadline to turn in the book to get the other half. I can't make it off that."

Madge set her cup down as well. "Listen, we turned down your publisher and I tried shopping to other editors but if you are stuck to this six-figure advance . . . you may have just written your last book."

Keesha crossed her legs in the charcoal wide-legged pantsuit she wore with fuchsia heels. She came dressed for business because she meant business. Her savings were already drying up making her share of the bills. She hated swallowing her pride and firing the part-time maid she had hired—the one Corey warned her she could not afford. They still had a mortgage, car notes, Kimani's private school tuition, credit cards, personal loans. Gas was high as hell. Groceries were bananas. Clothes were a hard screw. And then there was Diane still sucking on the teat whenever she got ready. And that still wasn't all of her bills. Hell, Uncle Sam got his off the muscle.

Keesha began flexing her foot in agitation.

The bills were steadily stacking and the money was steadily drying up.

"I also spoke to the production company this morning when you were headed in," Madge said, her Long Island accent prominent.

Keesha noticed this time she did take a sip from the cup. She steeled herself.

"The length of time they purchased to try and acquire backing for the film has passed and they are not going to make a new offer to extend the contract."

"So no movie."

Madge shook her head, sending her dry and brittle bob swaying back and forth around her slender face. "No movie," she said.

Keesha was no virgin and she thought she knew how it

felt to be fucked but this was a whole new level that she did not like.

"I didn't turn down the offer from your editor. I just told them we would consider it for a week or so," Madge said, lighting a Marlboro Light.

Keesha felt a strong craving for a Newport—almost as strong as she used to crave dope—but cigarettes were a no-go now too.

Bzzzzzzzzz . . .

Keesha checked the cell phone sitting in her lap. It was Shawn. She sent his aggravating ass to voice mail. The last thing she had time for was him, his dick, or his assertions that the baby could be his.

"Keesha, the goal is to keep putting books out, build your audience, write better and better books with each new one," Madge said. She dipped her head so low that her glasses almost slid off her nose. "Take the lower advance. Write the best book you got in you and make your money on the back end. With the right book sales we're back in better negotiating waters. You feel me?"

Keesha actually smiled at her agent's attempt at Blackness. Keesha knew she meant to lighten the mood. It just barely worked. "Okay. Take the deal," she said, feeling like it would have been easier to pull teeth without Novocain then pull those words from her.

Madge put away the liquor bottle and walked to her adjoining bathroom to flush the liquor from the two cups they didn't drink. She walked back over to follow Keesha to the door. "Go and enjoy lunch and I'll call you when the deal is done," she said, opening the door.

Corey stood up and dropped the magazine he was reading as he waited. His eyes studied her face as Madge walked back into her office and closed the door. "What happened?" he asked as they left the building.

"I fucked up. My advance is getting slashed and I ignored every motherfucking thing you told me about saving money and planning for the future. I fucked up," she said.

He wrapped his arm around her shoulders as they stood in the foyer of the building. "Trust me, it will all work out," he assured her. "You see these shoulders? I got it."

Keesha's guilt cloaked her. This man had no clue about the confusion she was bringing into his life with the baby. *I have to tell him the truth. I have to. I will not do to my baby what my mother did to me. Fuck that crazy shit.*

"I got a surprise for you," he said, opening the glass door and letting her walk out onto the side street first.

They walked to the corner and hailed a cab. As soon as she was settled on the seat, Corey whispered something to the driver before he finally climbed into the back. Instead of driving into New York and dealing with parking, they had parked their car at Newark Penn Station, hopped on a train to New York Penn, and then caught a cab to Madge's office.

Keesha assumed they were just retracing their steps back home. Her assumptions were proven wrong when the cab pulled to a stop outside one of the entrances to Central Park. "Why are we at the park?" she asked.

"We're going on a carriage ride," he told her, climbing from the back of the cab to pay their driver, and then walked over to talk to the carriage driver.

She felt her phone vibrating in her pocket like crazy and as soon as Corey jumped out of the cab she pulled it out and put it on silent before she climbed out of the cab. She pulled the trench coat she wore over her suit around her thick body as Corey took her hand and led her to the carriage.

This some white people shit.

But she swallowed back her complaints at the roses and chocolates on the seat. Keesha let Corey help her up into the carriage and she picked up her gifts as she scooted over to make room for him.

The driver looked over his shoulder down at them and at Corey's nod the carriage took off at a leisurely pace.

Keesha couldn't lie. She had never done anything like something she'd seen in a movie, and the fact that he planned that ahead of time made her love him more . . . and feel bad for him even more than that. Corey was so crunk for Jesus over the baby. She hated that the truth of it all might destroy him.

They came to a stop beside a lake and Keesha had to admit that even just sitting by the water with her head resting on Corey's shoulders was relaxing. They went from all hood to all good.

"Keesha, I love you."

She sat up to look him directly in his face but her eyes fell down to the solitaire ring he held in his hand. *Oh God . . .*

He reached out for her left hand. "I know we have gone through some tough things but we came through it together and I just believe that we were meant for each other. And not just you and me, but Kimani and the new baby too. We were meant to be family and be there for each other. Thick and thin."

Guilt and love had her sandwiched.

"I couldn't imagine my life without you and I don't want to." Corey slid the ring onto her finger. "Will you marry me?" he asked.

Her shoulders slumped because this should have been a perfect moment. It should have been but it wasn't. Not with the weight of her secret overshadowing it all.

"Keesha?" he asked.

He was the only good thing in her life besides her child. She recognized that much too late. *I can't lose him. I can't.*

"Yes, yes," she told him, leaning forward to taste his mouth.

He held her face and deepened the kiss, their tongues circling each other before he drew hers into his mouth.

Keesha closed her eyes and gave in to the way he made her feel.

Lord, please let this be Corey's baby. Please.

* * *

Keesha and Corey were lounging on the sofa and Kimani was stretched out on the floor as they all watched *Coming to America* for the millionth time.

Brrrnnnggg . . .

She picked up the cordless where it sat on the back of the chair. She answered when she recognized their neighbor's cell phone number. "Hey, Jeremiah. What's up?"

"Walk over here when you get a chance and come by yourself."

Click.

Keesha frowned but she dropped the phone and stood up, sliding her bare feet into her slippers.

"Where you going, Bay?" Corey asked, his eyes barely shifting from the flat screen over the fireplace.

"Jeremiah's. He didn't say what's wrong but it must be something with him and his boo," she said, already easing around the couch and heading for the front door. "I'll be right back."

The sun was just starting to set and the sweater she wore barely did a thing to keep the fall night winds from biting against her. Before she could make it down her steps and across the drive, Jeremiah was already standing on his porch with a big red box in his hand.

"Is that an engagement gift for me?" she asked. "I didn't even get to tell you about it yet."

"Damn, so Corey proposed. Congratulations," he said with a smile that deepened his dimples. He came down the steps to hand it to her. "But we'll talk about that later. Let's get into this box that is for you. The deliveryman said to only give it to you when you were alone."

Keesha arched a brow as she eyed the red box and gold bow. "Who's it from?" she asked.

"They didn't say."

She turned and dropped down on Jeremiah's porch to undo the lid. She removed the card taped to the wax paper and then lifted the paper. "It's chocolate," she said, reaching for one.

Jeremiah politely reached out and took it from her hand to toss into the bushes lining his front yard. "An unsealed box that you were not expecting and have no clue who it's from, Ms. Everything-I-Eat-My-Baby-Eats."

"True," she agreed, opening the card.

"*So I'm never keeping secrets, and I'm never telling lies . . .*"

"Okay somebody likes Babyface," Jeremiah drawled sarcastically.

Keesha read the card to herself and then read it again.

I'm bored with you. Meet me at the Elizabeth Ballroom of the Hilton at Newark Airport at eight o'clock. Friday. Show up or I have another package to send Corey.

She honestly thought the e-mails she had been getting were spam and she ignored them all but here was a package with the same bullshit, delivered to her at her address and they clearly knew about Corey.

Was this some of Shawn's mess, she wondered, turning the lid over to pull the card from beneath the gold bow.

CANDY IS SWEET, REVENGE IS SWEETER.

"Who's it from?" Jeremiah asked.

"Some fool," she lied, tearing up both cards.

Friday night she was going to fuck Shawn all the way up. Oh shit just got real.

Chapter 19
Danielle

"*Danielle you went MIA on me. Give me a call when you get a chance.*"

Beep.

"Sorry, Omari," she said. She hadn't really spoken to him since she left the hospital.

"*Missing you on TV this week, boo-boo. Enjoy your vacay.*"

Beep.

"Miss you too, Nora," she said with a smile. Nora was the makeup artist from the show.

"*Danielle, this is Ming. I've been checking your mail at your condo like you asked and I have everything but a big red package with a gold bow they would only deliver straight to you. See you Monday. Bye.*"

Beep.

"Thank God for you, Ming."

"*Hey, Dani, this is Kent. I'm missing my cohost. These correspondents cannot compete. Quote me on it.*"

Danielle smiled as she logged out of her voice mail.

Kent's use of his on-camera catchphrase tickled her and she could use a laugh as she tried to make decisions that would affect the rest of her life. *Whatever is left of it.*

Mind over matter, Danielle, she told herself.

She reached for her bottle of water as she rested on a

lounge chair in a cabana on the beach. Over the last month she had been to see more doctors and specialists. She had learned so much about the disorder and she did take some peace in knowing that although the disorder could cause cysts in many organs of the body so far she only had complications with her kidneys. She was in the early stages and although there were treatments and lifestyles changes to extend the life of her kidneys there was no cure.

One day her kidneys would fail.

One day she would need dialysis.

One day she would die from it.

Danielle took a deep breath and pressed a hand to her forehead. Everyone lived to die one day but she hadn't even hit thirty yet and facing that was hard.

So far she had returned to work and had not disclosed her disorder to the producers but the first chance she got to take a full week off, she took it, because besides her physical state, she had to worry about her mental health, and that meant being in the company of someone she loved who also loved her.

She shifted her eyes out to the turquoise waters of Ocho Rios, Jamaica, and smiled at the sight of Mohammed emerging from the water. Her heart swelled with love for him and then filled with sadness that when she left Jamaica in the morning he might not see her again until she was in her casket.

Mohammed rung the water from the ends of his dreads as he made his way back to her. "You should swim. The water feels good," he said, his Jamaican accent even heavier since he moved back.

"Just enjoying watching you," she said, handing him a towel.

"You're in Jamaica," he said with a smile. "You need to get wet."

He chuckled as he stretched out on the lounge chair beside her and pulled her clothes, dampening the sheer cover-up she wore over a three-hundred-dollar bathing suit that she had absolutely no plans to swim in.

"Stop, Mohammed," she said.

He leaned up to look down at her with a playful glint in the brown depths of his eyes. "Stop what? Stop this?" he asked, playfully biting her cheek.

The bites turned to kisses as he settled back and then pulled her body slightly atop his. "I thank you for spending your vacation with me," he said, his voice serious.

Danielle tucked her hand between his side and his arm as she closed her eyes and listened to the rumble of his words inside his chest. "Thank you for making time for me last minute," she said softly.

"I thought I would never see you again, I thought you had forgotten all about me," he said, his hands massaging her leg in that intimate way that wasn't sexual. It was the touch of a man toward a woman he loved.

"Never," she promised.

His hold on her tightened.

She pressed a kiss to his chest.

"All week I've been wanting to ask you what made you come here. And since you're leaving me tomorrow, now is as good a time as any," he said.

She hadn't told him about her illness. She didn't want to burden him with her illness. She selfishly had just wanted to spend time again with the one man she ever loved while she was up and healthy enough to enjoy it.

"Just missing you and decided to take a chance you weren't loving someone else," she lied.

Mohammed shook his head and leaned up a bit to free his dreads to hang over the back of the lounge. "I'm not gone lie. I've had women in all these years. You know that," he said.

"Oh, I know," she told him with mock attitude, lifting her head from his chest to look up at him.

"And I've even loved a couple . . . but never the way I loved you, Dani," he said. "Never."

She believed him.

Danielle forced herself to look out at the beautiful landscape of the ocean and the skies blending together in the distance as she blinked to keep tears from wetting his chest.

"I gone miss ya," he said, his accent *so* thick.

Thick and sexy.

"I love ya, Danielle," he promised.

She leaned up, bracing her hand on his chest for support, as she looked him in the eye. "And I love you, Mohammed. Please don't forget that. Ever," she said with a sappy smile as a tear she couldn't deny raced down her cheek.

"What's wrong?" he asked, pressing a kiss to his thumb before he swiped the tear away.

And the dam broke.

Danielle pressed her face back to his chest as the tears fell, racking her body, stuffing her nose, and tightening her throat.

Several people walking by their cabana on the beach eyed them as Mohammed pulled her body up and then twisted onto his side to make room to lay her on her back. He held her chin as Danielle tried to tuck her face against him. "No, no, no. Don't cry. Don't cry," he whispered down to her as he pressed his lips to her cheeks.

His affection made her cry harder but Danielle fought for control because she always thought she looked a complete mess after a snot-inducing cry. Puffy eyes. Red face. Running nose.

It was not the image she wanted to leave the man with.

She took the dry hand towel he offered her and wiped her face but she drew the line at blowing her nose.

"Better?" he asked.

"Hungry," she told him, trying to lighten the mood. "Let's hit the buffet at the hotel."

Mohammed stood up and then held her hand to help pull her up to her feet. "Nah, my mama is cooking dinner."

Danielle pulled out her pair of jean cutoffs and pulled them over her bikini bottoms. She tied the ends of the sheer cover-up into a knot at her waist. "I don't feel like changing. This cool?" she asked.

Mohammed eyed her. "No, it's hot . . . but it's cool."

She playfully slapped his thigh with a towel before she stuffed the towels into the large straw tote and slid her oversized shades onto her face.

They left the beach and made their way to Mohammed's Jeep parked at the hotel where Danielle was staying. She smiled at how much it resembled the beat-down Jeep he drove back in Jersey.

She climbed into the passenger seat and pulled her foot up onto the seat, looking out the window as they left the luxury resort. Danielle had barely spent any time at the resort, Mohammed had become her tour guide, showing her his Jamaica. She almost felt like she knew the way to drive to his home on her own.

During the fifteen-minute drive she just enjoyed being in Mohammed's company and for many of those minutes she had no worries in the world. "What's your mama cooking?" she asked, glancing over at him.

"Jerk chicken, rice and peas and fried dumplings."

Danielle's stomach growled.

Mohammed laughed as he turned down a street crowded with homes painted in bright colors and parked in the driveway between a turquoise house and a red one. When Mohammed moved back to St. Ann's Bay he purchased the house next to his childhood home, where his mother still resided.

As soon as they climbed from the Jeep the bright white door of his mother's home opened. Danielle smiled when Mohammed's three-year-old son, Adric, came running toward them at full speed. He sprang up and Mohammed caught him easily before settling him on his lap.

Danielle's insides turned to mush when Adric reached out his arms to hug her around the neck as well.

"I missed y'all," he said.

"Yes, he did," Oni, Mohammed's mother, said, still standing on the porch.

During the majority of Danielle's week, everywhere they went Adric—and sometimes Oni—was right there with them and in the short time Danielle had fallen for them both. She had been so pleased to know that Mohammed had spoken of her to his mother and the woman hugged and welcomed her like an old friend.

Or a daughter-in-law.

As they entered the two-bedroom home, the smell of the food made Danielle weak at the knees. Oni already had the round table in the bright blue dining room laid out with food and a big glass jug of punch.

Danielle's stomach growled again. Her new nutritionist had her on a strict diet low in protein and sodium and high in fiber to try to ensure she didn't grow any more cysts, but Danielle knew she was going to set it aside and enjoy the feast his mother fixed for her last night.

Mohammed set Adric on the floor and he came right over to Danielle to stand between her legs and lean back against her chest. She pressed a kiss to his cheek, his shoulder-length braids smelling of the coconut and oil herbs Oni used. "I know a little boy whose name is Adric. I know a little boy whose name is Adric," she sang in a chant. "Hey little boy?"

Adric turned with a giggle and placed both of his hands on her cheeks. "Yes?" he asked, still laughing.

"What's your name?"

"Adric," he said loudly with a jump.

They played the little game often over the last week and Danielle would cherish how Mohammed's son had instantly gravitated to her. His own mother had died during labor and he never knew her. For one week of her life she knew how it felt to play the role of mother and that meant everything to her because her illness prevented her from ever having children of her own.

She smiled through the tears that threatened to rise.

"Come help me, Dani," Oni said, reverting to Mohammed's nickname for her.

Danielle winked at Mohammed and walked through the dining room and into the bright yellow kitchen. She washed her hands at the sink. "I am starving, Mama Oni," she said.

"*Tell* him."

Danielle turned and nearly jumped up onto the sink to find Oni standing so closely behind her. She was a short and thin woman with beautiful dark skin that was still tight and smooth for her age. Her bright eyes seemed to gleam beneath the colorful headwrap she wore around her braided hair. "Ma'am?" she said, looking down at her.

"You no well, child. Oni see all, you know. And you no well," the old woman said, pointing her finger up at Danielle as she chastised her.

Danielle felt a cold breeze rush over body. She opened her mouth to lie, but the words wouldn't rise.

"Tell him," Oni stressed again with one last long look before she left the kitchen.

Danielle turned back to the deep white sink and turned

on the faucet, bending down to splash her face with the cool water before drinking a handful. As she stood up straight, she felt a twinge across her back and massaged it deeply even though she knew it couldn't fix what caused the ache.

Tell him.

Chapter 20
Latoya

Latoya pressed another piece of gum into her mouth as she climbed back into her car from dropping Tiffany at school and Taquan Jr. at daycare. Once she came from under that cloud of pill popping, things became clearer and one thing that was vividly lucid was freeing herself up by getting *both* of her kids out of the house during the day.

Taquan was against it until Latoya got sick of his mess and dropped the baby right off at the church to spend the day with him while she ran errands. That was the end of *that* debate.

She still craved the pills but she was doing better.

Thank God.

She steered her car toward the church as she hummed along to "Never Would Have Made It." "Ain't that the truth," she said aloud, tapping her fingers against the steering wheel.

When she pulled into the parking lot of the church she was surprised there weren't a lot of work trucks already there. Taquan told her he had to be at the church all day to oversee the new repair of the heating system. She grabbed the breakfast she purchased for him from his favorite diner and left the car to enter the church. She paused at the doors to the sanctuary.

It really is a beautiful church.

Latoya felt overcome by it and everything it stood for. For her His spirit was just as strong now as when the choir sang and her husband preached. It was in the quietest of moments that she felt her connection to her faith. *Peace be still.*

The path of her faith had taken so many detours and pitfalls along the way. But even when she faltered she knew the Lord had never left her side. He had never left her behind. Never forsaken her.

"Thank you, Lord," she whispered, coming down the aisle.

She set Taquan's breakfast on one of the pews and moved to lift the hem of the red wrap dress she wore as she knelt at the altar. She prayed for her husband to not let ambition pull him any further from his devotion to God. She prayed for the well being of her children and her family. She prayed for the Lord to strengthen her youngest sister to make better decisions than she had in the past. She prayed for each of the childhood friends she missed so much sometimes that she wept. And she prayed for herself most of all.

Her tears wet her folded hands.

"I am not happy, Lord," she admitted. "Please show me the way. Please."

And that was the truth. She had her faith, her children, her husband, and her family. But truth be told, Latoya was lost and confused and living in a world too filled with hurt. On the outside she lived the life everyone thought she strived for. But on the inside she was barely making it day to day and finding reasons to smile. To rejoice. To be happy.

She rose to her feet and wiped the tears from her eyes as she retrieved Taquan's food and headed up through the pulpit to take the shortcut to his office on the upper level. She climbed the stairs but looked up in surprise as her husband's door opened and Olivia, the choir director, exited.

Latoya paused and took in the clinging and deep-plunging

V-neck sweater the woman wore with leggings and high-heeled ankle boots. She was the epitome of brick house with more breasts, thighs, and hips than she had waist. The outfit hid nothing. Not even the fact that her nipples were hard.

"Sister Sanders," Olivia said, her husky voice just hinting at the beautiful, soul-stirring gospel solos she delivered every Sunday.

"Sister Olivia," Latoya said, still watching the woman as she continued down the stairs in a way that was pure sex. "I wasn't expecting to see you around today. Do you have choir rehearsal?"

Latoya knew firsthand the appeal of a minister to many women. There was power and presence in the pulpit. On top of that, Taquan was a young and charismatic minister whose attractiveness could not be denied. Plenty of the women of the church—young and old—gave him an extra long squeeze or a greeting that was almost sing-song: *"Morn-ing, Rev-er-end San-ders."*

Latoya was very clear that there were whores everywhere . . . including the church. To her they weren't two women serving the Lord. Olivia was the same age she was and in that moment Latoya was eyeing her like a woman going after her husband.

Olivia came to a stop a few steps just above the one Latoya stood on. Latoya took another step up so that she wasn't eye level with the woman's obvious camel toe.

"No, no choir rehearsal until later tonight," she said. "The preacher needed me to do something for him."

"Oh really," Latoya said, feeling her ire rise. "And what was that, Sister Olivia, particularly in *that* outfit?"

Olivia looked offended and made a face. "Excuse me?" she asked.

"What is it you had to do for *my* husband?" Latoya said.

Olivia smirked as she came down the few steps separating them. "Perhaps you should ask your husband," she said, looking Latoya in the eye as she stepped down onto the same step where she stood.

Latoya climbed one step and then turned to look down her nose at the woman. "And perhaps you should find out what is appropriate clothing to wear inside a church?"

Olivia chuckled. "I'll do better, *First Lady*, when you do better."

Latoya felt her neck warm because she knew a lot of the members of the church and the church board thought her attire wasn't always appropriate. "I don't really care what you do as long as you keep it away from my husband. Clear?"

Olivia sniffed the air. "Do I smell insecurity?" she said cattily.

Latoya sniffed the air as well. "Do I smell your . . . funky behind?" she countered with a pointed look at Olivia's crotch.

"Funny, I get no complaints," Olivia said with a quick but deliberate look up the stairs to the closed door of Taquan's office, then turned and continued down the stairs.

It took everything Latoya had not to race down the stairs behind her and beat her ass. Instead she headed up the stairs and stormed inside Taquan's office.

He was putting away files in his file cabinet and looked up at her in surprise. "Hey baby," he said.

"Baby hell," she snapped, throwing the container of food onto his desk.

"Respect the house of the Lord, Latoya."

She made a face. "Don't play with me," she warned.

Taquan frowned. "What's wrong? What you all bunched up in the face about?"

"Are you screwing Olivia Monroe?" she asked, moving over to the trash can to look down for condom wrappers or any other proof. "Is that why you can only share your rod once a lousy week?"

Taquan moved past her to close his office door. "I am not screwing Olivia."

"Newsflash, Rev, you ain't laying it down on me that often either," she said, watching him as he came around to sit behind the desk.

He instantly stood up and came back around the desk to pull her body against his as he kissed her. Deeply.

Latoya fought hard not to touch him and clasped her hands behind her back even as she felt herself melt as he nibbled her bottom lip before sucking it gently. She moaned in pleasure and kissed him back, sucking the tip of his tongue into her mouth the way she knew he liked.

Taquan lifted his head and looked down into her eyes. Their mouths were still open and panting. "I am not screwing Olivia Monroe," he repeated, before he slid his hands down to her hips and jerked them forward to press his erection against her belly.

"Then why were you two here alone?" she asked, even as her eyes fell on his lips, wanting to taste them again.

"She came by before she went to work to talk to me about using the basement level as a daycare center," he said, giving her buttocks another massage before he released her. "I think it's a good idea but it would have to wait until after the renovations so the children aren't displaced during that time."

"And where are the heating people?"

Taquan frowned as he reclaimed his seat. "Hopefully they'll be here at eight like we arranged."

"But she said—"

Brrrnnnggg.

"Hold on, baby," he said, reaching for the phone.

Latoya picked up the container of food and opened it to see if the chicken and waffles were salvageable.

"I wasn't aware of that, Brother Banks," Taquan said, shooting Latoya a hard stare.

She locked her knees because she knew the call from the president of the church board was about her altercation with Olivia.

"I understand that," Taquan said. "I'm sure it was just a misunderstanding on both their parts."

Latoya rolled her eyes.

"And I appreciate the board's support of my plan for expanding the church. You know that."

She couldn't believe that slore had already hopped on the phone. *I thought it was Jesus on the mainline, not Brother Banks.*

"Let me talk to my wife and I'll call you back," Taquan said.

"One, she had no right being in your office dressed like that. Two, she insinuated that you and her were dealing. Three, she was disrespectful," Latoya rushed to say as soon as he placed the phone in the receiver.

"The church board can still kill the deal for the expansion, Latoya," Taquan began. "Was this really the time to be childish and confront a church member about sleeping with me?"

Latoya looked at him in disbelief. "I am the First Lady of this church but I am your wife first and that gives me the right to confront any woman I believe wants you," she said.

Taquan shook his head before lowering it into his hands.

Latoya watched him as he stayed that way for long moments. "She said I should ask you what you needed her to do—"

"Do you really think I care about some catfight in the stairwell?"

"What?" she asked, not sure she heard him correctly.

Taquan raised his face and looked at her with unbridled anger that had his shortbread complexion of skin flushed. "Do you really think I care about some catfight in the stairwell? Huh? Do you?"

Latoya took a step back from the fire and brimstone in his eyes.

"I could care less about what either one of you are stressing," he said, rising to his feet to point to the mock-up of the new church hanging on the wall over his chair. "That's what I stress about. So you will not destroy this for me. You will apologize to Olivia if that's what it takes for the board members to get over this."

"No, I will not," Latoya asserted. "I will not apologize. You will defend me because I am telling you that she goaded me."

"Get out, Latoya," he said, waving his hand at her dismissively. "And don't say two words to me until you admit you were wrong and apologize."

And just like that he went back to his filing and ignored her. In that moment, Latoya actually felt hatred for her husband as waves of anger, disappointment, and hurt flooded her. She fought the urge to give him a good Newark-style cussing out that made you sit in the mirror afterward and cry while you asked the Lord, "Why me?" But she just turned to run from the church.

As soon as she climbed behind the wheel of her car she snatched up her purse and dug around in it for her Altoids can. It didn't register for a few aching moments that the can and everything in it was gone. It had been pure instinct to turn back to her pills.

She craved them.

Latoya flung her purse onto the floor and dropped her head to the steering wheel as she gripped it tightly. *Fight it. Just fight it.*

Still trembling with her emotions she finally started her

car and drove home, wiping her frustrated tears with one hand as she drove with the other. She was surprised that she missed Taquan Jr. because at least he would have distracted her from her thoughts.

As she pulled up to their house she saw a local delivery van parked in front of it on the street. She turned onto the drive and climbed out just as the driver stepped down from his truck and up onto the sidewalk. She met him at the end of the walkway.

"Latoya James-Sanders?" he asked, holding a bright red box with a gold bow.

She smiled at the man who looked no more than a teenager as she nodded and then dug out a tip to hand to him.

"No tip," he said, handing her the box. "Everything was taken care of. You have a good day."

Latoya carried it as she turned and unlocked the front door. She tripped over one of Taquan Jr.'s toys and the box went flying out of her hand as she fell. She lifted her head just in time to see it bounce off the wall. The lid fell off and wax paper floated in the air as at least two dozen chocolate candies dropped to the floor.

"Shit," she swore. "Shit, shit, shit."

Latoya was surprised at how good it felt to curse.

As the wax paper finally landed the card taped to it unfolded.

"So I'm never keeping secrets, and I'm never telling lies . . ."

She made a face as she climbed back to her feet. "Good Lord, what now?" she asked, moving over to pick up the note.

GIRL TALK

The six people in the limo rode in silence with the rest of the processional following behind the hearse as it traveled through the streets of Newark to the cemetery. Everyone was lost in their thoughts, their grief, and their memories. The silence was necessary.

They passed by the Cooper's Deli where they had shared their mutual love for its oversized corned beef and coleslaw on rye with Russian dressing. The three friends all looked at each other and shared a smile.

No words were ever needed. They all remembered. None of them would ever forget.

Not that memory or any other.

As the processional pulled into the cemetery and parked, they all seemed to take a deep breath to prepare for leaving their friend behind at her final burial place. By the time they gathered by the gravesite the casket had already been brought from the hearse. They again clutched at each others' hands as the people they brought with them gave them support in a row behind them.

They barely heard the words of the minister as they each locked eyes on the casket. It wasn't until everyone began saying the Lord's Prayer that they spoke.

"Our Father who art in heaven . . ."

They accepted the white long-stemmed lilies from one of the funeral director's crew as he moved about the crowd passing them out.

They knew she wouldn't want her funeral any other way.

They stepped forward as a young lady began to sing a cappella as they lowered the casket. One by one they began to toss the lilies atop the casket.

As the soloist lowered her voice for a gentle refrain, the minister opened a small black book that said The Book of Commons on it and glanced down into it. "We commend unto thy hands of mercy, most merciful Father, the soul of this our sister departed, and we commit her body to the ground, earth to earth, ashes to ashes, dust to dust."

"I will always love you," one friend said.

"Be at peace," the other said.

"We miss you," said the last.

Chapter 21

Monica

5:00 P.M.

Monica was afraid.

She hadn't even gone into her office since she received that package. She hadn't been sure if the bastard would make a move before Friday. She didn't know who to trust and enjoyed the comfort being inside the walls of their home gave her. Plus she wanted to be around Cameron to make sure he didn't receive anything strange.

Her fear was not of her being hurt mentally or physically. The love in her made her a warrior and she wanted to protect Cameron from being hurt at all costs. She wouldn't allow it.

From her office in their apartment she swiveled to look out the window. Night was coming on fast and with the change in time, it was darker much earlier. It would be dark in the next couple of hours it took to reach eight o'clock.

Her phone was on silent but she could see the screen light up from where it sat on the edge of her desk. Turning a bit, she reached for it. A text. Biting her bottom lip she opened it.

JUST CHECKING ON YOU. EVERY-
THING OKAY. U MAD AT ME? IM
SORRY ABOUT LAST WEEK. UR
RIGHT WE WERE DRUNK.

Monica snorted in disdain and tossed the phone back onto her desk before she swiveled back around to eye the skyline. Fuck Usain. It wasn't his first text that week or her first time ignoring him. Until she met the sneaky motherfucker who had been fucking with her for months she wasn't trusting a damn soul. Nobody.

And she was going to that meeting because she wanted the bullshit ended tonight. She wanted everything laid out on the table so she could decide if whatever secrets he held on her—whatever revenge was being sought—were worth her time.

She stood up and left her office. Looking down the hall she spotted the top of Cameron's head where he sat on the sofa watching television. She headed in his direction. By the time she moved across the polished black floors and into their sophisticatedly designed living room, she was naked. Her clothes were on the floor in a path behind her.

"Damn," Cameron said as she stepped in front of him.

Monica smiled as his eyes took her in. Her smooth brown skin. The way her dark nipples were already hard and poking through the long layers of her hair. The baldness of her pussy. The shape to her long legs that still showed the effects of decades of being a trained dancer.

He tossed aside the paper he was reading and reached for her, pulling her down to straddle his waist. He pressed his face against her cleavage and smoothed his hands from her shoulders down to the curves of her buttocks. "What's this—"

"Sssh." Monica held a finger to his lips before she pressed her hands against his shoulders and pushed him back as she traced his lips with her tongue. She felt the shiver race across his body.

As she eyed him, she stood up on the couch and then placed one leg over the back of it and pressed her hips forward until his face was buried between her thighs. Cameron didn't hesitate to lay his head back on the sofa and guide her body forward more as he released his tongue and opened the lips of her pussy in one swoop.

She hissed in pleasure and her fingers dug into the cushions of the sofa. "Yes," she moaned.

He licked her core, enjoying the taste of her juices, and then circled her clit before he used just the tip of his tongue to outline and then pluck it.

Monica felt her legs tremble as he began to slowly pull and suck her clit like he was giving it CPR. She cried out and rocked her hips against his face, sending her clit a little into his mouth. And when Cameron brought his hands around to slide a finger deeply inside her she almost buckled on top of him. He didn't let up. He brought his arms up to wrap around her thighs and lock her body in place as he shifted from deep sucks of her clit to rapid-fire flicks of his tongue against it.

"Oh God don't make me cum," she begged with a whimper as she clutched at the sofa with a grip tight enough to tear the charcoal suede as she tried to free his grip of her thighs and her clit.

He released it with a final kiss and looked up at her with hot eyes filled with desire. "You don't want to cum all in my mouth?" he asked, his chest heaving as he struggled to breathe after her pussy damn near smothered him.

She shook her head, causing her weave to sway back and forth across her tender nipples as she sat down far back enough on his knees to free his hard dick from the khakis he wore. "I want to have the strength to ride you and you know a good cum makes me weak," she told him, leaning forward to lick at his mouth as she stroked the length of his dark dick with both her hands.

Cameron reached up to cup the back of her head and deepened the kiss as he reached around his dick with his free hand to play in her pussy. The way she sat across his lap left her lips open and clit exposed from where it was usually nestled away.

"Make love to me, Cameron," she said, filled with sadness at anything snatching him away from her.

He studied her face and then wrapped one strong arm around her waist and stood up to carry her naked body across the apartment and up the stairs to their bedroom. Monica clung to him with arms and legs like she would never see him again. She was glad he understood what she meant by making love. Fucking could be done anywhere and with any amount of clothing on. Making love was two naked bodies somewhere where they could stretch out and get lost in one another: a bed, a blanket on the floor, even the beach.

Cameron laid her on the middle of the bed and stripped as Monica stretched her body languidly with her arms high above her head. With his dick leading the way, he climbed onto the bed between her open legs. Again he feasted on her pussy with a sexy lick from her ass up to her clit. His kisses continued against her belly button and up to her neck with thorough stops at her stomach and both pointed peaks of her breasts.

She shivered as he sucked at her neck as she massaged him from the buttocks and across the wide expanse of his back. The first feel of him guiding his dick inside her as he kissed her deeply caused Monica to nearly cum. He was long and thick and the blood coursing through his dick, making it hard, also made it warm.

Cameron eased his hands beneath her, guiding her buttocks up as he began to slowly wind his hips, sending his dick against her rigid and wet walls like they had nothing but time to enjoy each other. Just in and out, in and out again, and then a vicious swirl caused his stick to swoop against the walls of her pussy.

She sucked hotly at his shoulders as her fingers dug tiny pits into his ass with each delicious thrust. Just nice and slow and ever so thorough. In and out. In and out. "Oh God, Cameron, I love you so much," she whimpered as he sucked her neck and continued the onslaught.

He raised her hips higher and shifted his body to the side to deliver thrust after thrust to a new spot in her pussy.

"Ah shit," she cried out, tightening her legs around his back.

More thrusts.

"I'm cumming. Oh I'm cumming," she moaned against his neck as spasm after spasm hit her body with each tiny explosion inside of her. "Don't stop. Please don't stop."

He didn't.

Cameron shifted his body to the other side and went to work stroking against another spot in her pussy.

Nice and slow. In and out. Over and over and over.

Monica couldn't stop the emotions as she came. Tears raced down her cheeks as she kept proclaiming, "Cameron, I love you so much. I love you."

"I love you too, baby," he said, bending his head down to kiss her and stroke her tongue to the same rhythm of his dick strokes.

"I swear I love you. Don't ever leave me," she begged, still shivering and lost to everything as she finally came sliding down out of her climax.

"Shit I'm about to cum," he said, his tone thick and anxious.

Monica built up all the strength she could, motivated by wanting to please him the way he pleased her. She pushed his shoulder and Cameron rolled over onto his back, bringing Monica with him. His dick was still planted deeply within her.

She began to work her hips in that same slow back and forth motion as she sucked deeply at his tongue. Each move pulled tightly on his dick. She felt it get even harder inside her just moments before his entire body went stiff with the first shot of his cum firing from inside his dick against her walls. She sucked his tongue but rode his dick at the same slow and steady pace meant to drain a dick and extend his nut. "Don't you forget, I love you. You hear me, Cameron?" she demanded, looking down at the sweet torture expressed on his face as he grunted with each shot of cum she milked.

"I . . . love . . . you too . . . baby."

She continued working her hips even as he fought for control.

"Shit," he swore, closing his eyes.

She finally brought the ride to an end and his body went slack beneath her. She shifted her body atop him to lay her head on his shoulder. She kissed the spot near his lips and closed her eyes, listening to the rapid beating of his heart. It matched hers.

Soon, Cameron was snoring softly but even a sex-induced nap eluded Monica as she thought of the night still ahead of her. She gently rolled off the bed and walked into the bathroom to take a shower before she quickly dressed in stretchy jeans and a long-sleeve white tee with flats. She pulled her hair back into a ponytail and grabbed a black leather jacket.

Walking out of her closet, she saw that Cameron was still asleep. She started to risk a kiss, but decided against it. It was better to leave while he was not awake to ask questions. She already told him earlier that she had dinner plans with a client.

She left the bedroom and headed down the stairs. In her office she retrieved the key to the top drawer of her desk from its hiding spot inside the mouth of the large elephant statue she kept on the floor. She unlocked it and removed the nine millimeter gun, checking to make sure the safety was on before she slid it into the over-the-shoulder bag she wore.

"Just in case," she said, leaving her office and then the apartment.

Whoever was playing around in her life didn't know that she wasn't in the mood for the bullshit.

For a second, she'd forgotten that she gave Sampson the week off too.

"Could you hail me a cab please?" she asked the doorman.

He quickly obliged.

Once she was settled inside a cab and headed into Jersey, she bit at her nails in nervousness. She had no clue what she was going to meet. She didn't even really know if she could use the gun she purchased the day after the box arrived but she refused to go without some protection. Thankfully they wanted to meet at a public place like a hotel's conference room and she could only hope whoever the bastard or bitch was that they weren't crazy enough to get physical in public.

After nearly an hour the cab finally pulled to a stop in front of the Hilton near the Newark Airport. She paid her fare and left the cab to walk inside the hotel lobby. She looked around, hoping she didn't seem too obvious and sketchy. She saw nothing or no one out of the ordinary.

She walked up to the front desk and couldn't even find the politeness to greet the short, stubby white man working the desk. "Elizabeth Ballroom," she said, wishing the mini Starbucks in the lobby was open.

"Straight down the hall and just follow the signs," he said with a polite smile.

Monica walked away and then turned to come back to him. "Do you happen to know who rented the space?" she asked.

"Let me check," he said, tapping away on his computer. "It says JDI. John Doe Industries."

Fucking excellent.

"Okay, thank you." She headed down the hall and followed the signs on the way. As she came to the double doors leading into the ballroom she visibly shook her body and hopefully the nerves and uneasiness she felt. She stepped into the room and froze before she deeply frowned.

Save for the four chairs lined up in a row at the front of the room, it was empty.

"I'm sick of these childish-ass games," she said. Refusing to go any farther into the room, she posted up on the wall by the door with her hand inside her purse.

Chapter 22
Keesha

"Okay, what else can go?"

Keesha looked across her desk at Corey and fought the urge to snap "You motherfucker." It would have been just her anger talking and not something she meant. "I just hate doing this shit, Corey," she said. "What's the purpose up moving on up like George and Weezy if you just gone fall back down like James and Florida in the projects?"

Corey laughed.

Keesha was able to break a smile. "I'm sorry but I will not give up my car and the house. It's too many motherfuckers back in the hood waiting for me to fall. I refuse. I re-fuse. Fuck that."

"So you gone live life worrying about what people think?"

"What I'm saying is if we have to live in this motherfucker with nothing but beds, no lights, and just eating Oodles and Noodles in this bitch to keep it then I'm cool with it," she said, putting her palms up and leaning back in her chair.

Corey shook his head. "Look we're not going to lose our house or the car or pull Kimani out her school. I'd work two jobs before I let that happen."

Corey's cell phone sounded off. "Yo."

Keesha turned her attention back to her computer screen. She pushed her bob back behind her ears as she read the e-mail. Her lips moved as she read it. "The deal is done. I'll let you know when the contracts arrive."

Well that's some good news. At least I will have another book on the shelves. I just need to bring it next time.

As she skimmed through her list of e-mails she rolled her eyes at the "secret, secret" bullshit Shawn tried to play her with. He had still been blowing up her phone all week but she ignored him. She was going to play it out by his rules and if he thought it was going to end up with them booking a room he was about to get his face cracked in embarrassment.

"What hospital they took her to?" Corey said, rising to his feet.

Keesha shifted her eyes to him and he looked away from her. Her heart stopped.

"We're on the way."

She stood up slowly. "What happened, Corey?" she asked.

He came over and tried to hug her. She knocked his hands away and leaned back to eye him. "What happened?" she repeated.

"Your moms got in a fight today with some lady over some bullshit and . . . and the lady shot her, babe," he said, his voice filled with his anguish.

Keesha felt only a little relief at knowing her daughter was safe. Kimani was spending the weekend with Keesha's father. "Where?" she asked, as she stood up and grabbed her keys.

"Huh?" Corey asked, his face confused.

"Where did she get shot?" she asked, as they left the office and walked down the stairs together.

"Outside her apartment building," he said as if she was daft.

She picked up her pocketbook from the table by the door as they walked out of the house. "No, where the bullet land?" Keesha asked. She turned when she reached the passenger door of their Benz and realized Corey wasn't behind her. He still stood on the porch.

"Why are you calm?" he asked. "Your mother got shot."

"Yes . . . I heard you."

Corey came down the stairs and the look on his face changed from incredulous to annoyed. "Damn, you a cold-hearted bitch sometimes, Keesha," he said, deactivating the alarm.

Boo-doop.

She opened the passenger door and climbed inside, settling her purse on the floor by her feet before she pressed both hands to the soft swell of her stomach again. "So you don't know where she got shot?" she calmly asked as soon as he climbed behind the wheel and closed the driver's door.

"No, I don't know. The ambulance is headed to UMDNJ now," he said, his voice cold as he started the car and reversed down the driveway before he settled back into his seat and fell silent.

Keesha closed her eyes. She allowed herself to enjoy the silence he angrily provided for the majority of the twenty-minute ride from South Orange to Newark. "Do you know how badly I want to smoke right now?" she asked, finally breaking the silence as he navigated congested South Orange Avenue.

Corey glanced over at her. "Weed?"

She licked her lips and shook her head. "A Newport. You know I don't smoke weed no more," she said, her voice still calm. "If I let myself freak the fuck out over this I will smoke a pack and that ain't good for the baby."

He pulled to a red light and reached over to press his hand over hers still setting on her stomach. "My bad, Keesh," he said.

She nodded calmly. "So you enjoy this Zen shit right here *because* as soon as I find out what's going on with my mother—and if she is okay—I am going to tear you a new asshole and be that coldhearted *bitch* you think I am," she said sweetly, turning her head on the headrest to smile at him.

Corey removed his hand and frowned.

"I'm dead-ass serious too," she said.

He nodded. "I know."

"Good," she said before turning her head and closing her eyes again.

Lord, let her be okay.

Keesha didn't know a thing about praying. She'd never been to church. Growing up, Diane never pressed the issue because she was too busy sleeping in from partying until dawn the night before. When Keesha became the adult she continued the cycle of partying hard Saturday night and sleeping in Sunday morning.

"We here, baby," Corey said. "You go in and I'll park the car."

She opened her eyes and through the slightly tinted glass saw the entrance to the emergency room. She placed her hand on the door but she couldn't move.

"Baby, you all right? I said you go in and I'll park."

Keesha had no idea what awaited her inside. She felt all kinds of cravings hit her as the nerves and fear she was fighting crept up on her. Dope, nicotine, shot of brown liquor, pickles and cheese. All of her vices past and current. She forced herself to calm down as she finally climbed from the car and made her way inside.

The blend of the smell of illness and the smell of the products used to keep the hospital sterile caused her to gag. She stood there breathing deeply hoping the baby wasn't about to send the fried chicken and fries she had for lunch up and onto the floor.

As the wave of nausea passed, Keesha continued to the admitting desk. "My mother, Diane Lands, was shot and the ambulance was supposed to bring her here."

"I am glad you're here," the woman said. "Room three. Straight through that door on your right."

Keesha headed toward the door.

"Keesha."

She turned. Her face filled with pure aggravation at seeing Shawn walking up toward her. "What are you doing here?" she asked him.

"I heard about your moms and came to check on you," he said, his eyes shifting down to her stomach.

"I'm good. Corey is here," she said, turning away from him.

He lightly grabbed her hand. "We need to talk, Keesha."

"Right now?" she snapped, feeling all of her calm quickly fade as she snatched her hand away. "Besides didn't you want to meet at the Hilton and reveal secrets and shit? Sending all those e-mails threatening me. Fuck outta here."

Shawn made a face. "I never e-mailed. I don't have no e-mail account."

Keesha studied his face and believed him.

If this fool didn't send those e-mails and that box, then who did?

Over Shawn's shoulder she saw Corey in the distance walking from the parking deck. "Look, I have to check on my mother. A'ight? And I know you feel this could be your baby but we don't know. I really feel like it's Corey's."

Shawn opened his mouth to protest.

She kept her eyes on Corey's figure even as she held up her hand. "Look we can't have a DNA test until the baby is born and that's over six months away. Could you please just chill 'til then and if the DNA proves the baby is yours then I will tell Corey the truth."

"I want to claim and take care of what's mine," Shawn insisted.

The emergency room door slid open and Corey walked up to them. He looked surprised to see his cousin. He dapped him.

"I heard about the shooting and decided to come through and check on my fam," Shawn said.

"Good looking out, cuz," Corey said.

"Come with me, Corey," she said, grabbing his hand and pulling him behind her through the door.

"Well, damn, bitch. Who taught you how to give shots?"

Both Keesha and Corey stopped dead in their tracks and looked at each other before they both looked at the closed curtain from behind which Diane's voice was vibrant and loud.

Keesha pulled the curtain back and they stepped into the small room.

Diane was laid on the bed on her side with a sheet partially draped over her hips. "There's my family. I told Junie to call you. Can y'all believe this *shit*?" she said.

Keesha's eyes skimmed over her mother's body. "I thought they said you got shot," she said, more than thoroughly confused.

"I did. In my ass," she said, chucking her thumb over her shoulder, pointing down toward her rear.

"Okay, I'm out," Corey said, turning and breezing past the curtain.

"These horrible nurses gone kill me before that bullet will," she said, looking over her shoulder to give the nurse a mean face.

"What happened?" Keesha asked as the nurse left the room.

"Frankie's old lady caught us in his car—"

Keesha's shoulders slumped. "Who is Frankie?"

"My side piece," she supplied, wincing as she shifted on the bed. "So anyway, she opened the door and boxed me. I jumped out the car and politely whipped that ass good—just ask anybody—and when I was turned to grab my keys from Frankie's whip he's long gone. My keys on the ground along with my bag of White Castles he just brought me. I bend down to scoop up my shit and pow, the trick shot me."

Keesha looked at her mother long and hard. She could hardly believe that it was a fifty-year-old grandmother talking like that and telling a story that no one should experience but especially not a fifty-year-old woman. And there was a complete absence of shock or terror about being shot. Diane made it seem like the woman nudged her in the ass instead of shot her in it.

My mother is crazy. Like for real.

"She better be glad she got locked up on the spot because I got a few more of these blows for her ass."

Like for real. Not ratchet. Not ghetto. Not immature. Just crazy.

"So you know I have to stay with y'all while I recoopate—"

Keesha eyed her. "While you what?" she asked.

"Recoopate."

"Diane, it's recuperate," Keesha said.

"Well, I'm gone have to do all *that* at y'all house . . . unless you can get your mama a nurse," she said.

Keesha sat her purse on the chair and leaned back against the wall. She had discovered that her mother was fine but she wanted all her vices more than ever.

* * *

"The Elizabeth Ballroom, please?"

The short and thick white man working the desk of the Hilton looked up at Keesha with a smile that just read "I'm paid to do this."

"Straight down the hall and just follow the signs," he said, that smile still in place.

She looked down the hall before she turned and headed toward it.

Keesha had convinced herself that Shawn was behind this meeting but he denied it. In fact when Diane was released and they took her back to their townhouse in South Orange, Shawn had followed them and was still sitting in the house with Corey when she left with the excuse of needing to go back to Diane's apartment to pack up some of her clothes.

So what the hell is this shit about? Revenge? Secrets? See, this some white people shit.

Keesha came to the door and opened it. There was a room big enough for a wedding reception with just four chairs sitting together in a row. "Hello," she called out, her hand clenching the door handle tight as hell.

"Keesha?"

She jumped back as Monica stepped in front of the doorway.

"What the fuck is this shit all about?" Keesha asked, pushing past her ex-friend to step into the ballroom. "You behind all this bullshit?"

Monica took her hand out of her purse and pointed the finger back. "Me? Hell you the one obviously," she balked.

They eyed each other.

"Look, somebody's been sending me e-mails and then I got a red box with some chocolates and a stupid Babyface remix of one of his songs telling me to come here," Keesha said, not missing one detail of the expensive clothes on Monica's back.

"So did I," Monica said.

The ballroom door opened and they both turned.

Chapter 23
Danielle

4:00 P.M.

Danielle walked into her New Jersey apartment, closing and locking the door behind her. She dropped her purse and keys on the sofa before walking into the kitchen to retrieve a bottle of water from the fridge. As she tipped her head back to sip the water she looked around at her apartment.

It's going to be hard to pack it all up.

Danielle had made the choice to not renew her lease in the next few months. She was moving out to Los Angeles once and for all. She weighed the pros and cons of the West Coast versus the East Coast: she would save thousands on the rent and utilities she continued to pay; she found a world-renowned specialist on PKD in Los Angeles; and most importantly, after spending that week with Mohammed and his family and falling completely back in love with him, the apartment was just a reminder of him and their relationship that she could not bear. When she kissed Mohammed good-bye that morning at the airport she had said her farewells for good.

Carrying the bottle, she made her way into the living room. She sat the bottle on the ottoman she used as a coffee table and picked up the remote to turn on the TV. She settled on VH1's perpetual run of reality TV show marathons. It didn't really matter. She really just wanted to break up the silence.

Danielle finally pulled off the burnt orange belted wool capelet she wore with jeggings and thigh-high camel-colored boots. She glanced at her watch.

Four more hours.

Her stomach clenched and she took a deep breath as she reached for her water and enjoyed a long, quenching gulp. Her new blood pressure medicine kept her running to the bathroom and she liked to make sure she wouldn't get dehydrated. "Like an old woman," she muttered, reaching in her Birkin for her iPhone.

She had missed calls but the first she noticed was from Omari. She still hadn't called him but every so often he would send a text or call to leave a voice mail that he wished they could reconnect. "I bet," she drawled, remembering the blow job she gave him in her LA office.

Danielle tapped her phone against her knee before she turned it over in the palm of her right hand and dialed his number. The man at least deserved some explanation for the end of their friendship—not the truth but something. It rang several times and went to voice mail.

"Hey, Omari, this is long-lost Danielle. I was in town until later tonight and thought I would give you a call and just explain things. I have to head out at seven for an appointment at eight but if you get this and you're not busy, give me a call back."

She ended the call and sat her phone on the seat beside her. She turned to lie back against the arm as she raised her legs up and crossed them at the ankles. She felt tired. She didn't know if it was jet lag or her illness but she could sleep for days.

She had gone right back to work on *The A-List* and flew out that morning right after taping. She was headed back on the first plane smoking as soon as her meeting was done. Danielle had no qualms about the fact that she flew into town for one night just to find out who was behind the upcoming blackmail. She had no choice.

When Danielle got home from Jamaica the doorman at her Los Angeles condo had given her the red box with the gold bow. The candies were melted but the message in the card was clear that someone was out for revenge and had secrets on her that they were willing to release to her network bosses if she didn't show up for the eight o'clock meeting.

She could still hear that fucking music.

"So I'm never keeping secrets, and I'm never telling lies . . ."
"So I'm never keeping secrets, and I'm never telling lies . . ."
"So I'm never keeping secrets, and I'm never telling lies . . ."
"So I'm never keeping secrets, and I'm never telling lies . . ."
"So I'm never keeping secrets, and I'm never telling lies . . ."
"So I'm never keeping secrets, and I'm never telling lies . . ."

Danielle had no idea she could dislike Babyface so much.

She just wondered who it was claiming to know her secrets and what they wanted in return to go against the music and actually keep them. She had all week to fret about it.

Like I don't have enough shit to worry about.

Needing a distraction, she dug into her tote and pulled

her iPad to swipe through the photos she took in Jamaica. A picture of Mohammed filled the screen and Danielle smiled, reaching to touch his face without swiping to the next photo. When her eyes became teary she sniffed, cleared her throat, and moved on through the series of photos. Again, she paused at one of her holding Adric as they came down a water slide.

She missed him just as badly as she missed his father. An actual pang of hurt touched her.

And she came to the photo of Oni holding a wooden statue during their visit to the craft market in Ocho Rios. Her eyes met Oni's in the photo.

Tell him.

Danielle closed the iPad cover and set it on the seat next to her now-sweating bottle of water. She shifted onto her side and tried to focus on the television.

Ding-dong.

Danielle was startled awake and she shot straight up, looking around. She hadn't even remembered falling asleep. She glanced at her watch. Almost three hours had passed. *Damn, I was tired.*

Ding-dong.

She looked at the door as if she could see through it. Uncrossing her feet she stood up and walked over to it, already knowing it was Omari. She opened the door with a smile.

Sure enough Omari was leaning in the doorway looking handsome in a chocolate overcoat, a wool brim, and dark jeans with boots. "Look who reappeared," he said with a smile.

Danielle smiled in return and moved a few steps backward to open the door and wave him in. "I've just been really busy," she said as she closed the door and watched him unbutton his coat before he sat down.

"I was in a meeting when you called. After your message I decided to come over instead of call," Omari said, lightly patting the seat next to him.

She picked up her iPad and bottled water to sit on the ottoman in front of him. "Still looking good I see," she said, crossing her legs.

His dark eyes took her all in. "Same here."

They fell into a comfortable silence.

"So what happened?" he asked. "I know we said no relationship but damn you just kicked a brotha to the curb. Used me up and threw me away."

Danielle cupped her hand over his. "It wasn't like that. Things got really stressful at work and I had to thin out my schedule," she lied.

Omari nodded in understanding as he turned her hand over and began tracing delicate circles in her palm. "I've missed you."

Danielle arched her brow. "Oh I know what you missed," she quipped.

"Hell yeah. Shee-it," he said. "But I also just missed talking to you and seeing that pretty face."

Life was all the curveballs. Here was another decent guy with a good job and an even better dick game willing to woo her. She could no more lead him on than she could Mohammed. "I'm moving out west permanently," she admitted. "I'm giving up my lease on this apartment."

"Wooow," Omari said softly, looking at her in surprise.

Danielle cocked her head to the side and pouted. "I'm sorry," she said.

Omari sat up on the edge of the sofa and released her hand to press both of his hands to her hips as he leaned forward and kissed her full on the mouth. Once and then again. "I could have fallen for you," he admitted. "But I understand."

Danielle closed her eyes as he tasted her mouth again. She couldn't lie—his kisses tasted and felt good. And there was a time when having two men at her beck and call would have made her proud. She would have used them for the time, their gifts and their dick even as she knew her health meant no promise of forever. Thankfully she had grown up. And it felt good.

She just wasn't that selfish person anymore.

So she gave him one last deep kiss that brought moans from them both, before she stood and held his hand to lead him to the door.

"If you change your mind . . ."

"I'll call," she finished.

Omari gave her one last kiss on the cheek before he turned and walked out of her life.

Danielle shut the door and turned to see he left his brim on the sofa. She started to call him but walked over to pick it up and inhale the scent of his spicy and warm cologne instead.

Glancing again at her watch, she shoved the hat, her cell, and her iPad back into her tote and slid her capelet back on over the long-sleeved fitted white tee she wore. Since the hotel was by the airport she planned on heading straight there after the meeting, confrontation, sparring match, what-the-fuck-ever.

With one walk through every room in the apartment, she finally turned off the lights, picked up her tote, and headed out of her apartment. She paid the car service she used to get from the airport to sit and wait to carry her back. As soon as she walked off the elevator, crossed the foyer, and came through the open door of the building, the uniformed driver hopped out of his seat and came around to open the back passenger door for her.

"Thank you," she said.

As he came around the SUV and climbed back in his seat, she told him, "The Hilton at the Newark Airport."

Danielle looked out the window at the already dark skies. She moved her foot back and forth rapidly as she fought not to let her anxiety overcome her. She tried to envision who could want revenge for something she did?

The last man she did wrong was Sahad Linx, the record label owner who walked in and caught her full of Mohammed's dick. Was it him? He had been pissed at her the last time she saw him at a restaurant in New York five years ago. She had considered contacting him directly but if it wasn't him she didn't want to look foolish.

No man would hold a grudge that long.

And then she considered that if it wasn't Carolyn then maybe it was someone Carolyn bragged to. *You cannot trust a cokehead. Especially a freaky one.*

Whoever it was sent the package to her Los Angeles address but wanted to meet in Jersey? Another damn riddle she contemplated all week long.

Danielle hated the idea of being watched, stalked, and monitored. How else did they know where she lived in Los Angeles? She shivered in repulsion.

This had to be about money because she just couldn't see anything else to be gained from it.

An accident on 1 and 9 tied them up. Danielle glanced at her watch as the driver pulled to a stop just outside the towering hotel. It was a little after eight. "I shouldn't be more than an hour," she told him as he held the door and held her hand to help her down.

"No problem."

Danielle walked into the stylish lobby and headed straight for the Elizabeth Ballroom. When she worked at the law firm there had been a huge banquet there. She reached the double doors and pulled the right one open and stepped inside.

"Danielle?"

She stopped, her heart still pounding with adrenaline, and she looked from the surprised face of first Keesha and then Monica. And then back to Keesha. And back to Monica.

For a moment she forgot her reason for even being there and felt overwhelmed by the sight of her friends. She turned and squeezed her eyes to keep from crying. So many times she had thought of them and wanted them near her as she fought not to look at life like it was ending. She missed them terribly.

"Did you get that red box too?" Monica asked.

Danielle took a deep breath and turned back to them, her face filling with surprise as she continued to blink rapidly. "Yes. That's why I'm here," she said.

"Me too," Keesha said.

"Same here," Monica added, crossing her arms over her chest.

Danielle looked around at the empty room and the four chairs. "So I assume we're just waiting on Latoya to get the party started."

Both women nodded in agreement.

Chapter 24
Latoya

7:59 P.M.

Latoya didn't know why she was concerned about her appearance for someone who wanted to wreak havoc in her life, but she was. As she stood outside the double doors of the Elizabeth Ballroom, she smoothed herself, made sure none of her short hairs were flying and the jean dress she wore was dust-free. With one last prayer to God she raised her hand to pull the door open and looked down at it trembling. She gripped the handle and pulled it open.

"We've been waiting on you."

She paused in the doorway at Monica, Keesha, and Danielle standing in the massive empty ballroom. Her eyes feasted on them. Keesha was a little thicker but still curvy with the same flawless dark skin that Hershey's couldn't make in a million days. Danielle was still a tall version of LisaRaye with the curves and light eyes and all. Monica looked the most different with her waist-length, bone-straight hair and clothes that were casual but pricey. Anyone could see that.

She genuinely smiled at them as she finally walked into the room and let the door close behind her. "You all didn't have to go through all this for a reunion," she said, walking up to them.

"We didn't," Keesha said.

Latoya let her perplexity show.

"Someone has been harassing all four of us for months and we all got the package of candy telling us to meet here at eight," Danielle said, moving across the room to grab one of the chairs and plop down into it.

"Whoever it is has it out for all four of us obviously," Monica said.

"Like who?" Latoya asked, moving to take one of the seats by Danielle when she caught Keesha's dark eyes leveled on her in assessment.

The doors opened and they all looked on at the tall and handsome man entering the ballroom dressed in a three-piece pinstripe suit that was tailored flawlessly, fitting his toned frame with perfection. The wide lapel of the jacket with a crisp spread-collared shirt and Windsor-knotted tie was off the pages of *GQ*. Even the briefcase he carried was the type of polished leather that had to cost four figures.

He smiled at them as two bodyguards entered the room to flank him. "Good evening, ladies," he said, his voice deep and filled with confidence.

"It was you, Usain?" Monica asked in disbelief, storming up to him with her hand ready to deliver a blow to his smug face.

The bodyguards stepped forward to block her path.

Latoya couldn't believe she was looking into the face of her church friend Marion. *But Monica knows him as Usain?*

"Usain?" Keesha added, rushing forward to join Monica in trying to swing on him. "That ain't no motherfucking Usain. That's my neighbor Jeremiah. You old slick gay bastard you."

"I can assure you that I am far from gay," he promised

her just before he locked his gaze on Danielle sitting there completely stunned by it all. "Am I, Danielle?"

"Fuck you," she said to him in a voice tight with anger.

He nodded. "You did and very well too. I thank you for it," he said as he smoothed his hands over his silk tie before placing them in the pockets of his pants.

"What are you, the fucking male Sybil?" Keesha snapped as she eyed him walking to the front of the room with swagger of a man used to being in control.

"No, that would be your mother. Who by the way *is* crazy as hell," he said, calmly pulling a remote from his pocket, dimming the lights, and lowering a large screen from the ceiling. "How's that gunshot?"

Keesha picked up a chair. One of the bodyguards made it across the room in no time to jerk it from her hands.

"And Monica don't even think about using that gun you brought last week," he said, never once turning from watching the screen lower and stop.

Latoya shook her head in denial as she sat there stiff as a board craving another of the pills in her purse. One trip to the doctor with a lie about back pain and she was back in business. She was ashamed of her relapse. Her weakness.

Things between Taquan and her had never been worse. Never.

He wouldn't forgive her for putting his megachurch plans at risk and she . . . she would never forgive him for cutting her out of his life until she finally apologized to Olivia. And even after she sat before her husband and the entire church board, he still treated her coldly afterward. She gave in to his demands and she was still being punished.

She turned to the only thing she could to cope and she knew her faith in God should be stronger but fighting the pain was too much. Living life on the edge of tears and feeling helpless had been too much to bear. She couldn't even remember the last time she prayed.

And now this circus unfolding before her. Discovering that a man she considered a friend and confidant was nothing more than a wolf in sheep's clothing. The devil in disguise.

It was too much.

She gripped and released the purse over and over, fighting her urge, fighting her demon.

Usain/Jeremiah/Marion/Omari laughed as he jerked at the cuffs of his sleeves. "You ladies have no idea how long I have waited for this right here," he said, turning as images began to flash across the screen.

All of the women gasped as snapshots of them filled the screen one after the other in rapid-fire succession.

"Sweet Jesus," Latoya whispered in shock, covering her gaping mouth with her trembling hands.

Monica pressed against the wall as the man she knew as Usain knelt to eat her.

He chuckled. "When you took that picture from me that night in your office I was just removing the camera I had put there earlier," he said.

Keesha getting dicked from behind by a tall and thick dude.

He glanced over at Keesha as he removed his jacket and rolled up his sleeves. "So which one was hitting the pussy better, your man or his cousin right here tagging the hell out dat ass?"

Danielle on her knees with her lips sealed around a man's shiny dick.

"You sick bastard," she whispered harshly, burying her face in her hands.

"You suck a mean dick," he said, using the remote to pause the photo just as the tip of his dick pressed against her inner cheek. "Swallow and all."

"Who are you?" Monica screamed.

"Good to the last drop, huh?" he said coldly, his eyes still on Danielle. "I thought I might get one last good blow this afternoon at your apartment—"

Danielle dug in her tote and snatched out the wool brim he had left on her couch. She flung it across the room at him. It landed near the tips of his polished shoes of the finest Italian leather. "You left this, you lying, sneaky, phony, posing-ass pussy motherfucker," she screamed, tears in her eyes.

He kicked the hat back toward her. "It doesn't match my outfit," he said, using the remote to resume the slide show.

The sight of Latoya stretched out on the church floor.

"That was smart of you pretending to catch the Holy Ghost so the church didn't know you were high off those pills you love," he said with a chuckle and slow, mocking clap. His eyes dropped down to her hands clenching and unclenching the handle of her clutch purse.

"Anytime you want to pop one of your pills you schemed from your doctor you just go right ahead," he said. "I know how it must feel to be a junkie and need a fix. Right, Keesha?"

Latoya felt the eyes of everyone in the room switch to her. She turned and raced to the door.

"Oh, no, don't you dare leave. We've only just begun, Mrs. Reverend Taquan Sanders," he called across the expanse of the room, his voice echoing and mocking.

Latoya froze at the door, her hand on the handle. Her addiction revealed. Her shame on full display. She dropped her head to the door.

She felt an arm on her shoulders and looked to see Keesha standing beside her.

"Excellent idea, Keesha. You really are the best one to help her since you know how it feels to fiend for it. Right?"

Latoya turned, shifting her eyes from other random shots of the four of them still flashing on the screen. "What the fuck do you want?" she said coldly, coming forward.

He frowned. "Language, First Lady. The Rev and that church board wouldn't like that," he said, throwing things she shared with him back in her face.

The man had weaved his way into all their lives for months and sat there sucking it up like a leech.

Latoya couldn't believe they all had been so stupid.

The lights in the room brightened and he picked up the briefcase he'd sat on the floor to pull out four files. He nodded as he tossed a file at each of their feet. "I don't need these anymore. Please know that there is barely anything about you that I don't know. Money talks and I got plenty of it."

Keesha swiped up her file and flipped through it. "No the fuck he didn't," she gasped.

"Yes the fuck I did," he said, clasping his hands together and looking so pleased with himself. "My private detectives are the best. Go ahead. Check it out. I had a ball. Better than anything on reality TV."

He pointed his finger at Danielle. "Having a lesbian tryst to start your career. The handyman boyfriend in the Bahamas who broke up you and Sahad Linx of all people. That motherfucker almost as rich as me. Almost but not quite."

Danielle shook her head back and forth as she glared at him like her eyes could burn a hole through him.

He turned to Keesha. "You really were so low to fuck Monica's man. I guess the dope made you able to look at yourself in the mirror. But then you top all of that by fucking two cousins at the same time and don't know who your baby daddy is. Damn you scandalous."

Keesha flipped him the bird. "You don't know shit about me," she snapped.

He snorted in derision and turned to Monica.

She kicked her thin folder and it slid across the carpet toward him. He stopped it by placing his foot down on the center of it. "You really messed up that therapist you were sneaking with. I didn't quite get to hit the pussy and see just what drove one fool to break your leg and the other one to stalk you and then eventually leave his wife. It tasted damn good though. Did you tell Cameron that you spread those legs for me?"

He turned back to Danielle. "Don't worry yours was good too," he said, chuckling.

She swiped at a tear that raced down her cheek.

He focused on Latoya. "You fight dirty for what you want. By any means necessary—including selling stories to the tabloids on your baby daddy. You really got to lay off them pills. You're starting to lose weight. Next you be selling ass for pills."

Latoya honestly didn't know if she could take any more of the humiliation from him. "What do you want?" she asked him again, her throat tightening with tears filled with anger, shame, and withdrawal.

He took his time unrolling his sleeves, buttoning his cuffs and sliding on his jacket. When he focused back on them his face was hard with anger. "Payback is a bitch and I owed you tricks. I mean I *really* owed you. Period point blank. Life is all about karma. And when it comes to karma sometimes it happens naturally and sometimes a bad motherfucker like me creates it."

He looked at each one with a line in his face born from bitterness. "You probably forgot the bullshit you pulled on me in high school. But I never forgot."

"High school," they all shrieked in disbelief before looking at each other in obvious bewilderment.

"You bitches don't even recognize me, do you?" he asked, his eyes glittering with anger.

Latoya squinted her eyes as she studied him.

Monica shook her head.

"Sure don't," Keesha said, closing the thick file folder that held her secrets.

Danielle crossed her legs and waved her hand at him. "This is your big moment. The big reveal of this childish bullshit. So have at it," she said.

He nodded. "You're right, beautiful, it is my mother-fucking day, plus I know you're tired from your disorder and so I won't keep you—especially you—any longer."

Latoya, Monica, and Keesha all looked at Danielle as she dropped her head in her hands and cried. They all instantly moved to stand around her. Latoya knelt by her side and gathered Danielle's hands into hers.

He walked up to them with his briefcase in hand.

"And by now all of your dirty little secrets that I already told you I would not keep have been sent to . . ."

They all looked up with hatred in their eyes for him.

"Cameron," he said, pointing it at Monica.

"Corey." He pointed to Keesha.

He pointed to Latoya. "The Rev."

"And your producers," he told Danielle.

She jumped to her feet and swung ever so quickly.

WHAP.

The sound of the slap echoed inside the ballroom.

The bodyguards instantly stepped forward. He held one hand up to stop them. "It's okay. She could never hurt me again the way I have hurt her," he said, flexing his broad shoulders in his suit. "Plus that blow job was worth a slap."

"How could you be so hateful?" Latoya asked him. "What kind of life is that if everything you are is built on a foundation of hatred?"

He looked at her like she was silly and nonsensical. "A damn good one," he said cockily.

"I want you to know that Xavier Lofton has *completely* wrecked y'all's shit," he said coldly, walking out of the ballroom without another glance back in their direction.

As soon as the door closed behind him and his body-guards, the stereo surround system kicked in.

"So I'm never keeping secrets, and I'm never telling lies . . ."

GIRL TALK

2000

The he steady thump of the bass seemed to hit the walls of the gym of University High as the last party of the school year raged on. The DJ mixed in DMX's "Party Up" just as Q-Tip's "Vibrant Thing" faded out.

"Y'all gone make me lose my mind up in here, up in here . . ."

Latoya and Keesha sat on the other side of the wall separating the gym from the locker room. There were just enough flashing lights streaming through the glass squares at the top of the double doors to keep them from being in total darkness.

"Here, Latoya. Hit that."

Latoya looked down at the blunt Keesha tried to hand her. "After I just sat and watched you lick it to roll it. No thanks," she said, turning up her nose as they sat on a wooden bench with their backs to the wall.

Keesha shrugged and took a long drag. The fiery tip of it burnt brighter in the darkness.

"Where are they? This place stinks," Latoya complained, as she rubbed her sweaty palms on the jeans Monica let her borrow.

"You'd stink too with all the funky asses that floated through this joint through the years," Keesha said, dropping the last end of the blunt under her foot to put it out before lobbing it into the trash can in the corner by the row of lockers.

The rear door squeaked as it opened and both girls leaned to the side to look down between the long rows of lockers to see Monica walking toward them. "They're

*coming," she said softly, stooping down to hide with them.
"Keesha, you smoked a whole blunt by yourself?"*

*Keesha giggled. "It's like Lay's, once you take one hit
you just can't stop."*

Monica sucked her teeth. "Shut your high ass up."

"For sure," Keesha said with emphasis.

*"Are we doing the right thing?" Latoya whispered,
feeling her nerves cause definite bubbles in her guts.*

*Monica nodded. "Yes," she whispered back with empha-
sis, turning to look around the lockers at the closed rear door.*

*Keesha raised one arm in the air and partied in her seat
to the sound of the party just outside the doors. "Y'all
gone make me act a FOOL up in here, up in here."*

*Monica and Latoya eyed her before they both rolled
their eyes.*

*"So we should let that little nerd get away with the lit-
tle stupid pranks he's been pulling on Danielle because she
wouldn't go to the junior prom with him?" Monica whispered.*

*Latoya thought of how long it took Danielle to be able
to sit down without it hurting from the thumbtack Xavier
slid in her chair. "It was so cute how he asked her to go
with his balloons and teddy bear," Latoya said, making a
sad face. "He had to build up all his little courage to even
try Danielle."*

"She didn't mean to laugh," Monica said.

*The rear door squeaked again and they all became si-
lent, moving further back into the darkness enough to hide.*

*"Nobody will bother us in here," Danielle said, pulling
Xavier's hand to step a few feet back from the doors leading into the gym.*

*Xavier was tall and thin. The oversized clothing he had
on looked more like he was wearing someone else's clothes
than trying to be in style. He was an okay-looking boy but*

his square fade that resembled the father's on the TV show
Moesha *and his acne just messed his entire game up.*

"You know I really like you, Danielle," he said, his
voice awkward and stilted and filled with the nerves he
was feeling.

"Aw that's so sweet, Xavier," she said before she stepped
close to him and leaned in to kiss him.

Xavier roughly grabbed at her butt as he released his
tongue and swiped it across Danielle's mouth.

Keesha, Latoya, and Monica all covered their mouths
not to make a noise as they looked on. It was not a pretty
sight to see Xavier awkwardly kissing Danielle with such
wet, slobby noises that echoed in the locker room.

His penis got hard and stuck out like a straight arrow
against the zipper of his jeans.

Danielle stepped back from him. Around her entire
mouth it felt sticky and wet but she smiled at him softly
and reached behind her to pull the peach T-shirt she wore
over her head. "Take your clothes off," she said, dropping
it to the floor.

"Oh shit," he swore, his eyes getting big as he stared at
Danielle's breasts in the black bra she wore.

He was out of all his clothes in no time.

The girls tried not to laugh as he almost fell trying to
pull his denims over his sneakers. He finally kicked the
shoes off and rushed out of his jeans and boxers.

Everyone's eyes got big at the size of Xavier's dick, including Danielle who stared at it for a few seconds with
her mouth open in surprise. It was large and thick and
hung from his thin body like it was heavy.

"Uhm uhm uhm," Danielle said, still eyeing it. "Well
damn, Xavier."

He smiled and wrapped his hand around it to wiggle
at her.

Keesha started to giggle but Latoya reached out to cover her mouth with her hand.

Xavier turned his head to look toward where they hid but Danielle stepped up and turned his face back toward her. She pushed him back against the door gently and pressed her lips against his again as he dick-pressed into her stomach.

That was the sign.

The girls all rose up and stepped out of the darkness just as Danielle reached and opened the door leading directly into the gym. She stepped back and all four girls pushed him out into the party. Danielle closed the door and locked it.

Soon the music stopped.

They stepped back just enough to still see into the party but not have their faces seen through the windows in the doors.

Xavier stood there in shock, dick hard as jail and naked as the day he was born. The crowd nearest to him backed away and formed a semicircle around him.

"Damn, big boy, what you up to?" the DJ joked on the mic, drawing more attention to the spectacle.

Everyone started laughing and pointing.

His hard-on disappeared and he peed himself.

Pure chaos reigned after that.

Xavier turned to try and open the doors, all of his shame so clear on his face as he banged on the doors.

The girls stepped back even farther into the darkness.

"He got a mark on his ass, y'all. Look," someone screamed loudly.

"We gotta get out of here," Keesha said, bending down to scoop up his clothes and sneakers. She dumped them into the trash can and raced down the length of the locker room and pushed through the rear door.

Seconds later the other three girls followed.

Chapter 25
Monica

8:59 P.M.

"I cannot believe that my entire relationship might be fucked over something we did in high school?" Monica said, breaking the silence as they all sat at one of the tables of the hotel's restaurant.

"My marriage too," Latoya admitted.

Keesha said nothing and just nervously bit at the acrylic tips of her nails.

Danielle turned to signal for the waiter. "Another glass of red wine, please," she said as soon as he appeared at her elbow.

Monica leveled her eyes on her. It was Danielle's third glass in just the minutes since they left the ballroom and the now annoying refrains of Babyface's "Never Keeping Secrets" behind. "Is it okay for you to be drinking, Danielle?" she asked.

Danielle leaned a bit out of the waiter's way as he sat the glass of wine before her. "Yes, I'm fine," she said, picking up the goblet and taking a deep sip.

Monica opened her mouth to protest but then she pressed her lips closed. They hadn't been friends in five years and Cristal had walked away from it, ignoring their calls and putting plenty of the distance she obviously wanted between them. Monica wasn't holding a grudge, she just had her own problems to worry about.

They all did.

She took a sip of her own glass of wine and glanced at Latoya. She couldn't believe after watching Keesha struggle to get clean from dope that Latoya the church mouse was popping pills. *She had God more than any of us. So why get high?*

Monica's eyes dipped down to Keesha's stomach. She was not at all surprised that she was fucking two men—and cousins at that. Although she'd forgiven Keesha for sleeping with Rah behind her back she had never really forgotten it. Her lips were as loose as her pussy. Running back and telling Rah during the sex and drug haze that Monica was cheating on him led to him beating her and breaking her leg in two.

Nope, I ain't surprised at all.

She picked up her iPhone from where it sat on the table next to her glass. No calls from Cameron. *Was that good or bad?*

"Am I the only one scared to go home?" she asked.

No one answered her as they all shifted in their seats. Their silence was telling though.

"It's weird that we let our friendship go and forgot all about our history together since high school and this vindictive asshole swoops right in and exploits our separation to destroy us," Monica said with a sarcastic half-laugh.

"That's for sure," Keesha agreed, pushing yet another piece of gum into her mouth to chew. "I thought he was my gay next-door neighbor but come to think of it I never even been inside that motherfucker's house."

Latoya shook her head. "Well now I know why he never came to church every week, he was off playing dress-up with the three of you," she said bitterly.

"And plotting to take us the fuck out," Keesha added around the wad of gum.

"And the big dick son-of-a-bitch pulled no shots because I've known him as the manager for Kelson Hunter," she said. "Oh shit, I forgot about Kelson."

"The actor?" one of them asked.

Monica barely heard them as she snatched up her phone and walked outside the restaurant located just off the hotel's lobby away from the table. She dialed Kelson's cell number, pacing as it rang.

"Hello," he said.

She paused at the coolness in his voice. "Kelson, hey this Monica—"

"Look, Monica, I'm not going to change my mind."

She frowned in confusion. "Excuse me?"

"Look I appreciate the work you've done for me already but I shouldn't be harassed for deciding to have my investments handled by another firm."

"What?" Monica snapped, drawing the many eyes of people in the lobby.

She held the phone away from her face and bent over to grip her knees as she forced herself to breathe. "Kelson," she said, pressing the phone back to her face. "Are you saying you fired me?"

"Are you saying you didn't get the certified letter I sent?" he asked. "It was signed for today."

She massaged her forehead. "I wasn't in the office all week. My assistant must've signed for it."

"It's just business, Monica," he said.

"No, that's more than fine," she assured him. "I'll get the letter when I go in Monday."

"And this is not because you picked Usain over me either."

That bastard told Kelson. She shook her head and

punched the air. "Kelson, where did you meet Usain?" she asked, coming to a stop.

"He's an associate with XXL Entertainment," he said. "Why?"

"You're still with XXL?" she asked. "I assumed you left them to work with Usain."

"Nope, they sent him to me, wanted someone to work more closely with me, like a liaison between the company and me," he said.

"Did you ever meet with him at his office?" she asked.

"Nah, we usually did lunch or dinner meetings and he always paid so I was like cool, you know."

Monica nodded even though she knew he couldn't see her.

"I hope the next one is as cool as Usain."

Monica arched her brow. "What's that?"

"He resigned this morning."

Had he ever worked for XXL or had he conned Kelson just to get close to her? Or did Xavier Long own XXL?

"All right, Kelson, I'll see about the transfer of funds and a full accounting report of your investments first thing Monday," she said, switching into business mode. "You have a good weekend, okay?"

"Seriously, this is not about—"

"Bye-bye," Monica said, sounding robotic as she ended the call.

She pulled up her contacts and her thumb floated over Cameron's name. She just wanted to know what she was going up against when she went home. *No, not yet.*

When she got back to their table Danielle was already halfway through another glass.

"Well, at least you didn't fuck him," Danielle said, her voice sounding tired and slightly slurred as she sat with her chin in her hand on the tabletop.

Monica slid back into her seat. "Or let him eat you

out," she added as she slid in on the end of their conversation.

"Do you think we can press charges?" Latoya asked.

"For what, being stupid?" Keesha snapped, picking up her vibrating cell phone to check the caller ID before setting it back down.

Monica glanced at the screen and saw Corey's face. "Congratulations on your books," she said, seeing how Keesha looked worried as hell. She was going to bite straight through one of her acrylic tips.

Keesha actually smiled a little. "Thank you."

"You got your book published?" Danielle asked.

"Actually my third one comes out next year," Keesha said.

They all looked surprised at seeing Keesha's bashfulness.

"I have to buy a box and see if I can get it on the show some way or at least tweet something," Danielle said, her eyes a mix of sadness and happiness all at once.

"And congrats on your TV show," Keesha said. "Kimani told me about it. She is so proud and went to school and told all her friends."

"You're on TV?" Latoya asked, reaching over with the hand not clutching her purse to squeeze Danielle's hand. "What show? What are you doing on it? That's great, Dani."

She smiled and took another sip of her wine. "Doesn't really matter now does it?" she asked, looking down in the depths of wine left in her glass.

Keesha bit at her bottom lip. "I could seriously hurt Xavier for this shit he did to all of us. I cannot go through this pregnancy—my life—without Corey. I know I fucked up but damn like . . . like what the fuck am I supposed to do?"

"You go home and you talk to him and you beg him for his forgiveness," Monica said, leaning forward to lock her eyes with Keesha's. "It's hard but people do have the capacity to forgive. Trust me."

"Xavier didn't," Latoya said, taking a sip of her water as she kept one hand resting atop her purse on the end of the table.

"If he's this fucked up in the head about it, thank God he didn't have a small dick," Danielle said with attitude.

"Chile please," Keesha said, releasing a heavy sigh before she went back to chewing on her nail.

"I am not done with Xavier Lofton," Monica said, her eyes glinting with just as much anger as Xavier had held in his own when he glared at them.

They all fell silent. All were lost in their thoughts. In imagining the worst and hoping for the best. In dreading going home to face the havoc wreaked on their lives.

Latoya stood up suddenly. "Excuse me," she said, walking away from the table.

Xavier Lofton had played with them all like pawns on a chessboard, sitting back plotting every move and laughing at every turn. For years his hatred and need for revenge had festered until he had nothing but darkness and evil to put back out into the world. Nothing good had come from it. His revenge—his hatred—of them had tarnished his life for well over a decade.

Monica wondered just how the effects of his game would overshadow their lives as well.

She closed her eyes as she tapped her finger against the screen of her phone. Sitting there and not knowing if the man she loved had been delivered a bomb that would completely tear down the foundation of their relationship? Not easy. Not easy at all.

And if Xavier Lofton thought he got to piss over their lives and walk away to enjoy his without a care in the world then he was sadly mistaken.

Chapter 26
Keesha

Corey knows about Shawn. Corey knows about the baby. Corey knows about Shawn. Corey knows about the baby—

Keesha glanced around the table as she bit at her cuticle bed. She winced as she pulled at a piece of skin too deeply and caused a pop of blood to fill her mouth.

The track lighting of the restaurant glinted off her engagement ring on her left hand. She shifted her eyes away from it. *My marriage is over before it even began,* she thought.

Everything it stood for had just been shitted on.

Corey knows about Shawn. Corey knows about the baby. Corey knows about Shawn. Corey knows about the baby. Corey knows about Shawn.

Keesha knew she had fucked up. And all of her chickens had come home to roost.

She crossed and uncrossed her legs under the table as Danielle motioned for the waiter. He came over to her right away.

Keesha couldn't blame her. She knew if she wasn't pregnant she might roll her first blunt in five years and get Bobby Marley wasted. Still, she counted the empty glasses crowning Danielle's place setting.

Keesha squinted her eyes as she watched Danielle

smooth her hands over her sleek ponytail. *I wonder what's wrong with her? Xavier the Ass hadn't divulged* that *when he vomited all their secrets.*

Keesha glanced across the table at Latoya. Her eyes drifted down to take in the way her left hand stayed pressed against her clutch sitting on the table. Her eyes shifted again to take in the tiny beads of sweat on her upper lip and the rapid blinking of her eyes.

Latoya needed a pill and Keesha knew that as soon as she got out of their company or even thought they weren't looking that she was going to get her fix. She had been there and the craving for the drugs was all the more intense when it was just sitting there near you but you couldn't risk taking it.

What happened to her? How did Ms. Hallelujah end up on drugs?

She looked at each of these women she shared so much of her life with.

Even after she betrayed Monica they had bridged the gap and chosen their friendship over Rah's abusive ass.

Danielle had always been the one to call for good advice or just someone to let you rant.

And Latoya was the one that it just was hard not to love.

So what happened to all of us?

Keesha reached in her purse and pulled out the king-sized pack of gum she carried to try and chew and pop her way through her nicotine cravings. She pressed her hand up against her belly. The curve of her unborn baby had barely raised her waist up a size but touching her belly and knowing she was growing another child inside her was comfort. It made her calm when she wanted to go crazy. It made her relax when she wanted to flex.

I am going to be a better mother to you than I was to

your big sister, she thought, looking up just as Monica shifted her eyes away from her hand on her belly.

Keesha sat up a little straighter, wondering what she had been thinking.

You're pregnant and two cousins could be the daddy and now they both know about it.

Keesha packed another piece of gum into her mouth.

Corey knows about Shawn. Corey knows about the baby. Corey knows about Shawn. Corey knows about the baby. Corey knows about Shawn. Corey knows about the baby. Corey knows about Shawn. Corey knows about the baby. Corey knows about Shawn. Corey knows about the baby. Corey knows about Shawn. Corey knows about the baby. Corey knows about Shawn.

Kimani's father was taken from their lives by death and Keesha had to scrimp, save, and strip to take care of her daughter. Now she was looking at going it alone again. Corey would leave her and she didn't want Shawn.

Shawn had been a distraction from the unhappiness she caused in her home. He had been nothing more than a reason to think of how out of control she had become. Shawn was nothing more than a reason not to admit to Corey that he had been right and she had been wrong.

I want Corey. Not Shawn. I want Corey. I love Corey. I need Corey.

But going home and finding out that Corey has left me will destroy me.

Keesha nervously pushed yet another piece of gum into her mouth to chew as she eyed Latoya's steady touch on her purse tighten into a grip.

She understood all too well the other woman's urge to forget all the bullshit by getting high. All too well.

Keesha thought of how they all had been played by Xavier.

Hell, no wonder I never met his boyfriend Marcus. That slick, lying bastard!

Monica picked up her phone and walked outside the restaurant.

Keesha almost choked on the wad of gum as her phone lit up and began vibrating against the table.

Bzzzzzz . . . Bzzzzzz . . . Bzzzzzz . . .

She picked up her phone. *Corey.*

Danielle and Latoya shared a long look.

Bzzzzzz . . . Bzzzzzz . . . Bzzzzzz . . .

"At least you'll know where he stands before you go home," Danielle advised.

Keesha eyed her. Danielle had always been the one to make sure everybody else was okay. To make sure everybody else got what they needed. When both she and Tiffany needed a place to stay it was Danielle who opened up her doors to them. She was the most giving of them all.

It felt good to know that had not changed but Keesha wondered if she had anyone doing the same for her.

Keesha picked up the phone and placed her wad of gum inside her napkin as she answered the call, her heart pounding so loudly and so hard in her chest. "Hey baby—"

"You're fucking Shawn, Keesha? In our house? Are you for real? You were fucking Shawn IN OUR HOUSE? Are you fucking kid—"

She hung up on him and sat the phone back on the table as she pressed her hand against her belly. A tear raced down her cheek as guilt flooded her. Fear flooded her. Shame flooded her.

She was drowning.

Corey knows.

"He knows?" Danielle asked.

Keesha nodded and wiped the track of her tear.

"That bastard," Danielle said, signaling the waiter for another glass.

"I cannot believe this shit. I cannot wrap my brain around this shit. I just can't. I can't," Latoya said, visibly trembling.

Keesha eyed her, wondering if it was her emotions or the pills talking.

Bzzzzzz . . . Bzzzzzz . . . Bzzzzzz . . .

Her eyes shifted back to the phone but she didn't answer. She couldn't answer. She could not deal.

"Corey asked me to marry him," Keesha said with a sad smile as she tapped her still-vibrating phone. "He rented a carriage and we rode around Central Park and . . . and we came to a beautiful lake . . . and . . . and . . . and while I'm sitting holding the flowers and the candy he gave me he asked me to marry him. It was out of a movie or something and . . . and . . . it sounds corny as *fuck* but it felt so good for a man to do that for me. It made me feel so special, so loved, *so* happy.

"And I didn't deserve it because I knew what I did to him, but I *wanted* it," she said, her bottom lip trembling. "I wanted it *so* bad, y'all."

Bzzzzzz . . . Bzzzzzz . . . Bzzzzzz . . .

Tap-tap-tap.

"And now it's gone," she said softly as she looked down at her engagement ring.

The phone stopped vibrating for a few moments before it kicked right back in. Corey was blowing up her phone with the same speed and intensity that Xavier blew up their lives.

Bzzzzzz . . . Bzzzzzz . . . Bzzzzzz . . .

Tap-tap-tap.

The icon for a text message filled the screen.

Danielle and Latoya looked on quietly as Keesha picked up her phone. She released a shaky breath as she opened it:

FUCK U! DON'T FUCKING CALL ME
UNTIL ITS TIME TO TAKE A DNA
TEST. FUCK U!!!

Keesha closed her eyes. Although it was just words his anger as palpable.

"I cannot believe Xavier is such a damn lunatic," Latoya said, as she rubbed her fingers against her palm and then dabbed at her sweaty neck with one of the cloth napkins.

Bzzzzzz . . . Bzzzzzz . . . Bzzzzzz . . .

Keesha felt a jolt as she eyed Corey's face filling her screen with another incoming text. She reached for her cell phone.

I HATE U. HOW COULD U DO THIS?

She sat the phone back down as her soul continued to ache. She bit at her acrylic nail again.

Her world was collapsing around her.

In another place and under different circumstances she knew she would enjoy being back in the presence of her friends. But it was hard to marinate in the old times and their unlikely reunion when she knew all hell had broken loose in her relationship.

Fuck you all the way to hell, Xavier.

Even as they all made idle chit-chat about their careers and accomplishments, still pulsing in the air around them was that vibe of trouble ahead.

Keesha eyed the way Latoya fidgeted in her seat but kept her hand on that purse like her ass was playing Twister. She was ready to snatch it from her.

She focused her eyes on her silent phone.

Corey gave up. He was so beyond done with me that he don't have shit to say to me now.

She picked up her phone and read Corey's texts again, shaking her head in disbelief at it all.

She had made the first fatal mistake by cheating on him, and choosing his cousin had been so disrespectful. She delivered up the bullets Xavier Lofton used to shoot her relationship to death.

Keesha looked up as Latoya stood up suddenly.

"Excuse me," she said.

Her eyes followed her as she stopped a waiter and then headed toward the restroom he pointed to.

Danielle and Monica glanced at her and then glanced away, lost in their own thoughts and problems.

Keesha stood up and quick-stepped across the restaurant and into the bathroom behind her.

Chapter 27
Latoya

8:59 P.M.

Father God, I know I have forsaken You again. Please forgive me.

Father God, my marriage may be over . . . and I don't really think I care. Forgive me, Father.

It wasn't that Latoya didn't want her marriage but as she'd proven with the same tactics she pulled to ensure she didn't lose custody of Tiffany to Bones, she couldn't deal with losing her children. Right now if Xavier was telling the truth—and Latoya had no doubt that he was—then he had provided Taquan enough proof for her to lose far more than just her marriage. *Did he send the evidence to Bones too?*

Latoya pressed her hand against her clutch sitting on the table beside her glass of water. She wanted so badly to take a pill and knock off the rising edge. *Just one would get me right. Just one.*

She felt so high strung and anxious. So unbalanced and lost. Sweat was already beginning to dampen her clothes. She felt it on her upper lip. Her pulse raced. *Just one would level me off and I could think.*

Latoya shifted her eyes away from her purse just as the

waiter brought Danielle another glass of red wine. *Everyone has vices to cope and maintain.*

She shifted on her seat, feeling the pressure of the folder she sat on. She hadn't dared to leave it behind in the ballroom and she didn't want it sitting on the table mocking her so she stuck it under her when she sat down.

Danielle's was inside her Birkin. Monica's was on the floor beside her seat. Keesha had folded hers and shoved it inside her purse.

The very past anyone would rightfully want to leave behind was right there being carried by them. There was no way they could leave it behind.

Latoya watched Monica and Keesha check their phones. She had left hers in the car. She doubted Taquan called. He probably hopped on the phone with the board to diffuse how his wife's addiction would affect his grand tribute to himself. *The church of Taquan.* She felt hysterical laughter bubble up inside her.

She closed her eyes and fought for it not to escape. *His ass doesn't even deliver the Word that great. TD and Joel have nothing to worry about. Please.*

Latoya patted her purse just as she opened her eyes. She found Keesha's eyes on her and she nervously swiped at the sweat she felt beading on her upper lip.

Everything in Keesha's eyes let Latoya know that she was well aware that Latoya was in the throes of a minifit. She blinked as she shifted her eyes away from her, unable to take someone who knew her finally seeing the secret she had hidden so well all these months. She was exposed.

There was a bittersweetness to that.

She was so invisible in her life that no one in it even saw that she had succumbed to a drug addiction. Not one. And she didn't know if that was more about them not thinking it possible for her to become an addict or their just over-looking her like a pretty window dressing.

She had no doubts in her mind that these three women sitting here with her, equally dealing with a plague from their past, would have seen the change in her. They would have given a shit.

Her husband did not.

She blinked away rising tears.

Just one.

In those moments right after Xavier took such pleasure in humiliating them her thoughts had been how Taquan forcing her to apologize to Olivia had been worse. Much worse.

The smugness on that woman's face had felt like cuts to her soul with a brand-new razor blade.

To hell with him. I just don't want to lose my children. The same way I sat right there and allowed my husband to convince me to lose myself. Who the fuck am I anymore?

No, I'm still here because it feels damn good to be in the presence of these women I never should have left behind.

She had trusted in a man she thought was a friend when these women had already proven themselves. Latoya thought about how much she divulged to the man she knew as Marion. She whispered her secret right into the devil's ear. *Just one. Just one.* She gripped the purse and wondered if she could sneak one. *I miss my Altoids can.*

Latoya shrugged as the rest of the women talked about some actor named Kelson Hunter. In her home, they only watched nonsecular TV. She had no clue who Kelson Hunter was.

She clenched and unclenched her hand in her lap as Monica walked out of the restaurant with her phone. From her seat she could see Monica pacing as she talked on her phone. She wiped the sweat from her neck as she looked around the restaurant for the bathroom.

Bzzzzzz . . . Bzzzzzz . . . Bzzzzzz . . .

Keesha picked up her phone.

Latoya could tell from her face that it was Corey. She glanced at Danielle.

The look they shared was evident. Corey had always been so good for Keesha. Keesha *and* Kimani. They knew the man had to be hurt. He had to be. Keesha had pulled the ultimate no-no. Although it was true you never knew what drove anyone to cheat, they knew that discovering your fiancée might be pregnant by your cousin was a lot to bear. Especially coming from someone else.

Bzzzzzz . . . Bzzzzzz . . . Bzzzzzz . . .

"At least you'll know where he stands before you go home," Danielle said to Keesha.

Latoya already knew where Taquan stood. It was all about how anything she did either fed or fought his ambition. She shifted in her chair as the need for a pill nipped at her like mosquitoes in the summertime.

"Hey baby—"

Keesha's eyes widened even as they filled with pain.

Latoya couldn't make out Corey's words but she could tell he was screaming at her.

Keesha ended the call and sat the phone back down. A tear raced down her cheek.

Latoya felt hopeless and helpless. There was no doubt now that Xavier had indeed gone through with it. No doubt at all. By now Taquan knew it all. There was no scab on her past unpicked.

What now?

Latoya felt her emotions slide into red-hot anger that made her entire body tremble with it. Everything was so senseless.

Xavier was the devil's minion.

I rebuke him in the name of Jesus.

As badly as Latoya wanted a pill she knew she might

have another fight ahead of her. Perhaps against Taquan and Bones. She didn't know.

The sound of Keesha's phone vibrating was the only sound at the table.

Danielle kept looking off into the distance with her face filled with sleep and fatigue and the effects of the wine she was still sipping. Keesha looked like she was fighting hard not to cry. Fighting and losing.

Latoya saw her pain so clearly and her heart literally ached for her as she watched on as Keesha looked down at her engagement ring. She didn't know what to say to make her feel better when she was in the midst of her own emotional typhoon. At any moment any of them at the table could be a hypocrite because they all had sins and griefs to bear.

As Keesha checked her phone, Latoya pressed her back against the chair with her hand still on her purse. *What am I going to face when I get home? Will I even have a home to go to?*

Latoya felt like her clothes were binding her, too close to her skin. Rubbing her the wrong way. She picked up the napkin holding the utensils she had no plans on using and pressed it against her neck.

The mix of her addiction and the aftereffects of Xavier were too much to bear. She had enough on her own plate without the secrets of her friends being shoved down her throat as well.

Latoya frowned as she could clearly hear Xavier tell Danielle: *"You suck a mean dick."*

And then he said Danielle gave out sex favors for her job on television? She frowned deeper at a vision of Danielle getting eaten out by a woman. She side-eyed her. *So Dani's a lesbian now?*

The man had not just lied to them and invaded their

lives. He used his fake personas to his advantage to sex Danielle and Monica. *Just sick*.

Latoya played with the hairs at the nape of her neck as she fought to resist the demon on her back. She knew that once again she had to fight it. Get strong. Do better.

For my kids.

Latoya felt overwhelmed by her thoughts and all of the questions running through her mind.

What am I supposed to do?

Will Taquan forgive me and understand that I need his love and support to fight this addiction?

Will Bones forgive me and understand that I did what I had to do to stop him from taking his child from me?

Will my parents ever truly forgive me for the lies and deception I fed them during my late teens and early twenties?

Latoya's mouth felt dry and she drank deeply of the ice water. Her fingers remained on her clutch and lightly scratched back and forth against the leather. She stood up and tucked her clutch under her arm. "Excuse me," she said, leaving them to stop the first waiter she neared.

"Where's your restroom?" she asked him, feeling tightly wound.

"The ladies' room is right over in that corner there," he said, pointing in its direction.

She followed where he pointed and headed toward it. "Thank you," she said, feeling her heart racing in anticipation.

As soon as she pushed the door open and stepped inside she opened the flap of her clutch and dug out her prescription bottle. The pills inside rattled against the amber plastic as she fought with trembling hands to get it open.

The bathroom door opened and Keesha stepped inside.

Latoya froze, her hands still trembling.

"Those pills ain't shit but the anchor weighing you down," Keesha said softly but earnestly, her eyes filled with sympathy and concern as she removed her hand from her belly and reached out to Latoya with her palm side up.

Latoya's hand clutched the bottle and she bit her bottom lip. "Girl, y'all don't know. I hate my marriage," she admitted in a hoarse whisper, her shoulders sinking as tears gathered in her eyes. "I'm just trying to make it. I'm just trying to start and finish every fucking day without losing my damn mind."

And that was the truth.

Keesha stepped forward and wrapped her hand around the one Latoya clutched the pill bottle with. "I swear to you this will only get worse before it gets better," she said, gently removing the pills. "And you can't do it alone. You can't just call on the Lord. You have to go to all those people the Lord blessed with the know-how to help addicts like us. Junkies . . . fiends . . . like us."

Latoya allowed Keesha to pull her into a tight embrace.

"You can call on me when you need to talk or you need someone to listen to you vent or you just want someone to sit in silence and just be there. I will do that for you because I know you are better than this, Toy," she said.

Latoya turned her head to the side. Their reflection was in the mirrors over the sink. Keesha was holding her tightly and letting her know she was not alone anymore. For the first time in a long time Latoya felt like someone had her back.

She released a long, heavy, soul-cleansing breath as the tears wet her friend's shoulder.

"Thank you," she whispered, knowing her battle had just begun but knowing she didn't have to fight alone.

Chapter 28
Danielle

Danielle had never let the pitfalls of her life lead to a pity party. Never. She grew up in foster care and faced things she had thankfully learned to bury. She yearned to know more about the parents she never met but never was successful. She wanted to attend college but couldn't because at eighteen she was solely responsible for herself and her bills. She just learned that one of her biological parents gave her a kidney disorder that would one day end her life far earlier than the current life expectancy.

She always tucked down her feelings, lifted up her chin, and made a way when there was none.

The one good thing in her life—the one unspoiled thing—was her job as the co-anchor at *The A-List*. Her newfound fame and fortune were just the added perks of working hard for something and winning it.

And now it's slipping through my fingers too.

Danielle took a deep sip of her red wine, enjoying the taste of it, even though she knew it wasn't good for her. One glass of red wine? Helpful, actually. Nearing four? Suicide.

She just didn't give a fuck anymore. The one man she

loved was in Jamaica and the one she thought she could care deeply for had revealed himself to be a poser who wanted nothing more than to pay her back for a high school prank. *Fuck you, Omari . . . Xavier. Whatever. Fuck you.*

"I cannot believe that my entire relationship might be fucked over something we did in high school?"

"My marriage too," Latoya said.

At least y'all have a husband. Who wants to marry a dying woman?

Danielle finished her glass of wine by tipping her head back and getting every last drop. No family. No kids. No husband. And now no career because she had no idea how they would handle news of a serious health condition and a scandal over just how she got started in journalism. She just wanted to do her job and enjoy the best of it. She had every intention of resigning as soon as her doctors told her it was too much on her body. She was going to give them plenty of time to hire a new co-anchor.

I fought hard for it and won. I just wanted to enjoy it some. That's all.

Danielle eyed her empty glass and then raised her hand to summon the cute waiter who served them. *I just want to go numb. I just want to go numb. I just don't want to feel this anymore.*

She crossed her legs and placed her hand in her lap as her foot seemed to swing back and forth on its own volition. She wanted nothing more in that moment than to be on the beach with Mohammed, her head on his chest and her legs entwined with his as they watched the sun set over the ocean. She could die peacefully right there in his arms. Mohammed knew the best and the worst of her. Whatever Xavier had in those file folders would not make Mohammed stop loving her. That she knew. That she took pride and solace in.

She reached for her goblet and smiled a little as she took a deep sip.

So fuck you, Xavier. Fuck you and your hurt feelings.

Not even the fact that he pursued and seduced her into his bed was that worrisome to her. No matter how he looked at it. She got just as good as she gave. He ate just as much of her pussy as she blew him. And they were tied nut for nut.

Sex as a weapon? *Wrong bitch, loser.*

But for him to know about her illness and still continue with his ruse? Xavier was one slack-ass man.

Danielle had no one to go home to. No one to even hurt with her secrets. All she had was her career and now that bastard was snatching that away from her. Her stomach twisted to think of the call she would get summoning her to the executive producer's office. There would be nothing she could do but sit there and take it, their polite request for her to pack up her shit and get the hell away from *The A-List* with her sex scandal.

A celebrity with sex drama? Reportable.

A celebrity reporter with sex drama? *Deuces, bitch. It was good while it lasted.*

Danielle sipped her wine and waited for the appropriate time to pull away from their reunion to have the driver take her the short distance to the Newark Airport. She stared off at nothing with her thoughts on how Xavier gloated and berated them while he strutted like a fancy peacock before them.

Motherfucker, you had to fake a new identity to get this pussy you been dreaming about since high school, you hurt-feelings little punk bitch.

That's what I should've *said,* she thought.

The punk bitch dressed up well. Money did a nigga good because the man playing dress-up in my life was one fine motherfucker who looked NOTHING like he did in school.

Once he identified himself in that ballroom she could just make out a little bit of similarity between his figurative before and after. She was sure he at least got his teeth fixed, Lasik on his eyes, some dermatology on his skin, and plenty of milk to do that body good.

Sadistic bastard. Just how far did that bastard go to ruin us?

Bzzzzzz . . . Bzzzzzz . . . Bzzzzzz . . .

Keesha picked up her phone.

Danielle set her wineglass down and looked at Latoya before looking back at Keesha.

She always was the wild one but two cousins? No way, who am I to judge. I sold a lick at my cat for my career. Tomato fucking tomahto.

Danielle winced and leaned back a bit at the sounds of Corey's angry voice echoing through the phone. Keesha looked crushed as she rushed to end the call and cut his tirade off before he was done.

Her eyes went to the diamond solitaire on Keesha's left ring finger. *Not bad, Corey. Not bad at all. Too bad Xavier just shitted all over it.*

She shook her head a bit and took another sip of her wine as the annoying sound of Keesha's vibrating phone continued. She fought the urge to pick it up and fling it against the floor.

She felt the fatigue of everything weighing her down until she could barely raise her arm to lift up her glass of wine. Even through her fatigue, her bottomless glass of red wine, and her own life's hiccups, Danielle could clearly see that Keesha didn't think she deserved to be loved. *And how can you respect and honor something if you don't know its worth?*

Danielle covertly checked her watch. She knew she had to be heading out to make her flight soon.

"Do you think we can press charges?" Latoya asked.

Bless her naïve heart.

"For what, being stupid?" Keesha said a little sharply.

And bless her cold one.

They all fell silent. They could just as well catch up on each others' lives but it seemed too hard for any of them to focus on anything but someone from the past completely destroying each of their futures.

There was enough doom and gloom around the table and she hadn't wanted to add to the oppressive weight of it by dwelling on her illness. She swallowed down her own issues to ensure she added nothing extra to their plates. *Just like I did in the past.*

And that didn't sit well with her. Ever since her days in foster care she had learned not to show her constant hurt and disappointment. Not to let anyone see what she really felt. She carried that trait into her friendships with these ladies, putting their feelings first as she buried her own. In time she had come to resent their reliance on her as the strong one, the problem solver, the Mama Bear.

I can't go back to that, she thought. *Especially now when I have less time left to honor myself and what I want and need for me.*

And she knew then that even as she yearned for them in the hospital the night she collapsed that she would not share her diagnosis with them. Everyone was deep in the forest of their own troubles and she wouldn't add this additional fret to their lives.

Five years had passed but she loved them too much to do that. Just like Mohammed.

Danielle pushed her half-filled glass of wine away as she forced herself to sit up straighter in her chair and as she glanced again at her watch. She not only had to go, she *wanted* to go.

"I am not done with Xavier Lofton," Monica said.

Danielle eyed her but she looked away. *I have a life to live and no time to focus what's left of it on Xavier.*

There was nothing for any of them do.

Live and learn. That's what.

Danielle felt sadness as she watched Latoya rise and walk into the bathroom. She knew she was going to deal with it all with her pills. Keesha turned to eye Danielle meaningfully and kept looking at her until she stood up and went to the bathroom as well.

Monica stood up to come and sit in Keesha's chair, which was to Danielle's right. "You okay? Is there anything you need? Do you want to talk about it?" she asked with true concern in the dark depths of her eyes.

And such a simple gesture of friendship even after five years of no contact was the straw that almost broke Danielle's emotional back. Her breath caught as she felt her tears rising along with the words she wanted so desperately to spill to someone. To tell someone that she was not yet thirty and looking death dead in the eye and knew she would not win.

"No, no, I'm good. I swear," she said, blinking rapidly as she picked up her Birkin and then reached past the folded file to pull out her shades to put on. She also removed the Tiffany platinum case holding her business cards. She removed three and pushed them into Monica's hand as she rose to her feet as well.

"Tell Latoya and Keesha that these are my numbers, and to call me to keep in touch," she said, her voice beginning to break. "I have to leave now to catch a flight to LA. Okay?"

Monica took the cards and also took Danielle's hands

into both of her own. "Give us a chance, Danielle. Give us a chance to help you," she said, her own eyes filling with tears. "To be there for you like you have always been there for us."

Danielle forced yet another of her *A-List* smiles and hugged Monica close before she turned and rushed from the restaurant like fire was on her heels.

Chapter 29
Monica

"Is there a package for Mr. Steele?" Monica asked the doorman in the foyer of their building.

"There was but I took it up to him about a couple of hours ago," he said.

Monica nodded and smiled as she turned from his front desk. She felt light-headed and had to force herself to take every step to the elevator. Every single step.

Xavier hadn't lied. He deliberately made sure the second batch of packages were delivered while they sat like lambs to the slaughter in that ballroom.

She dreaded this moment but there was no escaping it.

Monica rode the elevator alone as she tried to think of just what she would say to Cameron. But that was difficult when she didn't know just what he knew and by what method it was delivered. Just how bad was it?

As soon as she walked into their apartment and closed the front door she took slow steps across the foyer but saw Cameron sitting almost in complete darkness and silence. He was dressed in dark denims and a dark midnight navy shirt, sitting in one of the four chairs positioned around an ottoman in front of the ceiling-to-floor windows. He looked out at the city landscape with his chin resting in his hand.

Monica came to a stop behind the sofa.

"I see you made a friend," he said, never once taking his eyes from whatever they focused on outside the window.

"Cameron—"

He held up his hand and shook his head before tapping his ear before he raised his hand and pointed the remote toward the flat screen over their marble fireplace.

Seconds later the sounds of Monica moaning in pleasure filled the sound system while the video of Xavier eating her on the wall of her office filled the television. She diverted her eyes. "Cameron, let me explain—"

He whipped his head to look at her with his eyes so filled with pain that she felt weakened by it. He picked up a black leather box and walked over to her. "Explain what?" he asked. "Huh? Explain how this stupid shit got delivered to me at our home? Huh?"

He opened it.

"So I'm never keeping secrets, and I'm never telling lies . . ."
"So I'm never keeping secrets, and I'm never telling lies . . ."
"So I'm never keeping secrets, and I'm never telling lies . . ."

Monica rushed over to him and snatched the box away from him to slam it closed.

"Did he send this to me?" Cameron asked, stepping in front of her to tightly grip her chin as his eyes bore into her like black diamonds. "Huh? Is your lover making a play for you? Does he want you?"

Monica tried to jerk her chin free but Cameron's grip tightened. "You're hurting me, Cameron," she told him, bringing her hands up to try and pull downward on his forearms. They felt like bands of steel.

"Is he the reason you won't have my baby?" he asked, finally freeing her with a jerking motion that made her head snap back a bit as her hair swung back and forth across her shoulders.

"I would never leave you. I would never cheat on you," she told him, wanting to reach out and touch him but not trusting the heated anger that was clearly etched in the lines of his face.

He laughed bitterly. "So what's that?" he asked, slashing his hand across the air to point to the screen.

Xavier had to have looped the image because Monica knew their little interlude had not lasted this long.

"I was drunk and I apologize for making a horrible decision but I promise—"

"Your promises don't mean shit to me anymore, Monica," he said coldly.

Monica felt weak with anguish and allowed herself to lean against the high back of the sofa as she crossed her arms over her chest. "Cameron, please—"

"Who is he?" he barked.

Monica raised her head and looked at him. Was now the time to explain about Xavier and his schemes? It wouldn't change the fact that she had let herself be seduced by him. "I am not in a relationship with him. Never slept with him. I'll never see him again. I was drunk and angry at you and it was stupid and I ended it. I stopped him from—"

"Eating your pussy," Cameron supplied with a sarcastic shrug as he began to pace back and forth before her.

"Cameron," she said.

"Is this because I got laid off? Because I am still the one paying the bills in here," Cameron told her, stopping in his pace to pierce her with his eyes.

"You know what?" he said, throwing up his hands and

walking past her. "I can't stand to look at you right now. I'm out of here."

She reached for his arm. "No, please don't leave me. Please Cameron you don't understand," she begged, clutching to him desperately. "Please."

He shook her off and continued his steady pace to the door. Seconds later it slammed shut.

Monica stumbled back but stopped just short of falling to the floor. She took off behind him and rushed out of the apartment just as the elevator doors shut him off from her view. She felt desperate and kept pushing at the buttons like it would make the elevator go in reverse.

Wanting to reach him before he left the building, she took off down the hall and pulled the door to the stairwell so hard that it swung back and slammed into the wall. Her heart pounded and her hair flew around and at times behind her as she took flight after flight of stairs. At times she moved so quickly that she stumbled down the steps or slid into the wall of the landing as she pursued her man at a feverish pace that she refused to give up.

By the time she reached the lobby floor her throat was dry from her gasping for breath. Her heart felt like it was kicking with steel-toe boots to be free of her chest.

"Shit," she swore, her chest heaving as she fought hard not to collapse.

Monica licked her lips as she pulled open the door to the lobby and rushed across the beautiful marbled floor. An elderly woman with her dog on a leash entered the building and walked directly into her path. Monica's momentum forward could not be stopped and she tripped over the dog and its leash.

She cried out as she hit the floor and the dog cried out from its leash being jerked forward by her foot.

"Ju-Ju," the woman exclaimed.

Monica turned onto her back to undo her foot from the leash. "I'm sorry," she said, turning back over to climb to her feet and race out the doors of the front of the building.

She looked up and down the street for any sign of Cameron. She thought she spotted him a block up the street and took off behind him. Nothing short of rich white folks staring at her kept her from screaming his name.

Monica had barely made it ten or fifteen feet before a man stepped into her path and she collided into him like he was a solid brick wall. She stumbled back and shook her head. "Excuse me," she said, attempting to sidestep him.

He sidestepped with her.

Monica frowned. "I said excuse me," she said with attitude, looking up at him.

She gasped in shock as she realized she was standing before Rah, her ex-boyfriend who went to jail for assault for stomping on her leg and breaking it in two.

He was thicker in size and much meaner in demeanor as he grabbed her arm and roughly jerked her close enough to him to press a gun to her side. "I swear to God I would gladly blow a bullet in your guts and kill you, bitch," he said, his voice rough and his eyes wild.

She looked down at the gun as it gleamed from the streetlight above.

"I knew if I just waited around I'd catch Miss High Society all alone," he said, digging the gun in deeper as he led her to a van illegally parked around the corner.

"Why are you doing this?" she asked.

"Shut the fuck up, bitch," he said in a voice that just sounded like murder and mayhem.

He attempted to push her into the back of the van but Monica used the last of her strength to resist him. He reached out quickly and backhanded her. Monica fell backward into the van.

The gun.

Fuck this shit.

She moved back into the darkness of the van just enough to shield her from him as she unlatched her purse and pulled the 9mm out. She removed the safety.

Click.

He heard the gun before he saw it and quickly pointed his arm inside the van to point his at her as well.

POW!

Chapter 30
Latoya

On the entire ride home Latoya had clenched and un-clenched her steering wheel until she was sure she rubbed some of the color from the leather. When she left the hotel and went to the parking deck to claim her car the first thing she did was check her phone. Not one call from Taquan. And one from Bones.

Lord help me.

Craving a pill so bad, her body was filled with so much anxiety that she could strip and just sit in her car at the red light butt naked. She seriously felt like she was going to freak out. But she thought of Keesha and the genuine support she offered even as she knew her own world was colliding.

She had the number of the rehabilitation center Keesha went to and she was going to call it first thing in the morning. She knew that meant a long talk with both her husband and the father of her older child.

She activated the Bluetooth system of her car that was connected to her phone as she dialed Bones's cell phone number.

"Yo."

"This Latoya. I was calling you back," she said, forcing normalcy into her voice as she fought to control the trembling from the pills and the nerves she felt because she didn't know the reason for his call. *Has Xavier gotten to him too?*

"I know I'm not supposed to get Tiffany again for another two weeks but my moms decided to go to this big family reunion in Atlanta—"

Latoya felt waves of relief course through her. "That's fine. I mean she won't miss school, right?" she asked.

"Nah, we just flying down there for the weekend."

"Okay."

The line went quiet.

Latoya wiped her hands over her mouth and lowered the windows to let in some of the crisp fall night air.

"You a'ight?"

Latoya jumped in surprise. She assumed he hung up. "Yes," she said.

"A'ight then."

The line disconnected.

They never minced words and she was surprised he even took a second out of his life to check on her. *That was a first.* But again she understood and never pressed him or his mother for more.

So far Xavier had spared her with Bones. So far.

Latoya came to a stop at another red light and stared at her phone for a long time before she finally dialed Taquan.

"Latoya," he said, his voice filling the interior of the car.

"It's me."

"Are you on your way home?"

"Yes."

"Your parents are here," he said.

She closed her eyes and hung her head so low that her chin almost hit her chest.

"Why are they there?" she asked, rubbing her forehead with her fingers.

"I called them. We are all so disappointed in you and want explanations," Taquan said. "Is it true?"

"Is what true?" she asked, intentionally stalling.

"Someone sent a box here saying you were addicted to pain pills and pretending to be sick to get them from the doctor."

Latoya let her head fall back against the headrest. "I need help. I need your help. I need you, Taquan," she said, her voice filled with all of her emotions.

"So it's true?"

"You don't understand how unhappy I have been. You are so caught up in building that church but you forgot about me and my dreams and my hopes and what the hell made me happy," she said, her voice rising. "I just needed an escape. I need—"

"So it's true?" he asked again.

"Yes, Taquan. Yes. Okay," she said with emphasis slamming her hand down onto the wheel. "I didn't know I would get hooked."

"So you know how this will look if the church board finds out about it?"

The rest of Latoya's words faded. She sat in her car at a red light on a deserted street, shocked and hurt beyond belief. "Is that all that matters, what the church board thinks?" she snapped. "*Not* 'let me counsel my wife the way I go slave-running for everybody else in the church.' *Not* 'let me support my wife through this addiction and her recovery the same way I did my flock.' *Not* 'let me hold my wife and tell her that we are going to get through this together'?"

"You are my wife and I am the pastor of that church and you were raised to know better and do better and you know I would never abide by my wife doing drugs," he said, his voice angry. "You have continuously tried to block my path—"

"Go to hell."

"What did you say?"

Latoya laughed bitterly even as her heart shattered into a million pieces. The pain was so deep in her chest that she could barely breathe around it. "I said that you, Reverend Taquan Sanders, can go to hell. You are not God and you certainly are not my God and I live my life for Him—or at least I should be. I got away from that and so did you. See the body of this family is only as smart, strong, and gifted as the head. You do a great job leading your church but you are a horrible husband and I do not want to live in your life anymore."

"You would leave me?" he asked, his voice echoing into the car after a long moment of silence.

"You left me a long time ago," she told him, shifting her eyes to the streetlight as she willed it to turn green.

"You're not taking my son," he said.

"He's better with you . . . for now," she admitted, calling on every bit of strength she had. "I'm going into rehab in the morning."

Taquan fell silent again.

"You still there, Taquan?"

"Listen we need to talk. Come home—"

"Send my parents home, this is a family matter between you and I," she said, her voice insistent.

"Latoya—"

She shifted her eyes up to the rearview mirror as someone came up on her with their bright lights.

"Latoya, I do love you."

Her eyes widened as the lights came closer and she could hear the squeal of tires just seconds before the car slammed into the back of her vehicle. Latoya was rammed forward against the steering wheel just before the air bag ejected. Her car went lurching forward into oncoming traffic and both a pickup truck and a car slammed into the sides of her.

"Latoya . . . Latoya . . ."

Chapter 31
Keesha

Keesha frowned as she drove up on her street and saw several of her neighbors standing on the street outside her townhouse. They eyed her as her Benz neared and she turned onto the driveway. It wasn't until she climbed from the car and locked it that she heard the crash of furniture coming from inside the house.

She went racing across the driveway and up the stairs to unlock the door and enter the house. "Oh my God," she said, looking on as Corey stood posted up against Shawn as they circled each other like predators.

Both were shirtless and bruised, with blood coming from their noses and lips.

"Dirty trick-ass motherfucker," Corey said, bobbing and weaving before he swung suddenly and uppercut Shawn.

"Stop," she screamed, holding up both her hands.

They ignored her and Shawn lunged forward, wrapping both his arms around Corey's leg to pick him up and slam him over his head. Corey crashed into the wall and all of her framed pictures came crashing down to the floor with him.

"Keesha, that you?" Diane called down the stairs.

She turned and dashed up to the guest room, coming to

a stop in the doorway. "How long they been going at it?" she asked, reaching in her purse for her cell phone.

Diane was sitting in the middle of the bed on a large inflated doughnut to keep her from putting pressure on her bullet wound. "About ten or fifteen minutes. Shawn went to the store to get beer and it's been on ever since he got back."

"Why didn't you call the police?"

"Shee-it, I got a warrant for a bad check," she said, picking up her lit cigarette from the ashtray sitting beside her on the bed.

"You just mad she was calling for this dick soon as your ass left the house."

"That's *all* your broke ass good for," Corey shot back.

Keesha walked into the room and picked up the ashtray to move to the bedside table. She winced at the sound of glass crashing. *This is some hood shit.*

"Two cousins, huh?" Diane asked, releasing a stream of smoke.

"911."

"I need the police sent to my house. My boyfriend and his cousin are fighting."

"What's your address, ma'am?"

"Fifty Ball Street."

"There have been other calls placed about that residence and we already have a unit en route."

Keesha was not surprised. She ended the call.

"So which one is the daddy?" Diane asked, motioning her cigarette toward Keesha's belly.

Keesha just sat down on the edge of the bed and covered her face with her hands. She had completely forgotten in all of the Xavier fuckery that when she left the house Shawn was there with Corey.

"Now you know how I feel, right?"

She dropped her hands to her lap and eyed her mother.

"I wouldn't lie to my child for over twenty years, though," she snapped, not in the mood for Diane's particular brand of crazy.

Keesha took no pleasure in two men fighting over her because she knew at the end of it all she would end up with neither. She had destroyed any chance with Corey and she didn't know how she was going to recover from that.

"All I'm saying is you shouldn't be so hard on me now that my shoes are on your feet," Diane added.

Keesha reached over and took the cigarette, stubbing it out in the ashtray before she left the bedroom and went back down the stairs. It wasn't until she was halfway down that she realized the house was quiet. Too quiet.

She ran down to the living room and came to a stop at the sight of Corey's body laying in the middle of the chaos she caused with a shard of glass plunged into his heart. "Noooooooo," Keesha screamed in high-pitched terror as she ran over to him.

Keesha fell to her knees beside him and held up her shaking hands, unsure of what to do to help him. "Oh Lord, Corey baby, please," she said, her eyes frantic as the blood oozed from him and stained the carpet.

His eyes stared straight up to the ceiling and his chest was still.

"No, baby. No. No. No. No," she begged, tears flowing as she rocked back and forth and picked up his lifeless hand to press kisses to it. "I'm so sorry. I'm sorry."

"Keesha. Keesha, what's wrong?" Diane hollered from up the stairs.

"Co-Co-Co-Co," Keesha tried to call his name as she shifted up to press kisses to his face, his hand still in hers tightly.

She knew he was dead. Gone from her.

And she knew that her actions had caused it. Her betrayal. Her decisions.

She lay down on the floor beside him and pressed her head to his shoulder as she planted kisses onto his chest and cried uncontrollably. "Forgive me," she mouthed, unable to speak as panic and grief struck her to her core.

"I love you so much. I'm so sorry," she mouthed in between her kisses.

Kisses he would never return.

She looked at the glass in his chest and her entire body literally shook with tears and deep mournful moans that could never fully release the pain she felt. The guilt she felt. The absolute loss.

Something inside of her died. A place where sanity didn't dwell took prominence. She felt completely swamped by a world that would never feel or see light and goodness. In that moment she couldn't imagine the sun ever rising again. And if it did she knew she wouldn't care.

"Keesha!" Diane continued to call.

It was all just too much to bear.

The pills.

She sat up and opened the purse she dropped to the floor and pulled out the bottle she took from Latoya earlier. With one long look at Corey's dead body she emptied the pills into her hand and then swallowed them down. Gulp after gulp after gulp until there were none.

"Keesha, what's going on?" Diane screamed down again.

She lay back down next to the man she loved, pressing her head on his shoulder again and entwining her hand with his as she waited to join him in death.

Chapter 32
Danielle

Brrrnnnggg...

Danielle felt like she had just laid her head down on the pillow before her phone began ringing on the nightstand, not very far from where her head lay. She picked up one plush pillow and pressed it down on her head, hoping for some relief. Her plane from Newark had just landed, and all she wanted to do was sleep off the combined effects of drama, emotions, red wine, and bad kidneys.

Brrrnnnggg...

She flung the pillow from her head and reached out in the darkness until she felt the phone and picked it up. "Hello," she said, her voice filled with the sleep she wanted so very badly.

"Ms. Johnson, I hate to awaken you but you have a visitor—"

She frowned as she heard rustling against the phone's mouthpiece.

"Danielle, please tell your pushy doorman to let me enter, please."

She shot straight up in bed at the sound of Mohammed's unmistakable voice. Her heart tap-danced on her ribs. "You're in Los Angeles?" she asked, sitting up on the side of the bed to turn on the light.

"Yes, and I've been traveling all day and I'm ready to

see you," he said with that Jamaica lilt that really should be criminal.

She stood up and looked down at the white silk pajamas she wore and then yanked the silk scarf from around her head as she felt her excitement completely beat out her surprise. "Let me talk to George," she said.

The phone rustled again.

"Yes, Ms. Johnson?"

"Please direct Mr. Ahmad to my apartment," she said, tucking the phone under her ear to smooth out the linens on her bed.

"Enjoy your night," he said.

Danielle paused and arched her brow. "I will."

She ended the call and placed the phone back on the base before she left her bedroom and crossed the hall into her living room. Sniffing the air she retrieved a can of air freshener from the guest bathroom and gave the room a few bursts. She looked around, assessing what he would think of it. For three times the money of her New Jersey apartment she received one half of the space. Still, she had made sure that her stylish presence of clean lines and splashes of colors against neutrals was present.

She jumped at the sound of the doorbell even though she was expecting Mohammed. She finger-combed her hair as she made her way to the door. She pulled it open with a smile, completely forgetting in her excitement that she had planned to never see Mohammed again.

As soon as she opened the door she felt nothing but wind as Mohammed stormed past her. Danielle made a face and then turned to him as she pushed the door closed. "Well, hello," she said.

His jaw was tight.

"Do I love you?" he asked.

Danielle looked startled. "You're asking me?"

He ran his fingers through his slender dreads. "Okay,

do you think I love you?" he asked, his hands now on his waist in the linen shorts he wore with a matching V-neck tee.

Neither Jamaica nor Los Angeles weather paid attention to the fall season.

Danielle took a few steps closer to him. "I *know* you love me," she told him.

"Then why didn't you tell me about your illness," he said.

Danielle wasn't sure if the hardness to his jaw was from anger or pain. She looked down at the terra-cotta tile of the floor as she made her way to him. She didn't look up but she was so close that the coconut oil of his braids seemed to surround her. "I didn't want you to feel like you had to take care of me. It's not your responsibility," she said, tilting her head to the side as she looked him in his eyes. She crossed her arms over her chest.

"That wasn't your decision to make."

Danielle bit the inside of her bottom lip as she let him pull her into his embrace. He held her close even as her arms were pressed in between their bodies with his arms locked behind her back. She pressed her face into his neck and let her lips rest just a hair's breadth from his warm mocha skin.

"Tell me," he guided her with kisses to her cheek.

And she did. As they stood there locked in an embrace that was everything she needed Danielle told him everything. It felt good to release it. When she was done she felt a pressure lift from her shoulders.

"So I don't want you to see me dying," she told him truthfully, leaning back in his embrace to look up at him.

"No one knows God's plan," he told her. "But I know an old woman and a little boy that love and miss you. You need to be around family at times like these."

Danielle bent her head to her chest. "I don't have any.

They screwed and made me and gave me this *thing* to deal with and disappeared," she said.

"Family has nothing to do with blood. It's all about who cares about you and we care about you."

Danielle looked up at him. "It's not gone always be easy and pretty. It could be bad. Real bad and then it will get worse," she warned him.

"I'll be right there loving you."

"But I am going to die, Mohammed," she insisted, breaking his hold on her as she turned to walk away a few steps.

"And I will love you even beyond death doing us part," he said. "Come home with me, Danielle. Get out of this rat race and let me help you."

She looked at him, her eyes searching his. She had just decided to leave Jersey for LA full-time and now this man wanted her to leave LA for Jamaica.

"My job—"

"I'll stay here in LA with you until you can resign and give them fair warning to find another smart woman with a pretty face."

Danielle thought about that week in Jamaica. She could use a million more. Life was too short. Tonight Monica, Keesha, nor Latoya knew if their loves were still intact after Hurricane Xavier. But she still had the man she loved wanting to fight with her through whatever came.

"Okay," she agreed with a nod.

Mohammed walked over and gathered her into his arms again. "And my mama said to tell you that you're welcome."

Danielle just laughed and then took Mohammed's hand in hers to lead him into the bedroom for a proper welcome.

Epilogue
Ladies

Each of the ladies held a plate at the repast for Latoya's funeral but none of them felt like eating. It had been a long draining day and they truly just wanted it to be over.

What had started to be a horrible day of secrets, lies, and betrayals revealed had been made all the more worse by the news of her passing. Latoya had been instantly killed in the car wreck that night. The combination of getting hit from behind and then having her car shoved forward into traffic to be violently sandwiched by two oncoming vehicles had sent her home to the Maker.

And now her children could only live with memories they had of their mother. They wouldn't even grow up in the same home any longer. Tiffany was going to live with her father Bones. He had immediately come to his daughter's side at the news of Latoya's passing. It had been Bones who comforted her throughout the emotional funeral.

Danielle could only hope that both Bones and Taquan, who were far from friends, would work together to make sure Tiffany and Taquan Jr. stayed close. She knew Latoya would want it no other way.

Danielle tucked her hair behind her ear as she looked at Mohammed. She gave him a smile but she hoped he didn't see the sadness she hid behind it. Although her soul literally ached for the tragedy, the funeral was a stark reminder of her limited mortality. One day people would come to mourn her and Mohammed would have to deal with her death just like Taquan was.

"Do you think he'll be okay?" Danielle asked, shifting her eyes to where he sat by the window in the living room of Latoya's parents' home.

"Hearing how that last phone call between them went," Monica said, her eyes following Danielle's to rest on the minister who was so obviously dealing with the loss of his wife, "I don't know."

"Take it from me, you don't want to hear or see someone die," Keesha added softly, almost too softly, as she gripped and ungripped the cigarette lighter she held in her hand.

She furrowed her brows just as one lone tear raced down her cheek. That tear hardly represented her level of grief at losing Latoya, losing Corey, and losing her mind. She stared off into the distance at some spot as a vision of Corey's dead body flashed. Keesha winced as she felt a sharp pain that pierced her soul the way the shard of glass had pierced Corey's body.

Keesha felt a hand comfortingly squeeze her shoulder. She looked up. Surprise filled her eyes to see her daughter standing there suddenly. She forced a reassuring smile even as she felt a tidal wave of guilt wash over her that her daughter was so affected by her suicide attempt. Kimani was never very far from her and constantly stopped what she was doing to check on her. The daughter taking care of the parent.

Keesha squinted her eyes as she saw Danielle and Monica share a look that was filled with as much concern as she felt. The same concern she constantly saw in the eyes of her father, stepmother, her baby sister and even Diane. "I'm going back into therapy," she said, answering a question she wasn't even sure they were going to ask. "They said I had a mental break. I fucking snapped. So, uhm, yeah."

"I'm glad you got out of the hospital in time to make the funeral," Monica said.

Keesha nodded. "I'm glad I got out the hospital at all," she said. "My baby wasn't so lucky, you know?"

Monica and Danielle fell silent.

The pills had led to Keesha suffering a miscarriage and they just didn't know what to say to that.

"It's okay. Maybe it's for the best. I mean, I don't think I could have taken having Shawn's baby after he killed Corey, so God and those mysterious ways, I guess," she said, her voice sad.

But none of her sadness or tears was for Shawn. Yet another death and the only bright spot in the darkness Keesha felt over her life. She hoped that crazy motherfucker rotted in hell. He shot himself that night as he sat in his car, overcome with grief for murdering the cousin he had already betrayed. *They* had betrayed.

She couldn't overlook her role in the tragedy and it was that truth that had her walking the fine line between sanity and insanity.

Feeling Kimani's steady presence behind her, Keesha reached up to smooth the back of her daughter's hand. "I'm okay," she assured her.

But that was a bold motherfucking lie. She was far from okay. She didn't know if she would ever write again. They were all back living in Diane's apartment because the home she had once loved and was so proud of acquiring was now a bloody crime scene and a constant reminder of it all.

Latoya was dead. Corey was dead. Her baby was dead. And she had tried to join them all in death.

There wasn't shit okay about that.

Will we ever be okay? Monica wondered as she leaned back against the wall of the crowded dining room and crossed her arms over her chest.

Taking a life was not an easy pill to swallow and Monica was choking on it.

She still had nightmares about the sight of the bullet she fired from her gun, piercing Rah's chest as the bullet he shot at her burnt a thin scar across her cheek before firing through the metal of his van. His injuries had been far more fatal than hers. As she climbed from the van and watched him bleed out onto the sidewalk his eyes had still held a crazy and demented rage for her. She had rushed to kick his gun away from him as he struggled for just enough strength to raise his arm and fire it at her again.

Monica covered her mouth with her hand as she felt the urge to vomit.

Not from the memory of the smell of his blood.

Not from the sight of his body convulsing during the last moments of his life.

Not even from the reality of coming so close to the end of her life.

None of those things made the bile of her stomach switch into reverse.

It was the truth—a truth she shared with no one—that her fear of him was so intense and palpable that she stood there and let him die.

Monica released an audible breath that was heavy.

She shook her head to clear the image of her not even attempting to call the police until she saw his chest rise and fall with his final breath.

In that moment, with her cheek still burning from his bullet and the threat of his words still haunting her, she felt she had no choice. It was survival of the fittest. Period point blank.

For years he sat in prison blaming her for actually being daring enough to press charges against him for breaking her leg. How dare *she*? She had no clue that Rah was even free and stalking her. Monica shook her head. She'd had two loons on her path and didn't even know it. It was Rah who sent the harassing text messages. She had always assumed it was the same person blowing up her e-mail box. She assumed wrong and it almost cost her life.

Crazy motherfucker.

She brought her hands up to gingerly touch the small bandage still covering her cheek. She nudged her chin higher as she looked over at Cameron talking to Mohammed. In the last week since that horrible night they weren't back to a hundred percent but they were trying and that's all she could ask for.

The ashes from Rah's cremation were probaly spinning like a mini tornado at his ironic role in offering something for her and Cameron to lean on each other about. In some weird twisted way Rah had made their transition from her betrayal to Cameron's attempt at forgiveness easier. That night the phone call from the police had brought Cameron to her side at the hospital. The story of her kidnapping and shooting had shaken his stance. And the sight of her wounded face had softened his anger.

She looked up again just as Cameron removed his phone from the inner pocket of his tailored suit. His eyes shifted to hers momentarily before he took out a pen and picked up one of the memorial cards sitting on a table.

Monica frowned as he scribbled on it.

"We can't let another five years go by, y'all," Keesha said, looking down at her hand as she made a fist. "We're like family and a family is stronger together than apart."

Monica's heart raced as Cameron ended his call and walked towards her. She hated the panic she felt at a quick irrational thought that it was his ex-wife on the phone and he was coming to her to announce he was leaving her cheating ass behind.

"You're right. I'll be in Jamaica but we're just a phone call away," Danielle was saying.

"Excuse me, ladies," Cameron said, stopping in their midst to hand the folded card to Monica.

She took it as he turned and walked back over to Mohammed. Glancing down she looked at his dark slashing handwriting and her gut clenched so tightly that it felt like a stab. She looked up to meet Cameron's stare with a question in her eyes. He nodded his affirmation sharply.

"Come with me," Monica said, turning to head through the dining room and up the stairs to Latoya's old bedroom.

"What's going on?" Danielle asked as she closed the bedroom door.

"We made mistakes but it's time to let one motherfucker know he made the biggest one of them all," Monica said, pulling her cell phone from her Celine tote as she dialed the number Cameron had scribbled on the card.

Keesha and Danielle's faces filled with understanding.

Monica turned on the cell's speakerphone and held it out in the middle of their semi-circle as they stood in the old bedroom of their deceased friend. Her death and the shattering of their lives brought on by one man's quest for revenge.

It was time to give as good—or as badly—as they got.

Brrrnnnggg . . . Brrrnnnggg . . . Brrrnnnggg . . .

It went to voice mail.

Danielle reached for Monica's free hand and then for Keesha's as she felt so many emotions flood her.

Keesha's eyes brimmed with enough angry fire to burn a house down with one glare.

Monica looked at a childhood picture of Latoya on the bedside table. A tear fell easily. And then another. And another. "Xavier Lofton, you have no idea of the check your worthless ass just wrote and we are coming for you to cash that motherfucker."

"Unlike you, we got plenty of enough balls to let you *know* to watch your back," Danielle added with ferocity, leaning forward to speak into the phone.

Keesha used her free hand to swipe at tears as anger nearly choked her. "Sooner or later, your ass is ours. Trust and believe that, motherfucker."

Monica ended the call.

Beep.

*   *   *

From a plush seat on his private jet, Xavier leaned forward to press a strong finger to his iPad to exit his voice mail. He chuckled as he recalled the idle threats of his classmates. Their words were nothing but jokes to him. They were nothing but amusement to him.

What they had thought of as a silly school prank had completely shattered what little confidence he had. What little life he had as a teenaged nerd already feeling isolated and bullied. School had been unpleasant at times before "the incident" but after it had been a daily battle not to cry as he was called every inane nickname in the book. People laughed in his face and continued to play pranks on him to further humiliate and bully him.

Life at UHS had been pure hell.

And because students at nearby Malcolm X. Shabazz High used the same line of public transportation and had spread his story like wildfire, even the bus ride home was more of the same. Many times he made the forty-five minute walk home to try and avoid the embarrassment.

He took it for a full year, thinking the focus would shift

off of him, but it never did. When he found himself even comtemplating taking his life for a millisecond, he knew he had to leave his dream school behind.

Xavier dropped out of school and for him he had never recovered. Everything beyond then had taken him twice as much work and drive. Twice as much fight and determination.

But he succeeded . . . eventually.

He shifted his dark slanted eyes out the window at the beautiful landscape beneath him as his jet headed toward Paris. "Alright bitches, let the games begin," he said, lifting his snifter of brandy in a mocking toast to them.

ACKNOWLEDGMENTS

Thank you to God for my blessings. Thank you to the readers, bookstores, bookclubs, and vendors for your support as we continue on this journey together. Thank you to the hardworking staff at Kensington/Dafina for being in the Niobia Bryant business. Thank you to my agent, Claudia, for teaching me so much about this industry and always having my back. Lastly, thank you to the usual suspects for all that you do, whether personal or professional, to keep my mind right so that the words can continue to flow.

Love and blessings, y'all. Love and bountiful blessings.

NEVER KEEPING SECRETS

Niobia Bryant

ABOUT THIS GUIDE

The questions that follow are included to enhance your group's reading of this book.

BOOK CLUB DISCUSSION QUESTIONS:

1) Danielle, Monica, Keesha and Latoya were the best of friends since high school. None of them could imagine their friendship ending. Do you believe it's possible to outgrow a woman you once considered a friend? Give examples.

2) In any relationship there is usually some give and take. Do you think it's possible for a friendship to be one-sided the way Danielle viewed her friendships with the other women? Do you speak up and let the friend know or just leave the friendship alone?

3) Danielle was ambitious, so much so that she compromised herself for her new career in journalism. Although she did go to college and fought hard to get the position at *The A-List* on her own, do you think she could ever overcome the way she got her first job on television? Was it worth it? How far are you willing to go for your success?

4) If you were in Danielle's position, would you have moved to Jamaica to be with Mohammed or suffered through your illness alone to avoid being a burden to the one you love?

5) Monica entered her relationship with Cameron with insecurities about him still being married. Although Cameron presented his wife divorce papers before entering a relationship with Monica, do you think she could ever be able to fully believe he will not leave her the way that he left his wife? Is it possible for a man to be faithful and committed in one relationship when he has shown he was not those things in another relationship?

6) Monica was averse to having children because of all the years she put into growing her career. She

was in a committed relationship with a wealthy man. Do you think his financial status should play any role in her decision to have children or not?

7) Monica had a very short amount of time to decide to kill or be killed. What would you have done in her position as her ex, Rah, manuevered to take her life? Have you ever been in a dangerous situation with an ex and would you be able to do whatever it takes to be free of his violence, stalking or other situations?

8) Latoya fought hard for her relationship with the Lord. Her husband asked her to shun her friends because their relationship with the Lord was not as strong or visible as hers. Would you have done the same? Do you think it's possible to be saved and have friends who are not? Would you, in the name of honoring your husband, take his lead on every decision you made? Should Latoya have stood up to her husband more or was she being a good wife and even better First Lady of the church?

9) Latoya had always considered herself a doting mother who put her children first and would fight to any ends to keep them with her. Do you think her addiction to pills made her lose sight that the very existence of her addiction meant she was putting herself first? Do you think her actions were selfish? Do you think her husband's quest for power pushed her to it?

10) Do you think Taquan and Bones will work together to make sure that Latoya's children stay in contact? If they don't get along is it the grandparents' duty to ensure this? If someone you disliked had a child with the same person you have a

child with, could you put aside those feelings for the greater good of the kids?

11) Keesha had a lot of anger against her mother for the way she treated her and for her discovery that the man she was raised to believe was her father was not. Do you feel it's ironic that she faced the same dilemma as her mother to fess up to having two men who could have gotten her pregnant? Do you think being in the situation made Keesha more sympathetic to Diane? Should it have?

12) Keesha stated that she wouldn't want to have the baby of the man who killed her fiancé. Do you think her statement was harsh? Do you feel it shows Keesha fully sees her role in the tragedy outside of Xavier's involvement?

13) Keesha had a daughter and was pregnant at the time she chose to take her own life because of the death of Corey. Was she putting her relationship ahead of her children or did she truly have a mental breakdown that erased reasoning?

14) If you were Keesha would you be able to still live in the house where Corey was killed?

15) Was Xavier justified in his actions against the women? Had he let the need for revenge go too far? Have you ever wanted to pay back someone for doing you wrong in the past or is it best to let it go and let karma rule? Would you go after Xavier Lofton for revenge?

16) Do you feel Xavier is directly responsible for any of the deaths in the book (Latoya's car wreck, Corey's murder, Shawn's suicide, or Keesha's suicide attempt)?

Don't miss Naomi Chase's sexy and thrilling novel,

Betrayal

Coming soon!

Chapter 1
Tamia

*M*oaning *with pleasure, Tamia tightened her thighs around the sweaty, muscular back of her lover.*

He groaned her name, his hips pumping up and down as he drove into her. Deeper, harder, the slap of their naked bodies echoing around the shadowy room.

Tamia clung tightly to his shoulders, her nails breaking his skin as his thick, hard shaft pounded her core. He felt so good inside her, hitting all her sweet spots. It was as if they'd never been apart.

Staring into her eyes, he lowered his mouth until his warm breath fanned her lips. "You thought I'd let you walk out of my life?" he whispered, the husky rasp of his voice sending shivers through her. "Is that what you thought? Huh?"

Lost in sensation, Tamia could barely breathe, let alone speak.

He thrust faster, his dark eyes boring into hers.

"I'm never letting you go, Tamia. Never . . ."

Five hours earlier

Time ground to a halt as Tamia stared up at Dominic, stunned speechless.

She couldn't believe he was standing at her table, looking like he had every right to be there with his hands casually tucked into his pockets, a smile playing at the corners of his full lips.

As fury quickly replaced her shock, Tamia spat, "What the fuck are you doing here?"

His eyes glinted with amusement. "Hello to you too, Tamia."

"Don't 'hello' me, motherf—" Glancing around the elegant restaurant, she lowered her voice to an angry hiss. "I don't know what the hell you think you're doing, but we have *nothing* to say to each other."

"I disagree," Dominic said calmly. "I think we have plenty to talk about."

"I don't give a shit what you think." Tamia turned her head, darting an anxious glance toward the front entrance. The last thing she wanted was for Brandon to show up and see Dominic standing at her table. There was no telling what he would think—or do.

"You need to leave, Dominic. I'm serious."

"Why?" His eyes gleamed. "You expecting someone?"

Tamia scowled. "Not that it's any of your damn business, but yeah, I *am* expecting someone. He should be here any moment."

Or so she hoped.

For the past twenty minutes, she'd been anxiously waiting for Brandon to join her at Da Marco, the Italian restaurant he'd taken her to on their first date. She'd told him to meet her there at four o'clock. It was now ten minutes past the hour.

He's coming, she assured herself. *He's just running late.*

She didn't want to consider the alternative. That Brandon was at the justice of the peace this very moment exchanging vows with Cynthia. She couldn't bear the thought of it.

"Let me buy you dinner," Dominic drawled.

Tamia gaped at him, incredulous. "What part of 'I'm expecting someone' did you not understand?"

He looked amused. "Come on, Tamia. You don't really think he's coming, do you?"

Her eyes narrowed with suspicion. "How the hell do you even know who I'm waiting for?"

Dominic chuckled softly. "I think I can safely assume that you're waiting for Brandon. Which is unfortunate, since I heard through the grapevine that he's getting married today." He raised a thick brow at Tamia. "Did I hear wrong?"

She glared at him. "How did you know I'd be here?" she demanded, ignoring his question. "Have you been following me?"

"Of course not," he said with lazy amusement. "I had a business meeting this afternoon, but my client had to cancel. I was just about to leave when I saw you."

Tamia didn't believe him, not for one damn second. This was the same conniving motherfucker who'd once blackmailed her for sex. So she couldn't believe a word that came out of his lying mouth.

Before she could light into his ass, the waiter appeared. After topping off Tamia's water, he divided a friendly smile between her and Dominic. "Will you two be dining together this evening?"

"No," Tamia said so sharply that the man looked startled.

Dominic smiled at the waiter. "Give us another minute."

"We don't need another minute," Tamia interjected through clenched teeth. "He's not joining me for dinner. I'm waiting for someone else. In the meantime, I'd like to order the grilled scampi with orange honey salad."

"Excellent, *signorina*." The waiter shot a sympathetic glance at Dominic before moving off.

Tamia picked up her crocodile Dolce & Gabbana handbag, one of many expensive gifts Brandon had lavished upon her during their recent trip to Italy.

"I'm going to the ladies' room," she coldly informed Dominic as she rose from the table. "I expect you to be gone when I get back."

With that, she turned and stalked off, feeling Dominic's gaze on her ass until she rounded the corner and disappeared from view.

Once inside the empty restroom, she slipped into the nearest stall and retrieved her smartphone from her handbag. After taking several deep breaths, she pulled up Brandon's number and pressed send.

Her heart sank when her call went straight to his voice mail.

"This is Brandon. Keep it short and sweet."

Tamia inhaled a shaky breath, debating whether or not to leave a message. If he'd gone through with marrying Cynthia, there was nothing she could say or do at this point. But if he was somewhere having second thoughts, she had to at least *try* to get through to him.

The beep sounded, prompting her to speak or hang up.

Gripping the phone, she nervously moistened her lips. "Hey . . . it's me. I'm at Da Marco waiting for you. I hope . . ." She trailed off, not wanting to sound too desperate. "I hope to see you soon."

She disconnected, closed her eyes, and held the phone to her thudding heart.

Please don't let it be too late, she silently prayed. *Please let Brandon be on his way to the restaurant, not the courthouse.*

Drawing another deep breath, she stepped out of the stall and crossed to the row of sinks to inspect her reflection in the mirror. Her sleek bob was freshly straightened, her red lipstick was perfectly intact, and she wore a

Versace tapestry print dress that molded her voluptuous curves. She'd been delighted when the Italian saleswoman told her that the dress wouldn't hit the U.S. market for another four months. She enjoyed being ahead of the curve.

With a parting glance at her reflection, Tamia left the restroom and headed back to her table.

When she saw Dominic sitting there, a wave of incredulous outrage swept through her.

This motherfucker!

As she marched over to the table, he stood and smoothly pulled out her chair for her. Ignoring the chivalrous gesture, she thrust her hands onto her hips and spat, "What the fuck do you think you're doing?"

His lips twitched. "You might want to keep your voice down," he advised. "People are staring at you."

"I don't give a shit." But even as the angry words left her mouth, Tamia couldn't help glancing around. Meeting the curious stares of several other diners, she scowled.

Not wanting to cause a scene, she reluctantly sat down and allowed Dominic to push her chair back in. But as soon as he reclaimed the seat across from her, she began looking around for the waiter so that she could request her food to go.

"I ordered a bottle of Chianti," Dominic said, gesturing to the wineglass in front of her. "It's good. Have some."

"I don't think so." Tamia glared at him. "I thought I told you to leave."

"You did," Dominic said mildly.

"So why the hell are you still here?"

"I thought you could use some company." He raised his glass to his lips, eyes dancing with humor. "Were you able to reach Brandon?"

Tamia's face heated. "None of your damn business."

Dominic laughed, leisurely sipping his wine.

Tamia hated him with every fiber of her being. But not even she could deny how fine he was, with his hooded dark eyes, juicy lips framed by a trim goatee, broad shoulders and muscular six-four body attired in Armani. His lazy West Indian accent only added to his immense sex appeal.

But it didn't matter how fine he was, or that he was by far one of the best lovers she'd ever had. From the moment Tamia met him, he'd wreaked pure havoc on her life, ultimately causing her to lose everything. Now that she was trying to pick up the broken pieces and move forward, she wanted absolutely nothing to do with him. The sooner he got that through his thick head, the better.

Tamia took a sip of her water, glancing impatiently around the restaurant. "Where the hell is that damn waiter?"

"Probably taking care of our order," Dominic drawled.

Tamia's eyes snapped to his. "*Our* order?"

"Yeah." He drank more wine. "I canceled your salad and ordered dinner for both of us."

"Excuse you?" *The nerve of this motherfucker!* "Who the hell told you to do that?"

He smiled lazily. "We're both here. We might as well eat together. Besides, this will give us a chance to discuss my proposal."

Tamia's eyes narrowed. "What proposal?"

"Glad you asked. I'd like to—"

"You know what?" Tamia cut him off, holding up a hand. "I don't even wanna hear it."

He frowned. "Why not?"

"*Why not? Why not?* Hmm, let me see. Maybe because the last time you approached me with one of your so-called proposals, I lost my boyfriend and my job, and I went to prison for murder."

Dominic grimaced, leaning back in his chair. "All of that was unfortunate—"

"*Unfortunate?*" Tamia echoed in angry disbelief. "Getting

a speeding ticket is unfortunate. Falling on your ass in public is unfortunate. What happened to me was absolutely devastating, Dominic, and none of it would have happened if you'd stayed the hell out of my life. So, no, I have absolutely no interest in hearing your proposal, so you can just go fuck yourself."

Dominic hung his head, looking contrite for the first time since she'd met him. "I know I did you wrong, Tamia. That's why I'd like to make amends."

"How? You nearly destroyed my life, Dominic. There's nothing you can say or do to make amends for that."

"Maybe not," he conceded, "but I'd at least like to try."

"Why? To ease your damn conscience?"

"Nah," he murmured, watching as she agitatedly sipped more water. "This isn't about making myself feel better. It's about rectifying a mistake, righting a wrong—"

Tamia snorted derisively, shaking her head at him. "You are so full of shit, Dominic. And you're out of your damn mind if you think I'd be stupid enough to ever trust you again."

He looked at her with solemn eyes. "Everyone deserves a second chance, Tamia."

"Not everyone." She set her empty glass down on the table, then grabbed her purse and stood so abruptly she got lightheaded.

As she swayed for a moment, Dominic frowned in concern. "Are you okay?"

"I'm fine," she snapped.

"Maybe you should stay and eat something."

Tamia sneered. "Nice try, but I'd rather go back to prison than stay here and have dinner with you." She jabbed a finger at him. "You wanna make amends? Stay the fuck away from me."

With that, she turned and strode from the table without a backward glance.

Chapter 2
Brandon

Brandon felt like a contestant on one of those old game shows.

Except in this case he only had to choose between two doors, not three. And unlike a contestant on a real game show, he knew exactly what awaited him behind each closed door.

Or did he?

Over the past year he'd learned not to take anything for granted, because nothing was ever as it seemed.

Nothing.

And no one.

Behind Door Number One was Tamia, the woman who could have been his soul mate if things hadn't gone so horribly wrong between them.

Behind Door Number Two was Cynthia, the woman who'd gone from being his friend to his lover and, now, the mother of his unborn child.

Both women genuinely loved him and wanted to be with him.

Both gave him something the other didn't.

But he could only choose one of them.

Squaring his broad shoulders, Brandon took a deep breath and stepped through Door Number Two.

Three pairs of eyes swung toward him.

"*Brandon!*" Cynthia cried, beaming with relief as she lunged from the table she'd been sharing with her parents.

"It's about damn time you got here," Bishop Yarbrough blustered, glaring accusingly at Brandon. "Where the hell have you been?"

"Joseph," his wife gently chided.

He scowled. "I'm sorry, Coretta, but the boy is almost thirty minutes late."

Brandon divided an apologetic glance between his would-be in-laws. "I'm sorry for keeping you waiting."

"No need to apologize, Brandon," Coretta assured him. "We're just glad you're finally here."

Brandon smiled briefly before shifting his gaze to Cynthia. Her long dark hair was elegantly pinned up, her makeup was flawless, and she wore a white silk dress that flattered her slender figure.

"You look beautiful," he told her.

She smiled with pleasure. "Wait until you see my *real* wedding gown."

Brandon hesitated. "Can we talk for a minute?"

Her smile faltered. She shot a nervous glance at her parents, who exchanged troubled looks.

"Everyone is waiting, Brandon," Cynthia said anxiously. "Daddy already had to pull strings to get us a private room for the ceremony, and the judge has been—"

"This is important," Brandon interrupted.

She held his steady gaze for a long moment, then swallowed visibly and nodded. "All right," she agreed with obvious reluctance. "We can talk. But we really need to hurry, or we're going to have to reschedule the ceremony."

"And that won't be happening," Joseph growled, leveling a warning glare at Brandon.

He just looked at the old man.

"Come on, Joseph," Coretta urged, steering her scowling husband from the room.

Once the door closed behind them, Brandon and Cynthia stared at each other for several moments.

"I can't do this," Brandon said quietly.

Panic flared in Cynthia's dark eyes. "Can't do what?"

"I can't marry you, sweetheart. Not today."

"Are you serious?" she whispered, staring incredulously at him. "Please tell me you're not serious."

"I'm afraid I am." His chest tightened with guilt. "I'm sorry."

"*You're sorry?* You wait until the day of our wedding to tell me you can't marry me, and all you have to say for yourself is 'I'm sorry'?"

Brandon grimaced. "I'm not saying the wedding's completely off," he explained, walking toward her. "All I'm saying is that we can't get married today."

"Why not?" she demanded. "We're already here at the courthouse. We have the marriage license. Our family and friends are out there waiting—"

"Listen to me." Brandon cupped her face between his hands, his eyes boring into hers. "You know I wanted a long engagement. I shouldn't have allowed myself to be talked into a hasty ceremony. I need more time."

"Time for what?" Cynthia challenged accusingly. "Time to change your mind about marrying me? Time to keep whoring around with Tamia?"

Brandon shook his head slowly at her. "I've never denied my feelings for Tamia. They're not going to disappear overnight just because you want them to."

"I know that," Cynthia snapped. "But I also know that we have a baby on the way, and I have no desire to be a single parent."

"You won't be, I promise." Brandon's voice gentled. "I meant it when I told you that I'm committed to making this relationship work. But a lot has happened over the past year, Cynthia. I need more time to process everything, get my head on straight. If you really love me and want to be with me, you need to be patient with me."

"*Patient?*" Cynthia repeated incredulously. "I was in love with you for two fucking years before I shared my feelings with you! Was *that* not patient? And once we were together, I was patient with you while you defended Tamia during her murder trial, even though I knew it'd come back to haunt me. Don't you *dare* talk to me about patience, Brandon Chambers, because I've been nothing but patient with you. If I were any more patient, I'd be a fucking doormat!"

Brandon slowly removed his hands from her face and stepped back. "I'm sorry for everything I've put you through, Cynthia. I really am. But I've never tried to hurt you or deceive you. From the very beginning I've kept it one hundred with you. You're a good woman, and I truly appreciate the way you've been there for me these past few years—"

"Yet this is how you choose to repay me," Cynthia said bitterly. "By jilting me at the altar."

"I'm not jilting you," Brandon corrected. "We're still engaged, and we're still getting married. Just not today."

"Unbelievable," Cynthia hissed, rapidly blinking back tears. "I should have known you'd pull a stunt like this."

Brandon grimaced, guilt gnawing at his insides as he tucked his hands into his pockets. "We need to let our guests know that we're postponing the ceremony."

"*We?*" Cynthia shrieked. "Are you crazy? I can't go out there and show my face to all those people! *You're* the one who's calling off the damn wedding, so *you* should be the one to tell everybody!"

Brandon nodded slowly. "You're right."

Cynthia stared at him as he turned and started from the room. Reaching the door, he paused and glanced back at her. "I know you don't want to hear this again," he said quietly, "but I truly *am* sorry."

She held up a trembling hand, nostrils flaring with emotion. "Just go, Brandon."

"Cynthia—"

"*GO!*"

He gave her one last look of regret, then turned and walked out the door.

Dreading the task ahead of him, he made his way to the small room where their family members and closest friends were waiting for the ceremony to begin. Cynthia's father stood at the front conferring with the judge, who was frowning as he impatiently checked his watch.

The moment Brandon appeared, all conversation ceased.

Joseph glowered at him, while Coretta offered a relieved smile that sent a sharp stab of guilt through Brandon.

Squaring his shoulders, he walked to the front of the room. Ignoring Joseph and the judge, he scanned the faces gathered before him. His parents watched him with tense expressions, as if they were bracing themselves for the worst. His younger siblings, Beau and Brooke, were smirking with suppressed laughter, while Cynthia's four brothers looked anything but amused. His best friend, Dre, was staring at him with a mixture of wariness and sympathy.

Brandon glanced away, clearing his throat before he spoke.

"Thank you all for coming and waiting so patiently. Unfortunately, Cynthia and I won't be getting married today." He paused. "I'm sorry."

As a shocked silence swept over the room, Cynthia's mother moaned, "*Help me, Lawd Jesus.*"

And then she fainted.